Ruthless Tides

∘Book Two∘

H. M. Huntress

Thank you for coming on this journey with me.

Here is a Spotify playlist of songs
which remind me of *Ruthless Tides*!
*Please note this playlist is subject
to change at any time*

Scan the QR code with the camera
on your phone to listen now!

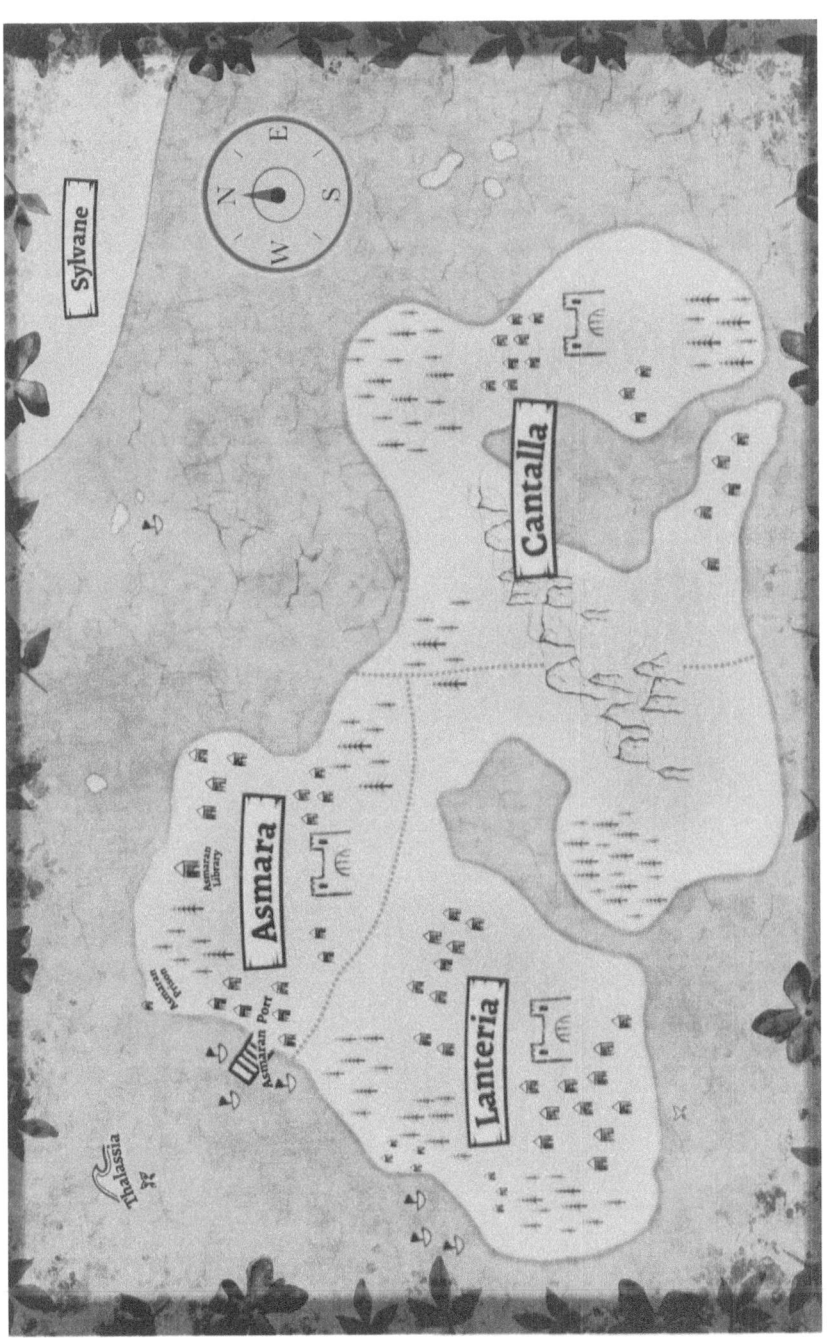

Pronunciation Guide

Character Names

Aurelia – Aw-rell-ee-ah
Humer – Hew-mer
Khali – Kaw-lee
Lia – Lee-ah
Neros – Nee-rose

Places

Sylvane – Sil-vane
Thalassia – Tah-lass-ee-uh

Lia

Blood pooled beneath my bare feet. I relished the feel of it, breathing in the tang in the air. There was nothing I wouldn't do to bring Viv and Jami home, including disposing of this traitorous mermaid who'd been following Finn and me. I recognized her as one of the mermaids who'd attacked me outside the prison after Viv and I visited Humer. Finn and I had lured her into a dark alley, and I hadn't hesitated to drive my dagger straight into her heart.

"We should go before someone happens upon us," Finn said, gripping my upper arm.

My gaze snapped to his and I nodded curtly. Leaning down, I pulled my jagged dagger out of the mermaid's chest, leaving a gaping hole and wiped the blood onto the mermaid's pants.

"Lia," Finn warned again.

"Right," I breathed, sheathing my dagger, and padding after him out of the alley. It wasn't far from where I'd taken out the man who had tried to jump me and Jami only a few days prior.

A lump formed in my throat. *Jami...*

1

I could still feel his lingering touch on my skin. The siren queen had taken him Neros knew where, and I would be damned if I didn't find a way to get him back.

We headed for the beach, ducking in and out of the shadows cast by the lanterns lighting the port to avoid anyone seeing us covered in the mermaid's blood. I had left my shoes on the beach, too focused on my task to bother grabbing them.

Laughter and music floated to us on the breeze from the hub of the port. My mouth twisted into a scowl, thinking of all the carefree people enjoying themselves that night.

The beach had been mine and Finn's home since we lost Jami and Viv. *No,* I chided myself. *Not lost. Not yet.* I'd found Viv once before when she'd been taken by Humer, I'd bring her home again.

Throwing back my shoulders, I kept my head held high as we stepped onto the beach. The sand stuck to the blood coating my feet. I went straight to the water, diving in and allowing it to wash me in entirety. My skin itched and my muscles contracted, anticipating a shift, but I resisted the urge.

When I resurfaced, Finn stood knee-deep in the water, washing his arms and hands. Only a few drops of blood had spattered on him. I'd gotten the worst of it.

"Brom wants a full report in the morning," Finn said, wading out of the water behind me.

"He'll get one." I flopped down on my makeshift bed in the sand, made of a rolled-up shirt for a pillow and a towel I'd swiped from a stall that had been set up in the port during the day.

"Have you spoken with Nix?" Finn asked, sitting beside me. He kept his legs bent and rested his elbows on his knees.

My mouth twisted. "Have you spoken with Marley?" I shot back.

2

Finn's jaw clenched and he stared out at the water.

We hadn't seen or heard from any of our group since the day of the attack. None of them agreed with the plan to trade the object of power, whatever it may be, for Viv and Jami. Brom was only working with us because we were letting him believe he'd still have a say in what happened to the object once we found it.

"They'll come around." Finn twisted his hands, clasping and unclasping them.

"We leave port tomorrow to start our search. They better come around fast or else they'll be left behind," I said, as if either of us needed the reminder. We'd been scrambling to find any hint on locating the island the map pictured. So far, we'd had no luck. We may have given the siren queen the fake map, but ours was equally useless until we had someone who knew where it was and could indicate where the Stones were on our map.

Our first stop once we left port would be the Asmaran library. There was a small inlet near the library we could drop anchor in. It was much faster to sail there than to travel on land.

I cleared my throat. "Do you think if we reached out to the king once more-"

"No. He won't help. All he cares about is the magical item. If we don't have it, he'll have nothing to do with the siren queen," Finn said. He hung his head between his knees, his hair sweeping over his face and concealing him from me.

I leaned back, laying my head on my makeshift pillow. The stars were shrouded by clouds, but I wished on them anyway, aching for Jami to be by my side, making fun of my wishing.

Finn settled into his makeshift bed beside me. "We should be hearing back from Jocelyn in the morning, and we'll

3

know if she's willing to help save her son." He'd sent a letter to Jami's mother, Jocelyn, the morning after Jami had been taken, hoping she might shed some light on the whole map situation. The map bore their family crest, after all.

"You don't seem too hopeful." A yawn punctuated my words.

Finn shook his head and closed his eyes. "Jami has always been the throw away child. His parents never paid much attention to him when he was young, I doubt they'll pay much mind to him now. If he's missing, all the better. One less son to fight over the estate when they're gone. Not that they'll be leaving anything to him anyway."

My heart ached for Jami in a way I'd only ever hurt for my sisters before. I'd had my fair share of childhood trauma, but I never let it affect me. My mother may not have cared for me, but she taught me valuable lessons in learning who to trust and who your true family is. Family is those who will stand by you through anything, no matter the consequences.

"I can't imagine anyone *not* caring about Jami. So, I'm choosing to believe that she'll help," I said, closing my eyes.

Finn grunted a laugh. "I guess we'll find out."

The waves lulled me to sleep until I heard soft footsteps coming toward us in the sand. I cracked one eye, expecting to see a drunken pirate from one of the many ships docked in the port, but instead, Khali was headed our way.

Finn and I both sat up.

"Mail arrived at the inn for you," she said, holding up an envelope. "From Lanteria."

I scrambled to my feet and met her halfway, eager for news from my sisters who had remained behind when we'd started our venture to Asmara.

"Thank you," I said, taking the envelope from Khali.

4

She eyed Finn behind me who remained seated. "I suppose the two of you haven't changed your mind yet?" she asked.

"We'll do whatever it takes to save Viv and Jami," Finn said, keeping his eyes trained on the waves.

I ignored them both as Khali went to sit beside him, and I read the letter.

Lia –
The captain will be happy to know that both of his men who were in critical condition have made a full recovery. We've since left the pirates behind to make their own way to Asmara, and we hope to arrive within a fortnight.

We'd be there sooner but we're taking a roundabout route to try and recruit as many shifters as possible for our fight with the siren queen, as you requested.

We're all still quite shaken by the loss of Bree, but I know she died for our people, as she would have wanted to go.

Stay strong and stay safe.

-Avery

Tears trailed down my cheeks. I missed Avery and all my other sisters I'd had to leave behind, but at least I would see them again soon. Bree was lost to us forever and I couldn't help but shoulder the blame for her death. I was the one who had brought all of them out here. Out of the safety of our home, and into the dangerous territory which was now being terrorized by the siren queen.

"Any news?" Finn asked.

I wiped my tears, straightened my spine, and turned back to him.

"Your two men who had been wounded are healed. My sisters are all on their way here," I recounted.

Finn grinned. "Good to hear."

"Khali." She cocked her head to look at me as I spoke. "I'll need you to let them know where we've gone once they arrive. They know to go to the inn."

Khali nodded. "I can do that. I'll keep rounding up an army for you as well. Goddess knows we'll need it."

"I appreciate it." A spike of guilt speared through me. The army would stand a much better chance if the siren queen never got her hands on the magical object I planned on handing over to her.

"I hope you two know what you're doing." Khali stood and began her walk back to port. "I'll be here when you return."

Finn stood as if he was going to follow her.

"Where are you going?" I asked.

Shoving his hands into his pockets, he answered, "I've some unfinished business to attend to."

I narrowed my eyes and shook my head. "I'm coming with you."

"Good. I'm going to need your help identifying my target."

"Target?" I bit my lip. I had a feeling I knew where this was headed. "It wouldn't happen to be the man who got away from attacking Jami the other night, would it?"

Finn's smirk told me everything. He turned on his heel.

I hurried to catch up. "If this interferes with us leaving tomorrow—"

"It won't. He'll be expecting me, and I wouldn't want to disappoint."

"I thought one murder was enough for tonight, but clearly I was wrong." I'd already killed one of Jami's attackers on

the night of the attack, and I didn't have any qualms about the one who'd gotten away meeting the same fate.

Finn

Losing Viv brought back too many memories of losing my mother. I couldn't seem to convince myself that I hadn't actually *lost* Viv, because it felt the same. She'd been torn from me as ruthlessly as my mother, and my heart ached to the point I wanted to drown my sorrows in whiskey and never wake from the stupor.

But I didn't have the luxury of that. Instead, I would go after the remaining man who tried to exact revenge meant for me on Jami, and then find the two most important people in my life before the siren queen decided to dispose of them.

We started at one of my favorite bars in Asmara, *The Broken Barrel.* I'd spent many nights drinking myself to oblivion there, and it had led to a few of my tattoos. I rubbed the eagle on my chest, thinking of Jami and internally validating my current mission.

Lia, though she didn't seem bothered by it, stuck out like a sore thumb with her bright green hair, tight corset, and leggings. Everyone else in the room resembled me and my crew on our worst days.

"Fancy a drink, darlin'?" A man with long, scraggly, black hair leaned back in his chair in front of Lia, blocking our

route to the bar. At least he was one of the cleaner looking guys in the room.

Lia smiled down at him and his eyes gleamed. I could only assume the nausea-inducing thoughts running through his mind and I wanted to punch him square in the jaw for it. I hoped he'd recognize me and back off, but his eyes were glued to Lia.

"I bet I could make a pretty girl like you—"

Lia slipped her foot against the back leg of his tipped chair, sending him toppling to the floor.

"Whoops." She pressed her fingers to her mouth in mock-shock and stepped around him, continuing toward the bar.

"Watch yourself, bitch," he growled.

I bent down, placing my arm across my knee and spoke low enough only he would hear. "Speak about her like that again and you'll lose a limb of her choosing."

Recognition flared in his eyes as he took me in, and his nostrils flared while he shoved himself to his feet and righted his chair.

"I'm just clumsy," he said quickly, taking off toward the door.

I smiled inwardly. It felt good to be back in my element.

"Coming?" Lia asked, raising her eyebrow as she watched me rise from the ground and rejoin her. "You didn't need to make him piss himself."

I lifted my shoulder and took a seat on one of the open barstools. Lia sat beside me, her feet tapping against the back of the bar and drawing the bartender's attention. He slung his rag over his shoulder and pulled out two glasses, filling them both with whiskey.

"It's been a while," he said, placing both glasses in front of me. "Good to see you're still up for terrorizing my patrons." He nodded to the door.

"Need to keep my reputation intact somehow, Leon." I sipped from my glass.

Lia reached over and snagged my second glass, but I didn't argue. I wouldn't be needing the second one tonight. We were on a mission.

"Have you heard talk of any dead pirates showing up in port?" I asked, lowering my voice.

Leon licked his lips and cleared his throat. "What do you know about that?"

"You tell me what *you* know first," I countered.

Bracing himself on the bar, Leon leaned in and said, "Captain Kerrigan is out for blood. He's offered a bounty for anyone who can bring him whoever killed his first mate."

I whistled low. *First mate.* I'd met Kerrigan a time or two and could vaguely recall his first mate who I'd apparently pissed off enough to make him go after Jami.

My gaze flicked to Lia who seemed smug as she sipped her whiskey.

"Any idea what happened?" I asked.

"Alistair was found shot dead in an alley a few streets over from here. Apparently, another pirate, Hugh, was with him."

Lia sputtered, whiskey dripping down her chin as she laughed.

"Sorry," she murmured. "It's an odd name for a pirate."

"Sorry about her," I said, returning my attention to Leon. "Go on."

Leon studied Lia a little closer but continued. "Hugh has refused to talk about what happened. Said that his days are numbered, and he's been holed up on their ship ever since."

I stuck my tongue into my cheek to stop myself from smiling. "Smart man."

"If he's on their ship, what's the plan?" Lia asked.

"Plan?" Leon asked. "Tell me what *you* know now."

"I killed him," Lia said, a bit too chipper. "And Hugh's next."

Leon's jaw dropped, but then he burst out laughing.

"Sorry, but I doubt you'll be able to get to him. Kerrigan is fast becoming the pirate to be most feared. No offense, Finn. It's just the way of the world." He wiped down a glass and put it on the shelf behind him.

Surprisingly, that didn't bother me as much as it once would have. But it also wouldn't stop me from exacting my revenge and insuring that no one thought they could get away with terrorizing my people without consequences. I had a reputation to uphold, after all.

"I'm not afraid of Kerrigan." I was smart enough not to think I could take on his whole crew alone, but thankfully, I wasn't alone.

"We can scale the ship and be in and out before anyone knows we were there," Lia said. "Nix has given me some pointers on blending in."

I glanced pointedly at her hair. "Nix doesn't have bright green hair."

"I'd obviously cover it," she said, shaking her head. "I've been around longer than you."

I often forgot about the hundreds of years that Lia and Viv had on me and Jami.

11

I clucked my tongue. "Either way. We're not scaling the ship."

Leon leaned across the bar and lowered his voice. "I happen to know that more than half of Kerrigan's men leave his ship every night when they're in port." He leaned back again and busied himself with wiping down the bar.

Ten minutes later, Lia and I were standing on the docks, staring up at Kerrigan's ship, *Wave Breaker.* It was a stupid name that he probably thought made it sound more menacing. A ship's name should *mean* something, in my opinion.

The port behind us bustled with people going from bar to bar, enjoying themselves a little too much. Down here by the boats, though, the sound was muffled and swallowed by the ocean waves. The lights were dim, and all we could see on the deck of *Wave Breaker* were a few shadows moving about. I only counted three men aboard and I doubted anyone belowdecks would be cognizant enough to fight.

"We're just going to walk up there, for all to see?" Lia asked, her hand on her hip. "Seems like a lot more trouble than simply scaling the ship, sneaking in, killing Hugh, and slipping back out."

I ground my jaw. "It's not about simplicity. It's about sending a message," I reminded her. "Unless you want Jami to be targeted again once we save him from the siren queen?"

She put her hands up in surrender. "Send the message. Tell me what you need me to do."

"Watch my back."

The first step onto the gangplank set my heart racing with adrenaline. It had been too long since I'd done anything like this, besides having to deal with Brom, but he was nothing compared to Kerrigan.

Lia stayed a step behind me the whole walk up to the ship and when we dropped down onto the deck, she stepped slightly to the right so I could see her in my peripheral vision, but she remained at my back.

"Oy!" someone shouted. "What d'you think you're doing?" Footsteps fast approached from the left and I turned as a tall, gangly man ran toward us. His dark hair was shaved, and he had earrings swung from the gaping holes in each of his earlobes.

"We're here for Hugh," I said, keeping my voice even and calm. "He should be expecting us." I didn't hide my smile.

The man before us had the sense to back up a step.

"You're Captain Finnian," he said, his hand flexing at his side where a gun was holstered.

I pursed my lips, flicking my eyes to his gun and tilted my head to the side. "Correct. So, you probably know not to try anything stupid."

A voice came from above us. "I should've guessed you were responsible for Alistair's death. He kept going on about some unfinished business he had with you." Kerrigan descended the stairs from the upper deck. "Bold of you to assume I'd let you live if you stepped foot on my ship."

He stopped at the bottom of the stairs; his pistol already gripped in his right hand.

"Let me finish this unresolved business and we'll be on our way." At my words, Kerrigan's gaze moved to Lia behind me as if he was noticing her for the first time. She raised her own pistol and aimed it at Kerrigan.

"I don't have much practice with these, but it worked fine for me when I killed your first mate," she said, her lips twitching with a smile.

"Captain?" The first man who had approached us spoke and I turned my head to face him. I'd almost forgotten he was there.

A red hawk caught my eye, perched on the rail on the opposite side of the ship and I couldn't help but laugh. Of course Marley would be close by for something like this. Kerrigan's gaze followed my own and I knew he recognized my crew member, as notorious as she was, and he heaved a sigh.

The shift came over me as soon as I willed it. In my experience, a single bullet from a pistol was a mere inconvenience in my shifted form. By the time any more rounds were fired, I'd have already taken out my target or disarmed the attacker.

Shaking out my mane, I stared Kerrigan down.

"Don't bother," Kerrigan said, holding a hand out to his other man. "Hugh's useless to us now, anyway. He's not worth the trouble of all this." He returned his own weapon to its holster and waved a hand to the stairs beneath the upper deck.

I stalked forward, a growl reverberating through me. Lia never wavered as she kept her aim locked on Kerrigan.

"This isn't over," Kerrigan said as I moved past him.

"It is if you don't want an entire ocean working against you," Lia said. "You may not recognize me, *Captain,* but I hold some sway with all of the sea."

"You're not the siren queen, so I think I have nothing to fear," Kerrigan retorted.

"I'll be sure to remember that once I've taken care of her." The absolute surety of Lia's tone had me believing her, even though I knew the odds of what she was saying.

I returned my focus to the task at hand and stopped at the first door before the stairs leading belowdecks. I let out a low

14

warning growl, hoping to terrify Hugh a bit more, not that he needed it from the sound of it.

Knocking down the door was too easy. The wood splintered and crashed inward when I threw my weight against it. I recognized Hugh curled up on the bed in the room and flashed back to the last time I'd seen him.

He and Alistair had been amongst a group of pirates from all different ships, playing cards in a tavern where I'd been sent by King Danforth to fetch a man named Phil I was supposed to interrogate and then deliver to the king. Phil was among those pirates playing cards, though he wasn't a pirate himself, from what I remembered.

"It's about time you showed up," Hugh said, his voice hoarse.

My instincts were warring inside me. A part of me wanted to rip this man to shreds for what he'd done to Jami, but there was another part that needed to know *why*.

I shifted back, surprising myself and Hugh.

"What was the unfinished business?" I asked. "Why did Alistair go after Jami?"

Hugh gaped at me. "I-I-"

"Tell me or I'll kill you slowly," I snapped, losing my patience.

"You were the one who killed Phil," Hugh said. "Alistair and Phil were planning on starting a life together, and he left with *you* and never came back. His body washed up on the beach a week later."

I dragged my hand over my face. Phil had been alive when I'd left him with the king. A little worse for the wear considering what I'd put him through, but alive.

I loomed over Hugh in his bed.

15

"If I find you anywhere near any of my crew, or anyone else I care about ever again, I will tear you limb from limb and keep you alive until the bitter end."

I forced myself to turn away from Hugh's rounded eyes and stormed out of the room, slamming the remnants of the door behind me.

"Lia," I said as I passed Kerrigan. "We're done here."

She kept her pistol aimed at Kerrigan until he was out of sight as we walked down the gangplank, and she lowered it to her side.

"That was fast," she commented.

"I let him live," I said. "Someone has to be able to tell everyone why they should fear me."

She tutted. "Seems a waste to me. But I'm trusting you."

Lia

After our eventful night, I was more than ready to sleep, even if it was on the beach again. I wondered why Finn had decided not to kill Hugh after we went through the trouble of finding him, but the haunted look on his face had told me not to ask. Yet.

Come morning, there was no response from Jocelyn. We slowly packed our bedding, hoping her response might appear, but nothing came.

Finn had hired a local mage to send a fire message to Jocelyn and asked her to respond by today. He knew there was a mage in their town in Sylvane who would be able to send a fire message back, but whether she'd want to respond was the question. Thankfully, a fire message would be able to find Finn wherever he was, but we needed the information as soon as possible.

"Hopefully she makes up her mind by the time we're done in Asmara. Otherwise, we're sailing blind," Finn said as we marched up the sandy bank toward the port.

I huffed in agreement.

We stopped at a stall, purchasing two cloaks, and pulled them on, keeping the hoods low over our heads to conceal

ourselves as we made our way to Brom's ship. It was imperative we remain as anonymous as possible from anyone who may be watching us for the siren queen. The previous night, I'd taken care of the mermaid assigned to watch us. With her gone, I wasn't too concerned anymore, but we couldn't be too careful. The siren queen couldn't know that Finn and I were on the ship or else she may revoke her free passage for Captain Brom.

None of our group met us at the docks as the pirates prepared the ship to leave. That meant none of them had come around to me and Finn's plan.

I took the first step onto the gangplank when a hand came down on my shoulder. I froze. Finn was already on board, but he watched from above.

"Lia," a somewhat familiar voice said.

A series of reactions sifted through my mind, none of them subtle, so I settled on turning and facing the man.

Recognition flared before it sank in who he was. *Jared Manes. Humer's brother.*

"How did you find me?" I asked, pulling my hood tighter.

"I followed you from the stall where you bought this." He pinched the fabric of my cloak and removed his hand from my shoulder. "I came here as soon as I realized my brother was taken, but I hadn't been able to find you. Until now."

I took a deep breath, trying to remain calm.

"I'd like to help you," he said.

"Help me?" I couldn't stop myself from laughing. "Just because you were helpful in the prison doesn't mean you've been forgiven for what you did to Viv." Anger burned in my chest.

The gangplank creaked behind me, and Jared's eyes flicked to someone else, his eyes widening slightly.

"Is there a problem?" Finn's harsh tone set even *me* on edge. I understood why Viv had fallen for him.

"I'd like to come with you. I've studied my brother's work and helped him for many years. He hid a lot of information from me, but I can at least supplement some of what you may already know," Jared explained in a hurry. "I want to find my brother, and you want to find your friends. We can help each other."

I narrowed my eyes and studied him. He seemed to be genuine, and we could use all the help we could get.

"Fine," I said. "But you won't talk to me or come near me unless you have something to say regarding the magical item or the siren queen."

Jared nodded. "Fair."

"And you won't leave my sight without permission," Finn added.

We boarded the ship with Jared in tow.

"You'll have to share a room with Finn, miss," a younger boy with blonde hair and bright, hazel eyes said to me. "Or else you'll have to sleep down below with the rest of us."

"That's all right, Jack." Finn put a hand on the boy's shoulder. "I'll be sleeping down below with you lot. This one too." He smirked and tilted his head to Jared. "The lady can have her own room."

Relief passed over me. It wasn't that I would mind sharing a room with Finn, but I needed my own space. Especially on a ship where I had to stay out of sight.

"Right this way," Jack said, waving his hand before him and aiming toward the stairs beneath the quarter deck. There was a door halfway down them on the left.

"Thank you, Jack." I shut the door behind me, opting to get myself settled in first rather than get to know the crew. Finn

had already met some of them when he'd been on the ship before, and everyone knew who he was. Being the Captain's son earned you that kind of recognition, or maybe it was his reputation which preceded him.

I didn't have a lot of things to unpack, but it was nice to have a stable place to stay for more than a night or two. We'd been on the move for so long and had barely spent any time in Asmara.

Sitting on the edge of the bed, realization washed over me that I was alone for the first time in a long time. Finn had been by my side since Jami and Viv were taken, and before that I'd always had at least one of my sisters with me.

A coldness crept in around me, creating an ache in my chest. No matter what, I had to stay strong for Viv. I could manage a few weeks of alone time to bring her home.

Someone knocked on the door and I hesitated, considering ignoring it, but I knew it would most likely be Finn.

"I've hardly had time to settle in." I opened the door and, as expected, Finn leaned against the wall in the stairwell.

He peered over my shoulder into the room. I winced, assuming he was imagining the time he'd spent with Viv in that room.

"Brom wants to see us in his cabin," he said.

Sighing, I stepped into the stairway and closed the door behind me. "He better not be trying to weasel his way out of our deal."

"Oh, I'm sure it's not that, *yet*. He'll wait until we're out to sea where we have little option but to go along with whatever he says."

Finn led the way to Captain Brom's room. It wasn't far from mine, which wasn't very comforting. Maybe I would take up sleeping belowdecks with the rest of the crew once I got to

20

know them better. It would certainly help curb the ache of missing my sisters.

"Whatever he says, go along with it. We can do what we want once we have the magical item. Until then, he must think he has our total cooperation," Finn reminded me. It was hard for me to take orders, but I nodded.

Finn knocked on the door to the captain's quarters and it swung open almost instantly. Callum stood inside, the man who had ridden with us into Asmara when we'd rescued Tabby and the twins.

"Nice to see you again," I said. He nodded in recognition.

"Have a seat," Captain Brom commanded from across the room where he sat behind his desk. "We have much to discuss."

"Indeed, we do," Finn said. We both sat in the chairs in front of the desk as Callum left the room.

Jami

I held Viv's hand tightly in my own. Her screams filled our closet-sized room. It took her longer to wake from her nightmare than the previous night. Sweat beaded on her brow and I waited patiently as she slowly woke.

"You're okay," I mumbled, only half awake myself. "I'm here."

Her breathing evened out and she squeezed my hand before releasing it.

The hard, tiled floor beneath us made it difficult for either of us to sleep, but we managed. There wasn't much else for us to do.

Since the siren queen had taken us, we'd been stuck in this room. I had no idea where we were, other than at the bottom of the ocean in some compound that allowed there to be air underwater. It had been at least a few days since we'd been brought down here, but I couldn't be sure exactly how many because no sunlight reached these depths.

The room we were in was empty and the gray walls bare. There wasn't much to look at except when we'd been afforded our trips to the bathroom down the hall.

22

The hallway leading to the bathroom was entirely made of glass, allowing us to see out into the dark abyss of the ocean. Every time I went out there, I nearly had a panic attack at the thought of being beneath the water. I had to keep telling myself it was an illusion. Magic. Even that didn't work most times.

"Three items, three locks, three..." Humer mumbled from across the room. Swift knocks accompanied each of his words. He'd been stuck in here with us, never speaking any kind of sense.

Viv shifted and I glanced down. She stared into the surrounding darkness. A small light seeped in under the door from the strange orbs of light lining the halls, but other than that, we had none at night.

"Maybe he'll say something of worth eventually," she said.

"I hope not. I'm sure *she's* listening in case he does." I shuddered at the thought of being watched. It seemed highly likely since we were here for one reason: to help the siren queen find whatever magical object was going to ensure she took over the seas.

Shuffling indicated Humer had risen and begun his pacing. A dark shadow moved a few feet away. He'd done this every night, and most of each day, since we arrived.

I closed my eyes in hopes I could sleep for a few hours and temporarily escape this waking nightmare.

A thud outside our door woke me right before the orb lights flicked on overhead. Hope bloomed in my chest that we were about to be rescued, but when the door opened, our same guard, or captor, stood there. Her black hair was shaved close to her head, and her eyes were almost as dark as her hair.

"Rise and shine," she growled, throwing three towels onto the floor before us. "You get to bathe today." She wrinkled her nose as if there were a stench in the room. There very well could have been; I wouldn't know. I'd grown accustomed to all the smells of our little closet.

"Lovely," Viv said, rising from the floor. She held her head high and grabbed one of the towels, handing another to me. She avoided looking at Humer, who still slept huddled in the corner parallel to us.

Our captor spoke again. "Afterward, I'm taking you to the queen. She's ready to ask some questions."

Viv's gaze met mine and fear sparked there akin to my own. There was no telling what the siren queen would do to us if we didn't answer her questions, but we couldn't give her any information. Not only because we truly had no more knowledge than her, other than knowing her map was a fake, but because if we helped her at all, then we would be culpable in helping her take over the ocean. I would never be able to live with myself if I did that.

Reaching into my pocket, I grasped for my lucky coin, but came up empty and remembered I'd given it to Lia. Old habits died hard.

As Viv and I waited in the hall, we heard a grunt from the room as our captor kicked Humer to wake him. From the bulk of the guard, I had to assume that kick would leave quite a bruise on Humer's frail frame.

"Get up and get going," the guard snapped.

Another guard watched Viv and I in the hall. She was much smaller than the first guard, but no less intimidating. Her silver-streaked black hair had been shorn bluntly at her chin, making even her hair seem dangerous.

"Let's move," she said, her bright green eyes flicking from us to Humer who stumbled out of the room. "We're already running late."

The first guard reappeared and brandished a long rod-like object at us. I assumed it was a prod of some kind. When it glowed at the end and buzzed, my suspicions were confirmed.

The shower room was next to the bathroom, and there were only two stalls. Humer was ushered into one, barely able to stand on his own at this point.

"You first," I said to Viv. There were no curtains on the stalls, so I stood in front of the one Viv occupied, back to her, to shield her from the others. They seemed too preoccupied with their own conversation to care about us.

"Murray got back last night," the smaller woman said to the other guard. "Said she lost contact with her eyes in the port."

My ears perked at that. *They must be talking about the Asmaran port because who else would the siren queen care enough to watch, but Lia?*

"Can't trust a mermaid to do a job right," the taller woman grumbled.

I couldn't help myself as I asked, "Aren't you both mermaids?" Their eyes snapped to me, and the taller woman's lip curled, while the other's head tilted.

"Don't speak to us, human filth," the taller woman growled.

I narrowed my eyes and pressed my mouth into a thin line, trying to keep from lashing out.

"We're sirens," the shorter woman said. She glanced up at the ceiling and continued. "Inside this underwater vessel is the only place we look like this."

The tall one's head whipped to the shorter one. "*Esme.*"

"The magic which allows us to appear human only works in enclosed spaces," Esme continued despite the other's obvious ire. Esme turned her face to the other woman and smiled. "You're such a stick in the mud. They're prisoners, Raf. Who cares if they know who we are?"

Raf sighed, as if this was a common problem she dealt with.

Viv tapped my shoulder. "Your turn," she said, taking my place in front of the stall. She'd already put her old clothes back on. It seemed a bit pointless for us to be showering to get rid of the smell, since they weren't giving us new clothes, but I wouldn't complain. At least it was something.

Raf and Esme gave away no more information as I showered.

The next room they brought us to had a domed ceiling made entirely of glass, or some other transparent material that held up against the crushing weight of the ocean. Nausea swirled in my gut as I stared up at the water that could easily engulf us if the dome failed to hold up against it.

"The prisoners, my Queen," Raf said. She and Esme bowed to the siren queen, and Humer followed suit. Viv and I remained upright.

The siren queen, unlike her guards, was not in a human form. She remained as terrifying as ever as she sat in a throne-like chair behind a long, black, marble table. Her pitch-black eyes watched us, and a slow smile revealed her pointed teeth.

Beneath the table, her tentacles never seemed to stop moving. One moved up, flipping her stark-white hair over her shoulder.

"Come closer, my pets." Her voice scraped against the inside of my skull, pulling on my will, and making me heed its

call. Viv moved beside me, even though I knew she was unaffected by the lure of a siren song.

And then a thought occurred to me... *I'm usually not affected by it either, and yet ...* That was a problem for another time. Right now, we had to get through this meeting. I thanked whatever Gods were out there that the siren queen believed me unaffected by her song because of Brom.

"I want to make sure this is in fact the map which will lead me to what I seek." She waved a hand over the table before her, indicating the unrolled map there.

"You doubt it?" I asked, pretending to study it. Of course it was a fake. I'd been there when Finn had handed the replica to Captain Brom to give to the siren queen.

Viv appeared bored beside me.

"I have someone who will be able to tell me for sure. Bring him in," the siren queen commanded. From the side of the room, two guards opened a door and I had to do a double take as Roland strolled into the room.

"Roland?" My eyes widened in disbelief. "How are you alive?" He appeared well taken care of. His red hair was slicked back and tamed, cut to follow the line of his clenched jaw.

Roland's gaze flicked to mine before returning to the siren queen. He was the tallest of us brothers, but only by an inch or two. As the middle child, he'd always tagged along with our oldest brother, Charles, whenever he tormented me. Or maybe Roland had been the true aggressor. I couldn't remember clearly anymore. Either way, his presence now could not mean anything good for me.

"He is alive because he has valuable information. The only reason *any* of you are alive," the siren queen stated. "Except for Vivianne, of course. I have plans for you." The smile she gave Viv made my skin crawl. I wanted to put my arm

around her and try to protect her, but I knew there was no point in it. The siren queen had the advantage here.

The siren queen turned her focus back to the map and my gut twisted. Roland would know the map was a fake. He'd had the real map in his possession for Gods knew how long and he had no reason to know we'd switched them on purpose. Not that he'd ever lie to save my life anyway.

Roland stepped up to the table with his hands clasped behind his back. Leaning over, his dark brown eyes roved over the map for a few seconds and leaned back again.

"It's the real map," he said. A small breath released from me as relief flooded me. For whatever reason, my brother had lied. "That is my father's island." He pointed to the one pictured on the map.

Our father's island? I knew from our family crest stamped on the map that our family had something to do with the island, but I'd never thought the island actually *belonged* to our family.

"Good. We shall start the hunt for it now." The siren queen rose, her tentacles snaking back in from beneath the table and making a slurping, cringe-inducing sound.

Esme followed her out of the room, leaving us with Raf and Roland.

"Back to your room," Raf commanded, waving her electric prod toward Humer who, for the first time, wasn't spewing some nonsense about three locks, or three of something whenever the island was mentioned. He appeared thoughtful as he followed Raf.

Viv went next, and I waited for Roland to start walking before I caught up with him.

"Why did you do it?" I whispered, trying to remain vague in case someone was listening.

28

Turning his head toward me, Roland cocked an eyebrow. "You're my brother." He kept walking, veering down the hall in the opposite direction, and didn't look back.

Nix

Lia scrubbed the blood from her skin in the water. I'd been about to take out the mermaid myself before Lia and Finn caught sight of her, and I'd had to stay back. I didn't want Lia to know I was following her. She'd be pissed.

Whether Lia liked it or not, she was the princess of Thalassia, and I couldn't let her go gallivanting around with pirates without backup. No matter what I thought of her plans.

A rustle sounded behind me in the trees and I snapped my head back to see a red hawk landing on a branch. Rolling my eyes, I faced forward again. Finn and Lia were walking back up the beach.

"I don't need your help, if that's what you're thinking," I said, knowing the hawk would not respond. "I am perfectly capable of stalking my princess on my own."

The rock I crouched behind covered me well enough, and I made sure to stay near the trees so I could blend into their shadows.

Another rustle came from behind me, but this time I didn't turn. I kept my eyes trained on the beach.

"I'm not here for your princess, or because you are incapable of anything," Marley said, resting a hand on my

shoulder. My heart rate increased but I kept my expression neutral. "I'm here to keep an eye on my captain."

Marley came to stand beside me. Like myself, her clothes were magicked to shift with her. She was only about an inch taller than me, which wasn't saying much for either of us, but I always felt as if I had to look up at her.

"They're going to figure out you're following them, sooner or later. If not before they board the ship, then most definitely once you are all on the ship together." Marley scanned the ocean.

"You doubt my stealth abilities?" I asked.

Marley hadn't grown up with me as my sisters had. They all knew better than to doubt my ability to become almost invisible. It helped that I was smaller than most of them, but it had a lot to do with getting comfortable with being overlooked. As a spy, being overlooked became a life-saving ability rather than a nuisance as it was for many. I liked to live life on the outskirts of every interaction.

"I think you've grown too confident in your stealth abilities." Marley leaned against a tree, kicking her foot back and cushioning her head with her hands. "I think you're entirely capable of going unseen on the boat, by Finn and Lia anyway, but I don't think that's going to happen."

I allowed myself a second to admire her as the moonlight reflected in her dark green eyes and made her pale skin glow.

I bit the inside of my cheek to stop myself from saying something I'd regret and instead said, "Do you want to bet on that?"

Marley pushed off from the tree and clapped her hands. "Oh, yes. I'd absolutely *love* to."

It wasn't too hard to get onto Brom's ship unnoticed. I dressed myself as a pirate, having swiped a pair of breeches which were supposed to cut off just below the knee, but they were a little longer on me. As for the tie front tunic, Marley had an extra she gave me. It was baggy and didn't cut as low as the men's ones, so I wouldn't have to bind my chest. Not that I had a lot to bind.

I wore a tricorn hat that I could hide behind when necessary, and I tucked my braided hair up underneath it. A few black tendrils wisped around my face, but otherwise, it was contained. No one asked questions as I helped a fellow pirate carry a barrel of gunpowder aboard.

Marley had it easy. She could fly behind the ship, landing on debris or nearby land to rest. Though, a hawk in the middle of the ocean might be a red flag if she were spotted.

"Do you think we'll actually find the scepter?" the man I helped with the barrel asked me. I cleared my throat before answering, trying to keep my voice low and indistinguishable in case Lia or Finn were nearby.

"Scepter?" I asked.

"I've heard the magical item the siren bitch wants is a scepter. None of this crown or necklace crap," he said, spitting off to the side of the boat to punctuate his words.

"Huh," I huffed, remaining noncommittal. I didn't want to give any of the crew a reason to talk to me again.

We set the barrel down to the lowest deck, and I headed up a floor to the crews' quarters. I picked a bunk toward the frontmost part of the ship, where there were only a few other hammocks. There were some hanging above others, leaving more room for provisions in half of the space.

Phase one, complete, I thought to myself, smirking as I imagined taking my winnings from Marley. It wasn't often I made bets on anything, but when I did, I won.

It wasn't long before I heard commands being shouted above me. I hadn't spent much time on ships, so none of the directions meant much to me. I was a fast learner, though, and didn't worry about anyone catching on that I had no idea what I was doing. Most of my time would be spent out of sight anyway.

"Fancy meeting you here," Marley's voice caught me off guard and I whirled around to find her lounging on a hammock a few rows away from mine. She wore a similar outfit to my own, but it looked much more natural on her since it was her common attire.

"Shouldn't you be flying around outside or something?" I asked, pretending not to be affected by her sudden appearance. No one had ever been able to sneak up on me before. Well, not in a long time. When I was younger, my dad did it often to teach me how *not* to let it happen.

"I thought it might be a bit more comfortable for me in here," she said, waving an arm around in the air. "I miss being on a ship." Closing her eyes, she took a deep breath as if enjoying the scent of stale alcohol, gun powder, and body odor.

I crinkled my nose.

"You almost look like you belong here," Marley said, smirking.

"Thanks, I guess." I sat on my hammock. Thankfully we were the only two in the bunk area. Everyone else had probably gone to the main deck to receive their orders and prepare to set sail, or whatever else they did before heading out to sea.

"I overheard them saying we're making a pit stop so Lia can check out Asmara's library." Marley stared up at the

wooden boards overhead. "I'd be interested in checking that out myself."

"The witches will never give her the information she wants if they know her true motivations," I mused. "But Lia already knows that. She'll tell them what they want to hear."

"You don't think they'll actually go through with it, do you?" Marley asked, not for the first time. It was something we'd been wondering since Lia announced her plan of trading the object of power for Jami and Viv.

"Lia is headstrong and lost in her feelings of grief right now. I hope she'll come to her senses, but I can't know for sure."

"Will you try to stop her if she decides to go through with it?"

I hesitated, unsure *what* I'd do. I wanted to save Viv and Jami, too.

In the end, I shook my head. "No. I'm nothing if not loyal to my princess."

"What of your kingdom? They're the ones who will suffer most from the siren queen gaining that kind of power," Marley pointed out, as if I didn't already know what Lia would be condemning our home to.

"I owe Lia my life. Without her, I'd be rotting in Thalassia's dungeons. My parents may have raised me to be a spy for the king, but that doesn't mean that's what I planned on using those skills for." I blew out a long breath. After all my father's training, I'd disappointed him by telling him I didn't *want* to be a spy for the king. He disowned me and I had to use the skills he'd taught me to take care of myself with a black mark on my name, until Lia had taken me in.

Marley scoffed. "Whatever that means."

34

I rolled my eyes. "It means I was a troubled youth, okay?"

"What, you mean you would have turned out like a *pirate?* The horror." Marley wiggled her fingers at me.

I opened my mouth to respond and then shut it again. Maybe she was right. Maybe I would have become a pirate if Lia had never stepped in and brought me into her group.

"I'm going to see what's going on upstairs, or above decks, or whatever it's called," I said, standing from my hammock.

"The main deck," Marley corrected.

I grunted in response, heading for the stairs.

At the bottom of the steps, I heard an all too familiar voice coming toward us.

"You can have any hammock you want," a different, younger voice said.

Finn responded. "I doubt that will go over well. I may just wait to see what's left open tonight."

I shoved Marley sideways toward the closet beside the stairs.

The door opened as she turned the handle and we practically fell inside, closing it softly behind us and making almost no noise, even in our haste.

"That was unnecessary," Marley said, her chest heaving against mine.

Heat bloomed in my cheeks, and I kept stock still as we waited.

"This does bring back some memories, though." Amusement colored her tone.

I shook my head. "Of hiding in closets?" I asked, hoping she couldn't sense how her nearness was truly affecting me.

Every place her body touched mine was tingling and all I wanted to do was pull her lips down to mine...

"Not hiding, per se." I could hear the laugh in her voice. "Though I wasn't keen on being found."

"Do you think they're gone yet?" I asked, trying to distract myself and pressing my ear against the door. I could still hear footsteps, but I couldn't tell if they were on the stairs, or level with us.

"This," she said, flicking my hat up and off my head. "Doesn't suit you as well as the rest of the outfit."

"Hey!" I gasped, trying to keep my voice down. I caught my hat before it hit the floor. "I need that, despite your thoughts on the fashion of it." My braid had dropped down over my shoulder and Marley plucked it up between her fingers.

"Why not just cut your hair? It's a nuisance."

I lifted my chin to stare at her and her own shorter, dark red hair poking out beneath her hat. It suited her well, but I preferred my longer hair for myself.

I snatched my braid back, inhaling sharply as my fingers grazed hers. A smile pulled at her lips, and I leaned toward her before reminding myself this was not the time for that.

"I like my hair, thank you very much." I flipped my braid out of reach.

Marley lifted her shoulder. "I never said I didn't like it. Just that it might make your mission a bit easier. But I'm all for whatever is going to help me win this bet. So, by all means, keep the hair." Even in the dark, her eyes sparked with mischief.

The door handle twisted and Marley, faster than I could come up with my own plan, moved her back to the door and pinned me against the shelves with her hands braced on either side of me, her lips crashing against mine.

Light poured into the closet as the door opened and someone cursed. "At least wait until we've made it out to sea," a man grumbled. "Damn new recruits can't even keep your hands to yourselves long enough to swab the decks."

Keeping me blocked with her body, Marley chuckled and pulled back, grabbing a bucket and mop, and passing it to the man in the doorway.

"'pologies. Can't seem to keep my hands off this one," she said, moving with him out of the closet and shutting the door enough so I had time to right myself with my hat and tuck my hair back under it.

My heart was hammering so fast, and my hands shook as I replaced the hat on my head. I couldn't make myself stop smiling as I still felt Marley's lips on mine and the taste of her lingered. *Red wine and whiskey.* She must have been drinking from her flask earlier.

I stepped out of the closet, shutting it behind me, to find that Marley and the man had disappeared up onto the main deck.

My heart finally calmed as I climbed the stairs, but the smile didn't leave my face as I stepped out onto the deck into the fresh air.

Viv

I took a deep breath. Another day of being trapped in the same tiny room as Humer. Every time he moved, I flinched. Even my nightmares were filled with his presence, whether he featured in them or not.

Whenever I was granted the escape of sleep, I found myself back in that underground laboratory Humer had kept me in for two years before Lia found me. He wasn't always the one working on me or tormenting me. Sometimes it was the siren queen, and once ... it was even Finn. That nightmare left me shaken and sweating.

"Vivianne," Humer spoke my name, and my scars tightened in response.

I refused to look his way as I pressed a hand to my lower abdomen where my scars were hidden beneath my corset top.

"My favorite test subject." He shuffled closer and I stiffened.

"Don't take another step," I warned. I had no idea what I'd do to stop him, maybe claw out his eyes, or his heart. It was a tempting thought.

Humer chuckled. "You don't threaten me, Vivianne."

38

Jami moved beside me, waking up from his nap. "Back off, asshole," he grumbled, his voice still groggy from sleep.

Laughing again, Humer shuffled back. I finally looked at him and he stared back, a gleam in his eyes.

"The queen will search until the day she dies, and she will find them," he said, his voice lowering as if he thought someone was listening. It was the most cognizant he had seemed since we were thrown in here.

I cocked my head in interest. "What is it?" I whispered, hoping no one was paying attention to us, if they were even listening.

His eyes flicked to Jami. "You know. You were there when it was hidden."

Jami's brow furrowed and I watched him carefully. A part of me wondered if he'd been lying to us the whole time about not knowing anything regarding the map or the magical object, but his face gave away everything. He knew nothing, and even if what Humer said was true, he had no memory of the object.

Shaking his head, he said, "My family never traveled outside of Sylvane."

"And yet ..." Humer trailed off, a glazed look taking over as he settled back into his strange daze. "Three items, three locks, three ..." Back to his usual babbling, though he never said what the last group of three was.

"That was strange," Jami said, wrapping his arms around his knees and pulling them to his chest. "Maybe he'll give us some *real* information."

"Doubtful," I muttered.

Before all this, I'd thought I'd crumble being this close to Humer again, but surprisingly, I wasn't too affected by it,

besides the fact that his voice made my scars ache and my insides twist.

I was half convinced none of this was even real. Maybe I'd died in that battle with the sirens, and this was my personal hell. Then again, if that were true, I'd be under Humer's knife rather than stuck in a room with him. And Jami wouldn't be there. Probably.

"So that was your brother." I changed the subject.

Jami sighed. "Yeah. That was him. Well, one of them. Roland." He reached into his pocket as if looking for something but pulled his empty hand out, flexing it instead.

"I thought your brothers were assholes." Lia had told me about them briefly and they hadn't seemed very brotherly to me, though I wouldn't know since I'd never had brothers.

"They were, or are." Jami shook his head as if it didn't make sense to him either. "I don't know. They tortured me as a child, so, yes."

"Brothers!" Humer cried out, making us both jump. "That's it." He settled down again.

"What's gotten into him today?" Jami scratched at the stubble growing on his chin.

"Well, he has a brother of his own," I said. "Jared Manes. Lia and I met him at the prison. I wonder what happened to him in that explosion."

"Jared?" Humer cut in. "No. Not that brother."

"Does he have others?" Jami asked me rather than trying to talk to Humer.

I shrugged. "I've no idea." There had been another man helping Humer all those years ago, and I'd never thought to ask Jared what happened to him. For all I knew, he could still be tormenting shifters.

"Brothers, brothers, brothers," Humer repeated as if trying to jog his memory.

"What do you think Lia and Finn are doing in Asmara?" I asked Jami, doing my best to ignore Humer as he continued mumbling to himself.

Jami leaned his head back against the wall, staring at the ceiling as if he might see through it to the surface where our friends were.

"Knowing Lia, she's hunting for you." His eyes flicked to me, and he smiled. "And knowing Finn, he's also hunting for you."

My heart pounded hearing Finn's name. I missed him more than I'd thought I would. Almost as much as Lia.

"If I thought that's what they were doing, I would say they're hunting for you too. But I know Lia and the other mermaids, and they'll be hunting for the object of power. That's the best way to ensure they bring down the siren queen *and* get us back." I truly wanted to believe they were coming for us first, but no one had ever been able to track down the siren queen's lair, and it would be a waste of time for Lia and Finn to try.

"Hush, they're listening," Humer said, his eyes tracking something invisible on the ceiling. "Tick, tick, tick."

Before Jami or I could respond, our door opened and Raf walked in. "We're about to be moving, so this is your courtesy warning. I don't recommend standing or walking around too much." She sneered and slammed the door shut behind her.

"Huh," I huffed. "Wonder what that means ..."

I ran a hand through my hair. It kept swooping in front of my eyes and tickling my cheeks.

"Bree thought we might be able to talk to the sirens and see if they wanted to end the queen's reign as well," I said,

keeping my voice as low as possible. "There is a natural order among them, and the siren queen has disrupted it by attempting to extend her reign indefinitely." It hurt to talk about Bree, and a solid lump stuck in my throat as I fought back tears. Before she'd died, she had given us a warning from the siren queen. *Stay out of the water.* We'd ignored the warning and we'd paid the price.

I'm sorry, Bree. My chest ached from the memory of her bleeding out in front of me and made it hard to breathe.

"I remember her saying something about that," Jami murmured, extending his hand, and placing it on my shoulder. His touch made me tense, and I wanted to brush him off, but I knew he was only trying to help. "I'm so sorry we lost her."

I coughed, trying to dislodge the lump in my throat. "She knew the risk of coming with us. But it doesn't make it any easier." Jami had lost Cole that night too. It should never have happened, but the siren queen had been a step ahead of us.

"Maybe Bree was right." Jami lowered his voice even more. "What if there is someone here who is willing to help us?"

I didn't dare respond or voice my thoughts, but I'd been wondering the same thing since we arrived. Maybe Bree had been right, maybe we had hope.

A horrible screeching sound made us all clap our hands over our ears. Beneath us, the floor rumbled, and the entire room lurched forward. My head slammed against the wall and from the groan beside me, I knew Jami's had too.

"I guess that's what Raf meant when she said we'd be moving. I didn't think she meant the entire fucking structure," Jami said.

I blinked stars from my vision and looked at him, realization dawning on me. "That's how no one ever finds the siren queen's lair. It's always moving."

"Sereida," Humer whispered, followed by some nonsensical mumbles and, "Always on the move."

"What?" I'd had enough of his ramblings.

Humer slapped his hands on his thighs. "We could have changed the world, Vivianne. You still can." He leaned forward, staring at me intently.

I scrunched my nose and hugged my arms around myself.

Humer rocked forward onto his knees. "I never had the chance to find out if we were successful, but I *know*."

"What the hell are you talking about, old man?" Jami snarled. "Leave her alone if you can't speak any sense."

Leaning back against the wall again, Humer lifted his chin to stare at the ceiling. I watched him carefully, afraid he may jump into motion at any second.

"Shifters can only reproduce with other like shifters," Humer spoke as if reading from his notes. I stiffened as he continued, my nails biting into my palms from how hard my fists were clenched. "What if they could reproduce with *any* shifter? Mix genes and create even more powerful breeds?"

"You're insane," I said, my voice shaking. "There's a reason shifters weren't created to be able to reproduce with other shifters. The gods knew what they were doing."

Humer laughed and blinked slowly, dropping his gaze to mine. I shuddered.

"I don't believe in any gods," he said as the vessel lurched again and we all shifted. That time I avoided slamming my head into the wall.

43

If Humer thought he had been successful with me ... I didn't want to know what that meant. It wasn't a bridge I was willing to cross yet.

"With the three I'd have been able to perfect my work ..." Humer trailed off. "Three items, three locks, three brothers." He devolved back to his rambling, but he had actually finished his set.

"Three brothers?" I asked, gaze flicking to Jami. "Do you think he means you?"

Jami's eyes widened. "I've no idea. Considering my family has something to do with these magical items being hidden, I guess it's possible."

"The siren queen must know, since she seems to be collecting you and your brothers."

"She's only missing Charles." Jami scowled. "I hope he doesn't show up here any time soon."

I leaned against him, resting my head on his shoulder. "As much as I'd like to say he won't, the siren queen seems to be pretty adept at getting what she wants, even on land."

Jami groaned. "Then maybe I should prepare myself for another family reunion."

Lia

Two of Brom's men accompanied me to shore in a long boat. My hood hung low, almost blocking my entire field of vision, but we couldn't be too careful.

My body ached to be in the water, and it took every ounce of resolve not to trail my fingers in it as we rowed to shore.

It had been a while since I'd visited the Asmaran library and the witches who watched over it. I used to spend a lot of time there when I was avoiding home. It held all the oldest books on the continent, maybe even the world.

The beach came up fast, and I climbed out of the boat, leaving the two men behind. They'd wait for me to return since the witches would never allow them in the library.

Sand and salt clung to my skin making me homesick. I took deep breaths as I walked up the beach toward the trees.

Though Khali didn't entirely approve of my new plan, she had reached out to one of our mutual friends so I could get a ride to the library. Otherwise, it would be quite the trek.

"Rising from the sea; a goddess, a *princess*," the familiar voice greeted me. Ryder rose from the rock he'd been sitting on.

"It's been a long time, Lia." He swept into a low bow, a cocky grin on his face.

Weariness seeped into me at the sight of him. It *had* been a long time and so much had happened. Ryder opened his arms and I stepped into them, letting him embrace me and soaking up his warmth.

"Khali said you're trying to take on the siren queen," he said, releasing me.

I edged back and wrung out the hem of my shirt which had absorbed water from the spray of the ocean. "Sort of." I didn't have the energy to tell him any more of the truth. "Are you going to help me get to the library?"

"What are friends for?" he asked.

One of the best things about Ryder was he didn't ask too many questions. He had enough secrets of his own, so he never expected me to share any of mine. It was one of the many reasons we'd called it quits on our relationship years prior. Friendship better suited both of our needs.

"Not to rush this reunion, but I'm in a bit of a hurry," I said, making him laugh.

Walking away from me, Ryder strolled on the beach, shifting into a full-sized, bright blue dragon, and stretched his wings toward the sky. The men in the long boat hardly reacted, which made me think slightly higher of them.

Ryder shook his long neck and leaned his head down so I could climb onto his back.

I nestled into the divot between his neck and back as I had many times before. The muscles beneath me bunched as he launched us into the sky and a small squeal escaped me. Air rushed past us, making my eyes water and my hair go wild around me. I ducked down, laying my chest flat against Ryder's neck to keep some of the wind from buffeting me.

"This is just as amazing as I remember," I said, my words lost to the roaring of the wind.

The beating of Ryder's wings soothed me as I watched the world pass by below us. Flying had a similar sensation to swimming through the ocean. Both were freeing in their own ways, and the wind almost felt like water rushing past me. It soothed me, until thoughts overwhelmed me. I wondered what was happening to Viv and Jami. Was the siren queen torturing them? Trying to pry information from them? Had she already discovered the map was a fake and taken out her anger on them?

We started our descent, and I realized we'd already reached the library. A trip which would have taken hours on foot took mere minutes in the sky. The massive spires stretched up toward us and Ryder banked left, avoiding them. A giant round, stained glass window sat in the middle of the intricate castle-like structure.

Ryder landed in the grass beside the library, waiting for me to slide down his front leg before shifting back to his human form.

"Well, that was fun," he said, rolling his shoulders and cracking his neck. "It's been a while since I let anyone ride me like that." He winked and I rolled my eyes.

"Don't get any ideas. We're friends now, remember?" I had made it clear when we'd broken things off that we'd never be anything more, and he'd never find me in his bed again. I'd only broken that promise once.

He was smart and kept his mouth shut as we approached the library's front door. Before we reached the door, it swung open as if to welcome us.

"Thank you, Shannon," I called out.

47

Instead of Shannon, though, Justine appeared before me, stepping out from behind a cart. "Shannon is in Sylvane." Her copper-red hair was pulled back into a bun and she wore a light gray dress which swept down to the floor, trailing behind her.

"Well, that's a shame. I was hoping to catch up with her," I said. It was true, Shannon had always been my favorite. "But it's nice to see you, Justine."

"Hmph." She raised an eyebrow and appraised me before turning her hazel-eyed gaze to Ryder. "I thought you ditched the dragon?"

"This is Ryder. Ryder, meet Justine. The head of the library, and Shannon's confidante apparently." I waved my hand between the two of them. Shannon had been the only one I'd told about Ryder, so I knew she'd shared the gossip with Justine. I didn't blame her. The witches spent most of their time in the library and needed something to make their days a bit more exciting. I was always happy to provide that entertainment.

Justine cocked her head and crossed her arms. "You know we don't let just anyone in here." Her gaze rested on Ryder.

Putting my hand on Ryder's bicep, I leaned closer to Justine. "I'll vouch for him, and if he steps out of line, I give you permission to ban him for life."

She sniffed. "I don't need your permission for that, but fine. Why have you come? Does it have anything to do with the siren queen's attacks?"

I nodded. "Yes. I need to find any information you have on objects of great power. Something which would help the siren queen take over the entire ocean."

Justine's eyes narrowed and she pursed her lips. "There aren't many objects which contain that much magic."

"So that means one exists, then," I said. "Tell me. It's the only way to save V—" I stopped myself. "Erm—the ocean." My eyes drifted to the ceiling, hoping Justine didn't catch my slip.

"I may have something." She lifted her hand into the air and at first, nothing happened. A few seconds later, a book came zooming through the room and straight into her hand. I'd seen it before, but it was always a little jarring to witness their power. My power was so different from theirs; it was almost like we were from different worlds.

I reached out for the book, but Justine held it out of reach.

"This isn't the book for you," she said, a smirk playing at her lips. "But you might find what you're looking for in that section." She pointed to a section far to the right where there were few bookcases. It seemed more like a reading area with all the tables and cushioned chairs there, but I wouldn't question Justine. She had been here longer than any other witch.

I turned to walk toward the section she'd indicated, but she cleared her throat and said, "I know your motives are impure, Lia. I may not know exactly what you are planning, but I know it's not for the greater good."

I fisted my hands at my sides and ground my jaw, trying to keep from snapping at her and saying something that would get me kicked out of the library.

"The siren queen took Viv and someone else I care greatly about." I matched her hard stare with my own.

"What?" Ryder said from beside me, but Justine and I ignored him.

Lowering her hand with the book, Justine clasped it before her and tapped her long nails against it.

49

"I won't keep you from searching for the information you need because I believe that with or without it you will find what it is you seek. But I *will* give you a warning. If you continue down this path, it will only lead to the destruction of all you hold dear, including those you think you are saving."

I held my hand out and gave her a blank stare. No matter what she said, it changed nothing.

Clutching her book close, she said, "When you're finished, you know where the return bin is." She turned on her heel and strode into the depths of the library.

Ryder followed me to the bookshelves and sat at a table nearby as I scanned the book spines.

"These books are ridiculous," I said as I read the titles. "Spells to Capture a Heart? Charms for Speed, Edible Magical Roots ... None of these are going to be of any use." I ran my index finger over the books, continuing to search for something that had to do with powerful magical objects.

"I could use that first one," Ryder joked. "It's rough out here for a dragon shifter to find love."

Kneeling, I looked at the books closer to the floor.

"You're simply too picky," I commented, only half paying attention to him.

"Hmm, I guess that may have something to do with it."

"Ha!" I grinned, plucking a book called *Objects Lost in Time* from the shelf. "This might hold something important."

I dropped it onto the table and sat across from Ryder.

"Seems like there's a lot of weight on your shoulders," Ryder said as he leaned back in his chair.

I ignored him, skimming the pages of the book for any mention of a powerful object.

To ward a person ... I paused and flicked my gaze to the top of the page. *Wards and Shields.* I remembered Humer mentioning how the island with the magical object was hidden.

"Of course," I murmured as I read. "A ward could hide the island."

"A ward?" Ryder asked, leaning forward to look at the page. "I've run into a few of them, quite literally. Some people don't even want anyone flying over their most prized possessions."

"You couldn't see it before flying into it? Wouldn't there be a shimmer or a haziness indicating magic?" I wracked my brain for everything I'd learned about wards in the past. It wasn't much, but I knew my father had used one on the royal treasury in Thalassia.

"No. Not even when I rebounded off them. It was like I hit an invisible wall. Everything seemed normal beyond the ward, but there was most likely something there I couldn't see."

I continued reading.

The best way to keep an item safe and ensure history forgets its existence, is to ward it. Otherwise, nothing can stay hidden forever. Wards can be put up for short periods, or an extended time. However, there are some side effects when a person is subjected to that kind of magic for too long. Long-term wards are best used on inanimate objects.

"I wonder if an island would be too large to be warded," I mused, skimming further down the page.

For long-term wards, a great amount of power is required to fuel them. For example, if you wanted a ward to last longer than a few days, it might deplete someone of their magic for the same amount of time, or longer depending on their skill level.

51

I propped my elbow on the table and rested my head in my hand. "To ward an island for this long would deplete someone entirely of their magic," I said.

"No one is stupid enough to do that," Ryder scoffed. "Once their magic ran out, their life force would go next."

"That's if the island is even warded," I sighed. "Let's see ..." I continued flipping through the pages but there was no mention of any object strong enough to take control of the ocean.

Huffing, I slammed the book shut and replaced it on the shelf. I continued scanning the books, moving to the next, and only other, shelf in the section.

Ryder rapped his knuckles on the table. "I wonder if they have any snacks here."

I whipped my head around and glared at him. "We're here for the books. *Not* the snacks." When I turned back around, I added, "But Justine does make some of the best homemade bread I've ever tasted."

Running my fingers over the spine, I halted, unsure what made me do so. Something about the book beneath my fingertips called to me. There was no title on the spine, but when I pulled it out, it said, *Secrets of Thalassia* on the front.

Oh. There were many things the world above the ocean didn't know about our kingdom, so I imagined there would be a plethora of secrets in this book.

I returned to the table, keeping the book in my lap as I flipped through the pages. It wasn't that I thought Ryder would care about any of Thalassia's secrets, but it felt wrong to have them out in the open.

As it turned out, there wasn't really anything in the book that stood out to me as a true *secret*. There was an entire chapter dedicated to the king's warded treasure vault, and

another explaining the rules of ascension. We didn't wait for one royal to die before the next ascended. The king or queen could simply decide to step down, or to rule alongside the next in line due to the longevity of mermaids.

I rapidly flipped through the pages until I came to one depicting three objects: a crown, a scepter, and a necklace. Straightening in my chair, I moved the book to the table and read the passage beneath the picture.

The Azurean Stones contain more power than any other magical object known to man or shifter. No one knows what form they take since they have only been recorded in history once. It is said the original queen of Sylvane obtained the three Stones as a gift from the kingdom of Thalassia—

"What?" I stopped reading, reeling back. "Why would I not know of these objects if we once *possessed* them?"

"All families have secrets; kingdoms are no different," Ryder commented, rocking his chair back as he stared at the ceiling.

It is said the queen had the Stones placed into a crown, but there is no evidence it ever made it back to her possession after being crafted. Many believe the Stones were stolen and redistributed among the sea-dwellers.

"Well, this is useless." I slammed my hand on the table in frustration.

"At least now you have an idea of where to go to find some answers," Ryder said.

"I'm regretting bringing you with me," I grumbled. "Your commentary is—"

"Unmatched? Amusing? Invaluable?" Ryder grinned. "What now, Lia?"

I closed my eyes, imagining the glistening underwater kingdom I couldn't return to until I'd dealt with the siren queen. "Now, I need to go home."

"But you can't go," Ryder said, and when I opened my eyes, he was leaning across the table, mere inches from my face.

"Aargh!" I reeled back, nearly toppling out of my chair. "Holy gods, Ryder!"

He laughed heartily, clapping his hands. We earned a harsh shushing sound from somewhere deeper in the library.

"I'm going to feed you to the sirens if you keep doing shit like that!" I hissed. "Now, come on. We have to find Justine."

I knew she couldn't have gone too far. She was always watching everyone in the library. It only took a few minutes of wandering before she found us, looking annoyed.

"You're done with your reading?" she asked. Her hands were clasped in front of her, and her brows were almost in her hairline. "And I assume you put the book into the return bin?"

I scrunched my nose and chose not to answer that question. "I need to contact my parents," I said. "It's urgent."

"And dangerous," Justine reminded me, as if I could forget.

I cleared my throat. "Yes, I know. It will be quick and then we'll be out of your library."

Justine ran her tongue over her lower lip and lifted her chin. "Very well. You will have *five minutes.* That is all I will afford. It's been a long time since Mai has used her gift, and I won't push her harder than that."

I nodded in understanding. Few witches had the ability to astral project, and it could drain their magic detrimentally if they did it wrong or too often. It would make it even harder for her to get through the protection seal shielding Thalassia from

the siren queen, but it was the only way to reach my parents. Even fire messages wouldn't make it through the dome.

Justine led us up a winding staircase to the second floor. Much like the first, it was filled with bookcases, but there was a narrow hallway to the left which led to Mai's room. Every other witch had a room in the basement of the library, but Mai refused to go underground after an astral projection gone wrong.

"Wait here." Justine put her hand up to stop Ryder and I from advancing as we approached the wooden door of Mai's room.

Knocking once, Justine proceeded into the room without an invitation. "Princess Aurelia requests your services."

A long sigh followed. "I will see her," Mai responded. Her voice sounded much older than she looked. She was the youngest of the witches, though not much younger than me. I wasn't sure how aging worked for the witches, but Mai didn't appear older than eighteen or nineteen.

Justine walked out of the room and waved a hand toward the door. "Only you, Aurelia," she said, putting her other hand up as she locked eyes with Ryder. "I shall keep your dragon company while you speak with your parents."

"Thank you." I walked into Mai's room, surprised by the changes she'd made. There were plants hanging in every corner and lining the shelves. In the center, she had a round bed with pillows propping her up as she lounged there in a silken robe.

Light streamed in from the floor to ceiling window on the right-hand side, making her hip length golden hair glow.

She locked me in place with her brown doe-eyed stare. "It's been a long time, Lia," she said, a smile transforming her face to the welcoming one I remembered.

Hurrying to the bed, I sat beside her and threw my arms around her shoulders. She chuckled and hugged me back.

"I'm so sorry to ask this of you," I said, pulling back and gripping her hand in mine. "But Viv's life depends on it."

"I have heard that before, you know." Sadness filled her gaze. It had been when I'd asked her to help me find Viv when she'd been taken by Humer. It was a last resort because of the dangers of attempting to astral project to someone's unknown location. The witch could become stuck in the place, neither here nor there with their body, which is almost what happened and led to Mai's new living arrangements on the second floor.

Guilt swarmed my gut, but I couldn't let it stop me. Astral projecting into Thalassia was much safer because Mai knew exactly where she was headed. There was much less chance of losing herself or becoming stuck.

"I am eternally grateful to you for finding Viv. This time, we won't be looking for her." *As much as I want to,* I silently added. "I need to reach out to my parents in Thalassia. I need you to ask them about the Azurean Stones which were supposedly given by Thalassia to the queen of Sylvane a long time ago."

"I can do that," Mai said. "But we'll need to light some candles."

I hugged her again. "Thank you, Mai. I promise someday I will have a way to repay you."

With a snap of her fingers, Mai's wheelchair moved from the side of the room to the edge of her bed. She held her arm out to me and I helped her from the bed into her chair. She'd been paralyzed from the waist down since before I knew her and none of the witches had discovered a way to heal her. She never seemed too bothered by it. I assumed she had long since come to terms with it.

"If you don't mind creating the circle." Mai pointed to a cabinet on the left wall. I opened it to find nothing but candles

lining its shelves. Grabbing five of them, I brought them to the projection circle which had been painted on the floor in front of the window. I placed a candle on each point of the star that overlapped the many circles.

Mai positioned her chair in the center of it all and snapped her fingers, lighting the candles instantly.

"Remember, do not cross into the circle while the candles remain lit," Mai warned. "I'll be able to hear you but try not to say anything unless I prompt you to, otherwise I may lose focus and snap back into my body too soon."

"Got it," I confirmed. I remembered all her warnings from the first time we'd done this.

"Okay. Here we go." Mai closed her eyes and placed her hands on her knees.

I watched her, entranced by the siren-like song she started humming. After a few minutes, her form became hazy, and I knew she had made it into Thalassia.

I wouldn't be able to hear what my parents said, or what she told them, but she would relay anything important to me.

"Queen Marisa would like to know how you came across the information," Mai said. Her fingers started tapping a rhythm against her knees.

"The Asmaran library. But that's not important. I need to know what *they* know," I said. We had little time. It had already been a solid two minutes at least.

"Queen Marisa has no ..." Mai trailed off. "King Lahara said the Stones were *stolen*."

"What? By whom?"

Mai hummed again and the tapping on her knees quickened. "Not the queen of Sylvane. They never made it to her. They were stolen from the royal carriage delivering them."

"So, they made it to Sylvane, but not to the queen?"

57

"Yes. And never seen again."

"Fuck." I dropped my head into my hands. We were back to square one.

"Stolen by a powerful mage is what King Lahara was told."

The haziness became denser around Mai.

"You can come back Mai," I said, though I wanted to know more.

"King Lahara says he loves you and wishes you luck on bringing down the siren queen. He trusts you and your sisters to win this war and keep Thalassia free." With that, Mai's eyes fluttered open, and her form became solid again. The candles flickered out.

I swallowed, shame threatening to eat me alive at my father's words. *If he only knew what I mean to do,* I thought.

"Thank you, Mai," I whispered.

"There's still time to change your course," Mai said, apparently reading me as Justine had.

"I can't—"

"I understand if you don't," she said. "Your mother ..." She cast her eyes to her hands which had stilled as soon as she'd returned to her body.

"You can tell me," I said, blinking slowly and rolling my shoulders back. "I'm under no illusion she will ever change her feelings toward me."

Mai nodded. "She was not happy to hear from you, even through me. She was prepared to turn me away before your father stepped in."

I had guessed as much. My mother yearned for me to fail, if only so I could prove her right that I was a good-for-nothing blight on the family. If she'd been able to have any more

children, she'd have exiled me from the kingdom and wiped my name from the royal records.

"Growing up with a mother like that, I understand why Viv means so much to you. She is your *true* family." Mai maneuvered herself out of the circle. "I might choose the same path if I were in your situation. However." She lifted a finger as she wheeled past me and met my gaze. "There is always another option, whether we see it now or not. Keep in mind that though all may seem lost, the siren queen is not all powerful yet."

"I'll keep that in mind." If there were any way I could save Viv without handing over the Azurean Stones to the siren queen, I would do it. But I highly doubted anything would present itself.

"Good luck, Lia," Mai said, and I knew I was being dismissed. Mai had her limits for social interactions, and I respected them.

"I'll come visit again when things aren't so dire," I promised.

"Bring Vivianne with you. I miss her face," she said, smiling.

"Will do."

I left her room, closing the door behind me. I was tempted to take the lift across from her room down to the first floor and ditch Ryder for his antics earlier, but I needed him to take me back to the beach. And I had no doubt he'd find me and make me regret trying to leave him behind.

"I assume Mai was successful?" Justine asked as I came across her and Ryder waiting beside the stairs.

I nodded but kept the information I'd learned to myself.

"Good, then the two of you can be out of my hair." She turned to descend the stairs.

Ryder laughed as he followed her. "Don't lie, Justine, you'd love nothing more than for me to stick around awhile and have me in more places than *your hair.*"

I groaned, but to my utter disbelief, Justine actually *smirked.*

"Ugh," I shuddered.

Ryder nudged me with his elbow. "Don't worry, we wouldn't leave you out." He wiggled his eyebrows.

I didn't deign to answer.

Justine saw us out, making sure we didn't linger, and closed the door without more than a quick, "Don't come back too soon."

"I can't believe Justine didn't hex you for joking around with her like that," I said as Ryder readied to fly. He was already in his dragon form, shifting as his eye that I could see twinkled.

When we reached the beach, he transformed back to his human form and wrapped me in a hug. I returned the gesture, surprised how much I'd needed that after talking with Mai about my mother.

"If you need anything, Lia," he said, pulling back slightly to look in my eyes. "I'm always here for you. No matter what."

"So long as it doesn't involve a three-way with Justine," I teased, though tears welled in my eyes. "Thank you."

He hugged me close one more time before releasing me and letting me return to the long boat. I'd pulled my hood back up as soon as we neared the beach, and it sunk low over my eyes once more.

"Time to go," I said as I climbed into the boat.

The pirates nodded and rowed us back to the ship.

Finn

Marley pretended I hadn't spotted her the second I'd stepped onto the ship. She told me it had something to do with a bet she'd made with Nix, who was trying much harder, and more successfully, to go unseen. I wasn't about to make Marley lose a bet, so I ignored her. At least she wore a hat while on deck to hide her bright red hair. That would be a beacon to anyone working for the siren queen that we were on board.

"How long have you been on Brom's ship?" I asked Jack as he practiced his knot tying on a loose rope. His legs were stretched out in front of him, the rope draped over them.

I kept my head low as I sat beside Jack, my knees bent so I could rest my forearms on them.

"Two years now," Jack said, shrugging. "Ran away on my fourteenth birthday and I found Brom looking for deckhands in the Asmaran port."

Jack reminded me of myself when I first boarded Captain Jorge's ship. I'd been two years older than Jack, but that didn't mean I was any wiser or more experienced. I was loyal to a fault and eager to please, until I learned the dark side of being a pirate. It wasn't all camaraderie and making money.

"Your parents?" I asked, figuring no *good* parent would let their child run off and become a pirate at the age of fourteen, unless they were pirates themselves or ...

"Either dead or gave me up when I was born. Either way, I don't care to know who they were." Jack grunted as he worked to untie the knot once more. "What's it like being Captain Brom's son?" he asked, pausing in his efforts.

I resisted the urge to roll my eyes. "I wouldn't know. This is the longest I've ever been in his presence. He didn't deign to visit when my mother was alive, and afterward, he scorned me for becoming a better pirate than him."

Jack dropped the rope and placed his hands on his knees. "Better pirates don't lose their ships and crews to the sea," he said matter-of-factly.

I couldn't argue with him. Better pirates also weren't fighting the urge to vomit from the anxiety of being back on the water. I'd succumbed once, when no one was around, over the side of the railing.

Being back out on the water had been difficult. Nightmares of the siren queen taking down our ship plagued me at night, and visions of her controlling my crew flashed in my mind anytime the ship rocked a bit too hard. I thought it might get easier day by day, but so far, I still felt trapped. Trapped in my own mind and trapped on this gods-damned boat.

Talk to me again in ten years." I stood, patted Jack's shoulder, and walked away. My hood threatened to slip down, but I tugged it back up and aimed for the stairs on the opposite end of the ship. I'd wait for Lia's return in the bunkroom, where there was no chance of me being spotted by prying eyes.

As I crossed the main deck, Brom stepped into my path and cocked his head at me.

62

"I have a task for you," he grunted, beckoning me back the way I'd come.

I looked to either side of myself and curled my lip. "You couldn't possibly be talking to me. Why would you think I owe you anything?"

Brom ran his tongue over his top teeth. "Boy, I could have you thrown overboard. Don't think for one second I actually *need* you."

"Lia would—"

"Do you want to find your dame or not?" Brom asked, exasperated.

I begrudgingly followed him to his room. To my surprise, he continued into his bedroom and past the partition blocking his tub from view. There was a shadowy figure already in the tub.

Halting, I snapped, "What is this?"

Brom sniggered as he dipped behind the partition and I heard splashing from the tub before his shadow tore something from the other figure and an ear-piercing scream ripped through the air. My hands covered my ears before I realized I'd moved.

"No one will hear you, dear," Brom said. "The beauty of having a mage at my disposal means this room is soundproof."

"*What is this?*" I asked again, stepping toward the partition.

"A gift," Brom said, reappearing in full view. "She may have the answers you need to find your lovely lady."

"Vivianne. Her name is Viv—"

Brom dismissively waved his hand. "You have two seconds to get over here and start interrogating this bitch or else I'm killing her myself and disposing of her. She's been in here since the attack, and I'm in need of a hot bath."

I huffed but held my tongue and stormed past the partition to find a siren hissing at me from Brom's tub. Unbridled hatred filled her black eyes and though her scaled arms were tied behind her back, I could still see her claws.

The large window behind the tub had the curtains drawn so no prying eyes could see what happened in this room. Though, I imagined the only eyes out in the ocean would be other sirens.

"The queen will have your heads for this," she hissed.

"She'll have our heads either way," I said, prowling closer. I understood what Brom wanted me to do, and I was happy to oblige if it meant any hint at where Viv might be.

"I won't tell you anything," she said.

"We'll see about that." My lion claws slid from between my knuckles, through my skin. The pain was as excruciating as ever, but I didn't flinch. Blood ran down my hands, pooling on the floor.

I'd done plenty of interrogations like this before in the name of King Danforth, and for my own purposes. It was what had spurred the start of my reputation. Following through on threats is what kept it holding strong.

"I'll ask once, and I won't ask again. You can make it easier on yourself and answer now, or just let me know when you're ready." I kept my voice calm and even. "Where is the siren queen's lair?"

The siren's lips curled into a grin, and she cackled.

I heaved a dramatic sigh. "No one ever takes the easy way, but I do always get what I want in the end."

She at least had the sense to grimace at that.

Crouching down beside the tub, I draped an arm over the side of it and tilted my head as I took in the siren. Her eyes narrowed and I waited as I anticipated her next move.

She lunged, teeth bared as she prepared to sink them into my flesh, but my hand wrapped around her throat first, pushing her back against the tub, my claws scraping the sides of her neck.

"There will be none of that," I said, squeezing once before ripping my hand away, ensuring my claws dug in enough to leave blood trailing down her neck into the water.

The siren thrashed in the tub, sending water everywhere and thoroughly soaking me. I released an exaggerated sigh before thrusting my arm into the tub and pinning her tail down with my claws. It won me a screech so loud I wouldn't be surprised if my ears bled.

Her screech turned into a melody in an attempt to entrance me, but my other hand wrapped back around her throat, quieting the sound, before it could take hold.

"Try that again and I will rip your vocal cords out, and then you'll have to spell your answer for me in your own blood," I growled. "I'm going to need a drink to get through this."

As if he'd anticipated my need, Brom appeared around the partition with a whiskey glass in each hand. The golden liquid was like a beacon. Relinquishing my hold on the siren and moving out of her reach, I gratefully took a glass from Brom and relished the burn as it traced its way to my stomach.

On principal, I'd never tortured a woman before of my own accord, and even though sirens were more monster than woman, it was still unsettling to me. Brom seemed to have no qualms, pulling up a chair to watch as I took a break and sipped my drink.

Blood stained the water in the tub red. The siren's eyes were closed, but the gills above her collarbones fluttered. Brom must have been replacing the salt water for her in the bath to keep her alive ever since the attack, but I assumed it wasn't the

same as being in the ocean. She wouldn't last long living this way.

"How much do your claws mean to you?" I asked, breaking the long silence that had stretched between us all.

Flexing her hands behind her back, the siren opened her eyes and stared at me, offering no indication if she was ready to talk or not.

I'd retracted my claws to wield my knife. It glinted in the sunlight shining through a small crack between the curtains.

"Do they grow back if you lose them?" I continued, crouching beside the tub once more. "It probably takes a while, right?"

Her entire body stiffened. I reached down, grabbing her wrists, and flipped her over, making her readjust so her cheek was pressed against the back of the tub as she glared daggers at me.

"If I took the whole webbed finger ..." I mused.

Brom chuckled darkly.

My knife was sharp enough it easily slid between where her claw merged with the base of her finger. A gasp escaped her, and she thrashed, but I avoided her tail.

"You'll never find her," the siren hissed. "Even if I told you."

In one swift motion, I severed the first claw from her index finger and she screamed.

For a single moment, Viv replaced the siren in the tub in my mind and I could hear her screams ricocheting through me.

I gasped and dropped the siren's wrists. Backing away, I turned to the wall and slammed my fist against it.

The siren, though panting as she tried to breathe behind me, laughed. "He can't handle it," she said between gulping breaths.

I whirled around, practically skidding on my knees as I dropped beside her again and hooked my arm around to press my knife to her throat.

"Are you in my head?" I asked, teeth gritted.

"I know how to make a man *suffer,*" she said. Her eyes fluttered closed.

This time when I grabbed her wrists, I took off her entire middle finger. Screw playing games. To her credit, her scream wasn't as loud that time.

"Finn, please." Viv's voice came from the siren's mouth. "Stop hurting me." The siren couldn't hold herself together though and dissolved into a fit of laughter.

Nausea punched my gut, and my head pounded a steady beat.

"I warned you about using your siren gifts against me." I pressed the tip of my knife against her larynx.

"The queen can never be found. Only those within the vessel know where it is at any given time," the siren said. Her words made no sense, though.

"The vessel?" Brom leaned forward in his chair.

"You may as well kill me now, because I have no idea where your precious Vivianne is."

Without hesitation, I did as she said and drove my blade into the base of her skull. The quickest way to kill a siren.

Brom burst out of his chair. "Why did you do that?"

I rose from my knees, wiping the blood-stained water from my hands onto my pants, and put my knife back into its sheath.

"She was *mine,*" Brom growled.

"She had no more information to give us," I deadpanned. I felt dead inside. We were no closer to finding Viv, and the siren had gotten inside my head. I could still hear

Viv's pleading voice. Even though it wasn't me causing her pain, she could be suffering under the siren queen's command. And I was powerless to stop it.

Brom's hand clamped onto my shoulder and I leveled my gaze with his. Whatever he saw there had him reconsidering his next move. He ground his jaw and turned on his heel, snatching his whiskey glass from the arm of his chair.

In a daze, I found my way belowdecks to the crews' quarters, washing up with a bucket and water, before collapsing into my hammock. I stared at the wooden planks above me, and eventually a head of red hair swam into my hazy vision. Focusing, I blinked at Marley who leaned over me.

"Decided to come out of hiding?" I asked, my voice gruff.

"No. Just making sure you weren't dead," she said, poking my arm.

"Satisfied?" I asked.

She shook her head and scrunched her nose. "You smell like rotting seaweed and blood."

"Good. Maybe it will deter anyone else from talking to me."

Marley shrugged and bumped into my hammock, setting it swinging. I rolled my eyes.

"*The queen can never be found. Only those within the vessel know where it is at any given time.*" I repeated the words to Marley, and she sucked in a sharp breath. She knew well enough to wait for my explanation before asking questions. "What do you think it means?" I asked, thinking about the siren's words.

"Sounds to me like you're not looking for a lair, but a ship."

"A ship?" My brows pinched together.

68

"A ship. An underwater ship." Marley danced backward, out of my line of vision, and by the time I'd sat up, she was gone.

Of course. An underwater ship. Why hadn't I thought of that? If the siren queen was always moving, no one would ever be able to pin her location down.

"She's back!" Jack hollered as he came barreling down the stairs. "Captain said to fetch you because the mermaid is back!" He turned around and raced up the stairs. I wasn't too far behind him.

Brom tossed me my cloak which I'd left in his room, and I quickly pulled it on. Lia was being helped back onto the ship and her lips pulled tight as she met my gaze.

"Before we pull up the anchor," Brom spoke with the two men who had accompanied Lia. "I need you to dispose of something for me on land."

I knew he meant the siren. If we dumped her in the water, another siren may come across her and we'd bring down the siren queen's wrath on us. We needed to stay off her radar for as long as possible.

"You," Brom pointed at Lia and hooked his thumb back toward his cabin. "You're coming with me and lion boy." He smirked at me before turning away. We followed him without question. I caught a glimpse of Tabby and the twins, Leo and Atty, peering through the rails from the upper deck. I cocked an eyebrow at them, and they moved out of sight. I hadn't seen them around since we'd boarded the ship, but I'd also been avoiding them. I wasn't sure how to act around them since they were technically my siblings, but I hadn't known they existed until a week ago.

Lia and I sat across from Brom at his desk.

"What did you learn?" he asked as two of his men carried a bundle out of his room. I swallowed back the bile rising in my throat and focused on Lia.

"Azurean Stones. That's what the magical item is, or items I guess if they were never put into a necklace or crown. There are three Stones, and they are said to have been stolen by a powerful mage on their way to the queen of Sylvane at the time. Long before I was even born," Lia said.

"What connects that mage to Jami's parents? Hundreds of years separate the two ..." I shook my head. It didn't make sense.

Lia mimicked my movements. "I've no idea. My father only knew of the Stones up until that point. Otherwise, they are a mystery."

"Your father?" Brom asked, his curiosity piqued. I imagined he had some ridiculous notion he might find a way to make a deal with the king of Thalassia to become king of the pirates or some nonsense.

Lia waved her hand to dismiss the comment. "It doesn't matter. I learned nothing that will help us."

I wanted to discuss the topic more, but not in front of Brom. So, I sighed in resignation and stood.

"No point wasting any more time, then. We should start searching for the island on the map." I pointed to the map on Brom's desk.

"It's most likely cloaked with a ward, so we won't be able to physically *see* it," Lia said. "That is one useful thing I learned, though I'm only guessing."

Brom groaned. "We can't do anything with *guesses*. I need a heading, or else we're not leaving this spot."

"We'll get you a heading," I said, putting my hand on Lia's shoulder. "Give us till morning."

70

Brom nodded his dismissal and we retreated to Lia's room.

We hadn't told him about Jared yet. Brom assumed he was one of my men, and I'd let him believe that. I'd bring him into the planning once I trusted him, and once I knew we were close enough that Brom couldn't use him for his own gains.

"Tell me you were able to learn more than what you told Brom," I practically pleaded with Lia as she slumped down onto her bed.

"Nope," she said, popping her 'p.'

"We're fucked," I grumbled sitting on the end of the bed and dropping my head into my hands. "And there's no way of pinpointing where Jami and Viv are. They're on an underwater ship. The siren queen's lair *moves.*"

Lia let out a groan to match mine and fell back against her pillows. "I'm assuming the dead siren in Brom's room is how you gleaned that little bit of info," she said. "I could smell the rotting seaweed as soon as I stepped back onto the ship."

I didn't bother confirming for her.

"We need Jocelyn to respond, or we have no way of finding that island," Lia said. "Ryder told me he's flown into wards so seamless they didn't even flicker when he struck them."

"The amount of magic that would consume ..." I mused, thinking of how hard it would be to maintain a ward of that magnitude for so long.

Lia sat up, and I craned my neck to look at her. She pulled her hair back out of her face, keeping her hands atop her head as she appeared thoughtful.

"An insane amount of magic," she breathed. "It's impossible. It must be another type of shield that doesn't consume as much. A confounding spell, or environmental type," she rambled.

"Or it's not as seamless. Maybe if we hit it with a ship, it will reveal itself," I suggested but Lia scoffed.

"If that were the case, it would have been found by now. We have to assume it's been shielded for twenty years or so, because that's about when Jami's family came into their money, right?" She locked eyes with me, hope glittering there. I noticed Jami's lucky coin clutched in her fingers as she ran her thumb over it.

"He was ten, so eighteen or nineteen years, yeah," I said.

"I can't imagine they'd want something so precious too far from home, or else they wouldn't be able to check on it from time to time," Lia continued, following her thought spiral. "So, we should sail for Sylvane."

"If we're wrong, we're wasting weeks of our time," I pointed out.

"Do you have any better ideas?" she snapped. The desperation in her voice was clear and I didn't have the heart to squash the little hope she had left.

"I'll let Brom know we're headed for Sylvane. Hopefully we'll hear from Jocelyn in the meantime, and she'll be able to give us a more precise heading."

Lia nodded and slouched back against her pillows. If anyone was going to figure out this mess, I would place my bets on her.

That night, Lia, Jared, and I sat in Lia's room on the floor with a crude recreation of the map drawn on parchment between us. Brom held the true map and wouldn't let it out of his sight.

"Recognize anything?" Lia asked, staring Jared down.

"This." He pointed to Jami's family crest in the corner. Lia had done a great job of drawing that. It was the one thing she

spent more than a few seconds on. "It was on some of the documents my brother had. He was obsessed with it and doodled it often."

"Okay." Lia drew out the word. "Anything else?"

"No. I never saw any maps in my brother's possessions. As you heard in the prison, though, he was obsessed with how to get to the magical object. There are three wards, or barriers, keeping it safe."

"As we've surmised." Irritation seeped into Lia's tone.

I cleared my throat. "Do you know what kind of wards?" I asked, trying to steer the conversation to something useful.

"One is a magical beast of some kind. Possibly a dragon, or a kraken, they sound similar, so I wasn't sure what he was muttering." Jared leaned over the map, tracing a line in the shape of a 'U' at the mouth of a cave. "I'd guess more likely it's a kraken. This looks like a good spot to keep one."

It was an inlet which looked perfect to sail the ship into to reach the cave. But if Jared was right, and there was a kraken there, we'd avoid it if possible.

"And the ward concealing the island itself," Lia chimed in.

"That would make sense," Jared said, circling the island with his index finger. "Marcus talked about fog a lot, so maybe that's what he meant. A fog that confuses whoever sails into it, and it makes sure they sail past the island every time."

"Marcus?" I asked, furrowing my brow.

"My brother," Jared clarified.

I pursed my lips. Viv had only ever referred to him as Humer; I'd never known his first name. I didn't like having anything else to humanize him. The first chance I got, he was dead for what he'd done to Viv.

Jared continued. "The third ward is on the magical item itself. Some kind of magical barrier, or spell, to deter anyone from taking it." He pointed to the center of the cave.

Lia groaned. "Still doesn't tell us *where* the island is."

"He mentioned three brothers, too. They seemed to be important to the whole thing," Jared said.

"Jami has two brothers, and his family crest is on the map," I pointed out. "It may have something to do with them. Which would explain why the siren queen wanted Jami."

"Why kill Roland and not take him instead of Jami?" Lia asked.

"We never actually *saw* Roland being killed. He was taken from the rowboat. It was everyone else who said he was dead," I reminded her. There was a very real possibility Roland was still alive, and in the siren queen's possession.

"We need to find the third brother then." Lia slapped her hands on her knees. "Where would Charles be?"

I shook my head. I hadn't seen Charles since the day Jami and I sailed away from Sylvane.

"We could ask Brom. Roland may have mentioned him and his whereabouts," I suggested. "Otherwise, I think we'll have to wait on Jocelyn's response for that as well."

"If you think of anything else," Lia said to Jared. "Find one of us immediately. Don't talk to anyone but us about this."

"Okay," Jared agreed.

Jared and I left Lia behind in her room to return belowdecks. I made him sleep in the hammock beside mine so I could keep a close eye on him, but I knew Marley would also watch him, even without me asking. I pretended not to notice her as we walked to our hammocks and couldn't help but laugh to myself as she gave me a one finger salute.

74

For once, the siren queen wasn't the monster in my nightmare.

Phil sat strapped to the chair in front of me, blood caking his blonde hair and dripping from the wounds my claws had made in his thighs.

"All the king wants to know is where your friends came across the large sum of gold," I drawled as I paced in front of the chair.

Phil coughed, more blood splattering across his shirt.

King Danforth allowed pirates to make port in Asmara, so long as they paid their dues. Like any other king, he needed some way to keep his kingdom running smoothly and keep the people happy and well fed.

Placing my hands on the arms of Phil's chair, I leaned in, closing my eyes for half a second, and when I opened them, it wasn't Phil staring back at me, but Viv. I wanted to reel back, to free her from the restraints, but the scene continued to play out as it had happened all those months ago.

"I told you all I know," she said, fists clenched and teeth gritted against the pain.

"No," I said. For some reason, though I couldn't move freely, my words were not trapped in this replay. "I don't want to hurt you."

"Then don't." Viv's fingers uncurled and grazed my wrist.

My claws slid out, and I tried with all my might to retract them, but I was not in control of this nightmare.

As I'd done to Phil, I slammed my claws down, through Viv's hand and the arm of the chair, ripping them free. Viv's screams had me gagging from the pain it caused me to hurt her.

"I can't stop this," I gasped.

75

"Yes, you can. Why are you doing this?" Viv sobbed and I let out a scream of frustration.

"Captain!" Marley shook me awake. "You're going to wake the whole ship," she warned in a hushed voice.

"Shit," I mumbled, half asleep. Rolling off my hammock, I rubbed the sleep from my eyes and stretched my arms over my head. "I need some air."

The cool night air took the edge off my nightmare, but nothing could erase Viv's screams as I'd used my claws on her.

I gripped my head in my hands and let the howling wind drown out the sobs that wracked me.

Nix

Lia looked bone-weary. All I wanted was to wrap my arms around her like we always did for each other. But I kept my distance. I sat in the crow's nest with one of the other pirates—Harlan, or Barrow—I'd befriended.

Whatever his name, he didn't talk much, which was perfect.

I bristled as Marley waltzed by Lia without Lia so much as lifting her head. She was so lost in thought; she hadn't noticed the familiar face swabbing the deck.

From the crow's nest, I could see Finn's younger siblings playing with Callum around the helm. They spent most of their time up there. Finn watched them from where he sat beside Lia. They both had their hoods up, but I spotted his gaze occasionally drifting back to the children. I wondered if he'd try to talk to them at some point.

"Jerky?" Harlan grunted. I was going with that name since Barrow didn't fit as well. Despite his graying, scraggly hair and dull brown eyes, he seemed as sharp as ever.

I took the jerky he offered and chewed it slowly. I didn't usually eat meat, but when you were stuck on a ship in the middle of the ocean, you took what you could get.

Once Lia and Finn disappeared belowdecks, I climbed down from the crow's nest. Marley met me as I reached the main deck and leaned against the mast with her arms crossed.

"Any good sightseeing?" she asked, smirking. All I could think about was our kiss from the day we'd boarded the ship, but I had no idea if it had affected her as much as me.

"More of the same," I said. "Ocean, pirates, gorgeous redheads swabbing the deck." I bit my lip to keep from smiling and turned my head away but kept her face in my peripheral to see her reaction.

As always, she had none.

Pushing off from the mast, she strolled by me, pausing to say, "Kegan does have a nice form, I'll admit, though I've got my eyes on someone else."

For a second, I was utterly baffled, until I realized there was *another* red head who had taken over for Marley swabbing the deck. His name must have been Kegan.

"Oh yeah?" I asked, but Marley was already walking away. She turned enough to wink at me and disappeared into the shadows leading down the stairs.

I slapped my palm against my forehead. *Idiot.* I could never tell if Marley was flirting with me or not.

Returning to the crow's nest for the remainder of the day, I let my thoughts wander to Viv and what horrors she may be facing. I needed to stay focused.

That night, a rowdy card game started on the main deck. Table and chairs had been set up with about twelve pirates gathered around. Only a few played at a time, and I couldn't really see from the crow's nest how they played, but it seemed fast paced from all the excitement.

An unmistakable head of dark red hair peeking out from beneath a hat stood on the outskirts talking with ...

"Liar!" I hissed under my breath. Harlan didn't react.

Slipping down the mast from the crow's nest, I wove around the back of the group of pirates until I was within reach of Marley.

" ... could be underneath us right now for all we know," Marley said.

"Doubtful. We'd be dead if that were the case, I'm sure," Finn responded, not taking his eyes from the card game. "I'm turning in for the night." He gave Marley a pat on the back before leaving her alone in the small crowd.

I closed the distance between us and waited for her to notice me.

Much to my amusement, she jumped a little when she finally found me beside her.

"How long have you been there?" she asked, her brow wrinkling.

"Long enough to know you've lost me my bet," I said, pointing an accusing finger at her.

"Lia still doesn't know you're here," she reminded me. "So, until then, our bet is still on. Feel free to push me into all the closets necessary to avoid detection." Her eyes sparkled and I stopped breathing for a second.

"What were you and Finn talking about?" I asked to distract myself from the feelings swirling around in my chest, making it hard to breathe or think straight.

"The fact that the siren queen's lair is constantly moving. That's how she's been able to keep it hidden all this time," Marley explained.

It made sense, but it didn't make our quest any easier. It would probably only fuel Lia's current plan of making the trade. There was little to no possibility of us finding Viv and Jami on our own.

"We'll find them, *and* we'll stop the siren queen," Marley said, nudging her shoulder against mine.

"You're only saying that so I don't pitch myself overboard," I mumbled.

She put up a finger. "One, I don't comfort people, so no, that's not why I'm saying that. And two, you're a mermaid. You can't drown." Marley laughed and I joined her.

"An unfortunate side effect of my kind," I teased.

"Do you miss the water, like I miss the sky?" she asked, her expression becoming somber.

"My body aches being so near the water and unable to shift." I stretched my arms in front of me as if that would dull the ache. "Why don't you fly for a while?"

Marley shook her head. "It would be a beacon for the siren queen. She knows surrounds Finn, and a hawk flying over a pirate ship is quite an obvious marker."

A cheer went up around us as someone won the card game. Everyone shifted, swapping seats for new contenders. I turned toward the railing and leaned my forearms on it, clasping my hands and squeezing them tight.

Marley turned to join me, her shoulder brushing mine as she mimicked my stance. She didn't move away from where our shoulders touched. I was always hyper aware of her when she was around, and it drove me a little crazy.

"It's going to be a couple weeks before we reach Sylvane," I said. "If we make it that far."

"I think the hope is we'll hit some kind of magical wall first, indicating the hidden island," Marley said.

"Lovely." I scoffed. There was little to no chance of that happening.

We continued watching the waves break against the side of the ship as it cut through the water.

Marley pulled her flask from her pocket, sipping whatever concoction she had inside. I tried, and failed, not to stare at her mouth as she licked a drop from her lips.

"Want a taste?" she asked.

"Mmm," I mused, licking my own lips.

Marley chuckled.

Shaking my head, I dipped my head to hide my blush and rested my chin on my arms as I returned my focus to the ocean.

"Your loss." She returned the flask to her pocket and pushed herself away from the railing.

"How did you meet Finn?" I asked to keep our conversation going. I didn't want to lose her company yet. Leaning back against the railing, she tapped her chin.

"It was either at a bar, or in a ditch outside one." She smirked. "He pulled me out of a ditch a time or two, and I can't recall if that was the first time we met, or the third. I wasn't always so pulled together, you know."

I glanced up, locking eyes with her. "In Sylvane?"

"Home, sweet, home." She cringed. "Or, it should have been. Now the sea is the only home I have. Nothing for me back in Sylvane."

I nodded in understanding. "I feel the same about Thalassia. If I had the choice, I'd never go back there."

"You always have a choice," Marley said.

I straightened, turning around, and propping my foot back against the side of the ship. "I serve Lia, and if she returns to Thalassia, so will I."

"Seems burdensome. I am loyal to Finn and will follow him to the ends of the Earth now, but if I ever decide I want to go or do something else, I'm gone," she said matter-of-factly.

The boat creaked and rocked as we hit a large wave, sending spray over us. Marley tilted her head back, closing her eyes, and took a deep breath. I admired her independence. I'd never be able to survive without my sisters, and I'd never want to. They were a part of me.

"I think I'm going to turn in for the night," I said, taking a step away from her, as much as I wanted to stay there with her all night.

Opening her eyes, she smiled at me. "Goodnight, Nix."

Jami

"I have to talk to Roland again," I muttered, trying not to catch Humer's attention. He was especially skittish today.

Viv shifted beside me and looked up at me. We sat shoulder to shoulder against the wall.

"We don't even know where the siren queen is keeping him. He could be anywhere," she pointed out the obvious. I'd been puzzling that out since I saw him.

"We're at the bottom of the ocean with no way of escape," I said.

"Speak for yourself." Viv nudged my shoulder with her own. "If I can get out of here, I can shift and swim back to shore."

"If you aren't recaptured first. But that's not my point. My point is that maybe they'll let us explore a little."

"Don't," Humer snapped. "Don't let them catch you."

Viv and I continued as if he hadn't interrupted.

"Esme seems the more lenient of our two guards," I said. "Maybe if we ask to stretch our legs, she'll let us."

Viv sighed. "Doubtful. Raf is always with her." She traced a crack in the tiles beneath us with the tip of her finger.

I patted my pocket, feeling for my lucky coin, before remembering again that I'd given it to Lia.

It had been a day since the vessel had started moving, and we'd only seen the guards once when they let us use the bathroom. It wouldn't be long before they returned.

"Shh!" Humer hissed.

A few seconds later, the door opened and Raf strolled in with Esme close behind her.

"Up," Raf commanded and waved the electric prod at us, motioning for us to stand.

We did as we were told, ready to be out of the closet, even if it was just to piss. "Walk." Waving the prod again, she pointed it out the door.

Viv led the way with me and Humer close behind.

"Zap, zap," Humer said, laughing as he walked.

"I have no idea why the queen thinks this guy is going to be of any use," Raf muttered.

Turning my head, I saw her and Esme out of the corner of my eye.

"She said he holds the key to finding the Stones," Esme said.

Stones. They knew what the magical object was.

"We have a map, don't we?" Raf grumbled.

Esme tutted. "Have you seen the map? It's impossible to figure out where the island it depicts is, and what we'll need once we get there. Apparently, he holds all that information."

"So why isn't the queen questioning him?" Raf asked.

"Listen to him for five seconds, and you'll know. She's waiting for him to stop talking nonsense," Esme explained. "In the meantime, we have Roland leading the way."

So, he must be around here somewhere. Hopefully he's not with the siren queen.

"How long are we going to be kept in a closet?" I asked, bracing myself for a shock. Surprisingly, it never came.

"Have a problem with your accommodations, do we?" Raf sneered as she came up beside me, her breath hot against my neck. I leaned away.

"I just find it interesting that my brother seems to be given much more freedom here than us, when he's also a prisoner." I had no idea if he was or not, but I'd find out.

Esme laughed. "Oh! He's got some nerve!" She danced up on the other side of me. "Your brother was never working against the siren queen, unlike the two of you."

"What about Humer?" I jerked my thumb at him. "He wasn't working against her either."

Esme shrugged. "He's crazy. We're not letting him around anyone else."

We stopped outside of the bathroom, Humer went first, as usual. I always tried to avoid looking out the long glass window into the open ocean, but I couldn't tear my gaze away. This time, we were moving, and more light filtered through the water. Fish and other sea creatures were visible, though swimming as fast as they could away from the giant contraption moving through their space.

My eyes shuttered closed.

I gasped for air as the pressure released from my shoulders, letting me go above the water, finally.

"You should just stay down, Jamesy," Charles said, from beside Roland, who had been the one holding me beneath the waves. Every time we visited the beach, on the one decent day of summer, they'd ensure to find a time to dunk me under and remind me how little they cared for me. I always tried to avoid them, but they found me every time.

"What good are you?" Roland joined in the jeering. *"No shifting, no magic. You may as well not exist."*

"Jami," Viv's voice broke through my thoughts. "Your turn." She held my shoulder and urged me toward the bathroom.

I shook my head to clear it. "Right, sorry."

After we'd all used the bathroom, our guards led us back to our closet.

"Would I be able to request a visit with my brother?" I figured I may as well ask. "I haven't seen Roland in almost ten years, and I'd like to talk to him."

Raf kept walking as if she hadn't heard, but Esme slowed and walked beside me.

"The siren queen might be interested in having the two of you together to look at the map, since it is your family's island. I'll suggest it," she said. "But don't expect much."

"Thank you." I decided not to get my hopes up. However, a few short hours later, Esme and Raf were back at our closet to escort me to the siren queen's room.

I hated to leave Viv alone with Humer, but she assured me she'd be fine. I knew she could take care of herself, and Humer was in no state to overpower her in any way if he decided to try anything.

Esme and Raf flanked me as I shuffled through the halls to the siren queen's room. The only sound was the echoes of our footsteps until Raf rapped her fist on the door and swung it open to reveal their queen.

The siren queen sat in front of her marble table again with the map laid out before her.

"This island is located on the other side of my ocean," the siren queen said to Roland as I walked in. "My vessel can

86

move faster than the average ship, but it will still take us a week to reach it."

Roland stood beside her, closer than I'd ever dare get, with his hand braced on the table as he leaned over the map. He knew it was a fake and yet studied it so intensely, as if it were real. *Maybe he doesn't know, but there is no way he doesn't.*

"Ah," the siren queen's eyes lifted to mine. "You've arrived. Come." Her voice reminded me a little of a snake. Low, drawn out, and breathy, as I imagined a snake shifter may sound. This time there was no pull toward her, she was not using her siren power, thankfully. I listened all the same and stood beside Roland, mimicking his stance and leaning over the table to assess the map.

"I'd never seen this map before a few weeks ago," I said.

"That's not true," Roland drawled. "You may not remember it, but you've seen it once before, when mother and father first acquired the island. It was nothing special then, of course. They chose to hide the Stones there and added all the wards that protect it."

My eyes widened. Roland knew much more about this than I'd thought he might. Of course, he was a few years older at the time the Stones were hidden, so it made sense he'd remember more of the details, though I remembered none.

In fact, other than the few memories I had of being tortured by him and Charles, I didn't have many memories at all from my childhood. Meeting Finn stood out, and a few happy memories with his small family, but that was it.

"A kraken lives in this inlet here. Don't let the size of the inlet fool you, it's much deeper than you'd imagine," Roland explained.

"I can deal with a kraken," the siren queen said, huffing a laugh. The hairs on my neck stood at the sound.

"I don't know what kind of ward is on the Stones themselves, that part is a little fuzzy in my memory," he said, shaking his head.

"Maybe my other prisoner will know when I question him." The siren queen tapped her long nails on the table, and I cringed. I assumed she talked about Humer, but there was a chance she meant Charles.

"What of our brother?" I asked Roland, but the siren queen spoke first.

"Yes, where shall I find him?"

Roland shifted beside me, pulling a hand back to run it over his chin-length, red hair. He and Charles both had inherited our father's hair color, while I'd gotten our mother's brown hair.

"I haven't seen Charles in almost as many years as you, brother," he answered me, and the siren queen watched him intensely. "I left Sylvane shortly after you, and never looked back."

"You had a picture of mother and father in your cabin on the ship," I reminded him. I hadn't even had that much.

Roland's head bobbed slowly.

"This isn't a family reunion," the siren queen snapped. "You're here to tell me about this island, or else I will return you to your rooms."

"Of course," Roland said, clearing his throat. He bumped against me, something dropping into my pocket as he leaned forward over the map. "There is a kraken here, guarding the entrance."

I didn't dare move to see what he had put in my pocket in case I caught the siren queen's attention.

"As you said. That might be a nuisance, but easy enough to deal with." The siren queen's tentacles slithered beneath the table and I cringed as one brushed my boot.

Roland nodded and continued, "There is some kind of ward blocking the entrance to the cave as well. Once inside, you'll have no problem getting to the chest that holds the Azurean Stones. You'll have to contend with the final ward, which none of my family knows. It was something the mage kept from us, or maybe we forgot."

I wanted to kick Roland for giving her all this information, but it wouldn't be of any use unless she actually *found* the island, which this map wouldn't lead her to. This island was a recognizable one located west of Asmara. I had no idea where the real island was.

"And we are headed in the right direction?" the siren queen asked, flicking her gaze between me and Roland.

Roland lifted a shoulder. "As far as I know."

As Roland spoke with the siren queen, I made the mistake of looking up at the glass ceiling overhead. The ocean loomed above us, threatening to come crashing in at any moment.

I gasped, my breath catching in my chest as I tried to remember how to breathe, and I reminded myself that I wasn't drowning as memories of being shoved under water by my brothers floated around in my mind.

Roland nudged my foot with his own, trying not to draw attention to my panic, maybe, or just because he was annoyed with me.

"Afraid of the ocean?" the siren queen teased, but her voice dripped with malice as she leaned toward me and sneered.

My gaze dropped from the ceiling, and I noticed Roland's pinched features almost made him look *guilty*.

"Only a fool wouldn't be afraid of the ocean," Roland said. "Or a siren." He smirked at the siren queen, winking at her as if they were in on some joke together.

I was surprised he bothered to speak up for me, though, even if he softened his remark by seemingly flirting with the most feared and gruesome woman in the sea.

The siren queen turned her attention back to me. "Do you have anything useful to reveal, or are you simply wasting my time?"

My chest constricted as I tried to think of something to give her so she wouldn't suspect I'd gone there just to see Roland.

"Yes," I drew out the word, buying time. I could feed her information she already knew. At least then I wouldn't feel like I was betraying our fight. "Humer has been mumbling something about three locks, and three brothers. I assume the locks are the wards that Roland told you about, and the brothers are ... well us."

One second I was staring into the siren queen's depthless gaze, and the next I was yanked off my feet and held upside down by one of her tentacles.

All my breath whooshed out of me, and my face heated as blood rushed to my head.

"You think I don't know what you're doing?" she hissed, her teeth becoming even sharper as she bared them at me. "I know where your loyalties lie." She moved me closer to herself until I was only a few inches from her face.

Whatever Roland had slipped into my pocket slid down, and I flexed my thighs, hoping to keep it from falling out.

"I-I'm loyal to none but myself. If I remembered anything else, I'd tell you." It was mostly the truth.

Another tentacle slithered over my body, wrapping around my neck, and squeezing. "If my song worked on you, I'd use it to make you slit your own throat. But instead, I'll let you continue to rot in your closet." Her scowl turned to a smile. "I can't wait to see the look on Princess Aurelia's face when I slaughter her entire kingdom, with you at my side."

I clawed at the tentacle around my throat, desperate for air as my lungs ached.

The siren queen dropped me, and I crashed to the floor, scraping my back along the marble table's edge. I gulped down as many lungful's of air as I could.

"Take him back to his room," the siren queen demanded of Raf, pointing at me. "I want to speak with Roland alone."

Raf brandished her electric prod at me, and I headed for the door with her on my heels. In the hall, Esme met us and walked in front of me.

Casually, I stuck my hands in my pockets, my hand curling around the object Roland had slipped into one of them.

A coin? I thought, clenching my jaw and running my hand over my face to disguise my confusion. My thumb brushed over the raised design on either side of the coin and instinctively I knew it was the same as mine. But what it meant, I had no idea.

Viv

Humer stared at me as the door shut behind Jami. It was almost as if he were staring *through* me as his dull, green eyes glazed and his expression remained impassive.

I inwardly recoiled from his gaze, but I didn't move an inch, trying to maintain a sense of ease and confidence that I didn't feel.

Deep breaths, Viv, I coached myself. *He can't hurt you here. He has none of his tools. Without them, he is nothing.*

My words did nothing to soothe the inner turmoil causing nausea to swirl in my gut, and a pounding began behind my left eye.

"The three brothers must give to the chest to open it," Humer whispered, his eyes suddenly clearing as he leaned forward. "Vivianne, I've missed you." His change of topic and tone took me off guard and I jerked back against the wall.

His chuckle raised goosebumps on my limbs.

"Do not fear me, my dear," he said, tutting as he shook his head. "Those days are long gone." He looked toward the ceiling and sighed. "My mind was stolen, and I can no longer practice as I once did."

Stolen. Whether it was captivity or age that had taken his sanity, it was long gone.

"How do you know so much about the Stones the queen is looking for?" I asked, though I loathed to speak with him.

"I've heard you speak of a Captain Finn, is he your latest infatuation?" Humer's eyes sparked with interest and my chest constricted. We'd been too cavalier speaking around him, thinking him too far gone to notice anything we said.

I ground my jaw, not deigning to respond.

Nodding his head, Humer continued, "It will pass. As all things do. You once desired me in that way."

My old intrusive thoughts made real. I leaned my head back against the wall, closing my eyes. An image of Humer the first night I'd met him flashed in my mind. The gods were certainly testing me with this ordeal.

Deep breaths. In. Out.

"You haven't changed a bit, Vivianne."

I opened my eyes and looked at Humer once more.

"Why are you doing this?" I asked, the words coming out soft and breathy, unlike the vitriol I wanted to spew his way for all he had done to me. "You said you didn't have a chance to test if I could bear another shifter's child, but you had plenty of chances. You tried on so many others ..." I closed my eyes, grief-stricken at the thought of all those who had died for his experiments.

"I've told you, Vivianne. You were my favorite. I wasn't willing to risk your life until I either had the Stones or could ensure my success with you."

I saw red behind my eyelids, and I couldn't stop myself from being sick. Thankfully, I had enough wherewithal to aim for the corner of the room, away from myself.

93

Humer tutted and when I looked at him he put a finger to his lips. A few seconds later, the door swung open. Only Esme entered, shutting the door with a soft *click*. Her eyes went first to the vomit on the floor, and her lip curled.

"Where is Jami?" I asked, worried he may be in trouble, and I wouldn't be able to help him.

Helpless, yet again, the thought nagged at me.

Esme shook her head, turning her attention to me. "He is still with the siren queen," she said, her voice hushed. "I was sent to check on the two of you."

That seemed odd. They never *checked* on us, except to bring us food or take us to the bathroom.

I decided to take a shot and trust my instincts. Bree had contacted at least one siren who wanted to end this siren queen's reign; there had to be more.

"Why do you work for her?" I asked, starting out with something innocuous.

Esme leaned her back against the door. "Because I'm a siren, and she's our queen," she said matter-of-factly.

"So, you're not ..."

"Just say what you want to say," Esme snapped, rolling her neck and throwing her hands up.

"Fine. It's no secret we want to end your queen's reign. What I want to know is whether you also feel she has overstepped in trying to extend her time as queen."

I held my breath as I waited for her answer and hope flared in my chest. It was dangerous to get my hopes up before she even indicated how she felt, but I couldn't help it.

Staring at the ceiling, Esme whispered, "Yes. She has overstepped by trying to extend her reign and for killing the one who was supposed to have taken her place."

94

When Esme looked at me again, tears filled her black eyes, and her grief was almost palpable.

I leaned forward, balancing my elbows on my knees. "The siren who she killed, was she the one who washed up on the beach? The one who talked with my friend Bree."

Esme nodded.

Bree had been right that some of the sirens may be on our side, or at least willing to help bring down their queen.

"I'm so sorry for your loss. If you truly want to end the siren queen's reign, then please, help us escape. If we can get out of here, we can take away some of the siren queen's leverage against our friends and help them find the Stones before she does."

Esme wiped away her tears. "I will help you escape," she said. "But I'm not doing it for you. I'm doing it because it's what Davine would have wanted. She died talking to your friend, trying to find a way out of this endless reign, and I won't let her have died in vain."

"If we escape, we're so far beneath the surface Jami and Humer won't survive the pressure," I said quickly, not trying to waste any time.

Esme nodded. "I will ensure it is timed right, when we are close enough to the surface that they will survive. But you'll need to be ready when the time comes. And then, you must promise me, you will use the Azurean Stones to end her once and for all."

I nodded. "Of course. That's what we all want."

"Good." Esme pursed her lips, seeming to consider whether she should say more, but instead she turned. Before leaving the room, she added, "I'll send someone to clean that up."

95

I inched away from the mess, almost having forgotten it was there.

Once the door shut behind Esme, Humer said, "A traitor to her own kind. Interesting. Truly."

I couldn't bring myself to care about what he said as hope continued to spread in me and finally, I could see a light at the end of our dark, depthless tunnel.

Until Humer spoke again.

"Never forget, no matter where you go, you belong to me, Vivianne."

I stared at him, horrified, but he'd shut his eyes and seemingly fallen asleep. Wrapping my arms around myself, I tried to hold myself together while I waited for Jami's return.

~

That night, once Humer had fallen asleep, I told Jami about my conversation with Esme. Someone had come almost immediately to clean up after me. I didn't tell Jami about that or Humer's comments.

"At least we know we're not being watched in here now. But how long can you drag two humans through the water with you? If we're nowhere near land, or another vessel, we won't be able to escape to somewhere safe before the siren queen notices we're gone and sends someone to bring us back." Jami voiced the concerns that had been forming in my mind.

"I'm hoping Esme is a good enough planner that she'll think of that." It was hard to put my faith in someone I hardly knew, especially a siren, but we didn't have much choice.

"There would also need to be a good reason for the siren queen to bring this vessel closer to the surface. I'm doubting anything short of us being in range of the island with

the Azurean Stones would cut it." Jami leaned his head back against the wall. "I'm not risking letting her get her hands on the Stones just to save myself. You can escape without Humer and me. He's not worth the trouble anyway."

I flicked my gaze to Humer. His eyes were closed and his features softened, almost making me think I'd imagined his veiled threat earlier. I shook off the thought and turned back to Jami.

"What if we can lead the siren queen *near* the island, to a spot we know the others will be, and we can help them find the island before the siren queen and destroy her with the Stones? Then is it worth saving your life?" I asked, the accusation clear. "Lia and Finn probably think your life is worth more than a little inconvenience."

Jami shook his head. "*A little inconvenience?* The siren queen has the entire ocean at her disposal! Do you really think we'd be able to escape her and find the Stones before she catches on?"

"I think it's worth trying." I jutted my chin into the air, not willing to take any more arguments on the matter. "Let's get some sleep, and maybe we can talk with Esme more tomorrow. If she can communicate with Finn and Lia, then we may stand a chance at making this work." I wrapped my arms around myself and closed my eyes. There was no way I would get any sleep with all the plotting and planning running through my mind, but I couldn't talk about it anymore. I needed some alone time in a place where I could have none.

Eventually, I dozed off for a few minutes, or hours, I couldn't be sure. But when I woke Humer hovered over me as he had all those years ago whenever he worked on me.

A scream tore from my throat. Jami, who must have been asleep beside me, was on his feet in seconds, his fist

connecting with Humer's face and sending him slamming into the opposite wall.

"What the fuck are you doing?" Jami asked, planting himself in front of me as he continued to face Humer, who appeared dazed from the impact of the punch and hitting the wall.

A wave of humiliation washed over me as I realized I had shrunk right back into my defenseless self that had been locked up by Humer for two years. I wasn't that person anymore. I could easily defend myself, and yet I'd needed Jami to come to my rescue.

"She is *my* test subject, Jared, step aside," Humer said.

A deep cold crept in around me. "He thinks he's back in his bunker," I said, standing beside Jami instead of behind him. I wouldn't hide from Humer any longer. "He thinks you're his brother."

I flexed my hands at my sides as Humer stepped toward us. Long, sharp, talon-like nails extended from the tips of my fingers. There wasn't much magic I could do without being in my mer form, but I had enough for this.

"Take another step, and I *will* kill you," I warned Humer. He shuffled forward anyway, lost to his delusion.

Too many things happened at once. Humer lunged toward me and I raised my hands in defense while the door to our closet opened and someone came rushing in, yelling about everyone needing to cooperate.

Somehow, Jami got between Humer and I, separating us, and the electric prod which had been used to threaten us this whole time finally found its mark. It brought Jami down to his knees as Raf struck him in the side with it, his entire body jolting.

"Humer is the one who tried to attack me!" I cried out, pointing to Humer, who had retreated to his corner.

"You think I care who started it?" Raf asked, far too nonchalant after having electrocuted a person. "I will happily use this on all of you if I have to." She swung the prod around in her hand and pointed it at me.

Lifting my hands, I retreated a step. I would be no help to Jami if I was incapacitated on the ground beside him. He remained on his knees, his head hung, and his hands fisted against the floor as he breathed raggedly.

"That's what I thought," Raf said, leaving the room and slamming the door shut behind her.

I dropped down beside Jami, putting my arms around him. His entire body shook, and he didn't make any moves as I tried to comfort him. It was all I could do.

"It wasn't as bad as I'd anticipated," Jami said after a few more seconds, breathless. "Though I'd like to avoid it in the future." He chuckled.

I removed my arms from around him and he looked at me with a clearly forced smile.

"You shouldn't have stepped between us," I said.

"And then you would have been the one electrocuted. What would Finn and Lia think if they knew I'd allowed that to happen?" he teased, but his body still shook.

I harrumphed.

Lia

I'd been watching Jared for a while, wondering what could possibly be going through his mind. He was helping one of Brom's men swab the deck, and his brow was furrowed as if he was in deep concentration.

Since our chat in my room, I hadn't spoken with him. All I could think about when I looked at him was how he had played a role in Viv's worst trauma and gotten away with it. He should have been beside Humer in that jail cell, and yet he'd been playing warden.

"Careful, you might burn holes into him," Finn said as he plopped down beside me on the stairs leading to the quarter deck. We both had our hoods up, though we were concealed by the railing in our seated position.

"I hope I do," I grumbled. "He deserves it."

Crossing one foot over the other, Finn leaned back with his elbows on the stair behind him. "That he does. But if he can help us get Viv back, I'm willing to work with him. He can suffer later." He smirked but I knew he meant it.

"Tell me something to take my mind off of him and Viv," I said, leaning forward to put my head in my hands.

100

Finn's sigh was long and drawn out before he said, "I can't think of anything *but* her, so I'm not going to be able to help you there."

With a frustrated groan, I stood and leaned over the railing, letting my arms dangle over the side. It was a risk, because if there were a siren beneath us, they might see my face, but I couldn't care at that moment.

Staring over the edge of the ship, I imagined myself sinking to the depths of the ocean, not allowing myself to shift, but to feel that weight crushing down on me. My mother would *love* that. Her weak, too-compassionate daughter finally proving her right, that I didn't deserve a place in Thalassia. She'd be the most upset with my plan to save Viv and Jami. Not because I'd be putting Thalassia at risk, but because I'd let my emotions get the best of me. Despite that, I'd show her how ruthless I could be and prove that loving someone enough you'd do anything for them wasn't a weakness, but a strength.

"What's going through your head, princess?"

I nearly jumped overboard when a familiar feminine voice sounded behind me.

"Nix?!" I cried, clasping my hand over my chest as I turned to her. My breaths came in short gasps as I tried to steady myself. "What the hell are you doing here?"

Nix bowed her head to me. "You know very well I couldn't let you go off on your own."

"Were you following us the whole time? Even before we left port?" I yelled, fury igniting the blood in my veins.

"Of course I have! I may not agree with your decision but I'm sure as hell not going to let you get hurt." Nix's eyes blazed with a fury that matched my own.

Before I could think it through, I wrapped my arms around Nix and pulled her close, my anger seeping out of me.

From Nix's rigidity, I could tell she hadn't been expecting me to hug her. A second later, though, her arms were around me.

"I'm sorry I followed you," she said.

"I'm glad you did," I admitted. "I've missed you." *And Viv* went unsaid, but it hung between us. Tears pricked my eyes; I refused to let them fall.

Finn still lounged on the stairs behind us, and I realized he'd known Nix was on the ship.

"You knew she was here this whole time and didn't tell me?" I snapped.

He sucked his lower lip between his teeth and lifted his shoulder in response.

Nix ran her hand down my arm, bringing my attention back to her.

"Marley and I had a bet going, so Finn agreed to let me play it out," she explained.

I stared at her incredulously. "A bet? You *hid* from me because of a bet?"

Nix tucked her chin against her chest, but it didn't hide her smile. I couldn't stay mad at her and wrapped her in my arms again, making her laugh.

"I'm assuming you've lost your bet?" I asked, laying my head on her shoulder.

"You are more important to me than any bet. As soon as I saw you needed me, I threw any care about that silly bet out the window. Who cares if Marley believes me to be a master spy? We both know I am, and that's what matters." I felt as if she were saying this more to appease her own doubts than mine. I never questioned Nix's skills, and she knew that.

Footsteps made me turn to find Marley approaching us with her hands on her hips.

"I should have known you wouldn't let Finn leave Asmara without you," I said, shaking my head.

Marley tilted her head to the side. "Yes. You should have."

We decided to reconvene in my room to discuss everything we'd learned so far and make sure everyone was on the same page. As it turned out, Finn had known Marley had been aboard the ship the entire time and had already been filling her in, and Marley had been filling Nix in. So, there wasn't much to catch them up on.

"So, hopefully we come across-" I paused as someone knocked on the door. My eyes flitted over everyone in the room. There was no one else I was expecting.

Finn opened the door a crack and moved aside, letting Jared into the room.

"Coins," Jared sputtered, as if out of breath. "Something my brother muttered about constantly along with the three brothers was three coins. I just remembered."

A few seconds passed before I jumped off my bed and ran to the dresser, pulling open the drawer and grabbing Jami's coin I had stashed in there for safe keeping.

"Coin!" I yelled as if we'd unlocked the whole mystery and not just a piece of the puzzle. "Jami's coin!"

Finn held his hand out to me, and I put the coin in his palm. He studied it and nodded.

"Could be," he said.

"Three brothers." I clasped my hands with a clap. "Three coins. This is one of them."

The boat rocked and Finn winced. I took the coin back from him and he sat on the bed, closing his eyes as his brow furrowed. I didn't have time to worry about him.

"But what do they do? Why coins?" I asked Jared, as if he might have more unlocked information stored in his brain.

He shook his head. "Marcus never mentioned that around me. But you'll need all three to get near the Stones. I'm sure of it."

Marley flopped down on the bed, jostling Finn. He opened his eyes and glared at her.

Turning back to me, Finn said, "Roland and Charles will have the other two, and Roland is either dead or with the siren queen."

"So, we need to find Charles. There's no point in finding the island if we don't have all three coins." My heart raced from all the adrenaline as things were falling into place. I could *almost* see a clear path to getting Jami and Viv back.

"You'll need to convince Brom to sail all the way to Sylvane then, because I haven't seen or heard from Charles since we left over ten years ago," Finn said, not sounding very hopeful.

Without hesitation, I walked out the door and up the stairs to Brom's cabin. Callum opened the door after one knock and invited me in to meet with Brom. I was surprised Finn hadn't joined me, but then again, he had appeared a little out of sorts.

"To what do I owe the pleasure of your company?" Brom sneered, steepling his hands in front of him on his desk. I didn't bother sitting as I held out the coin for him to see.

"We need to go to Sylvane to find Jami's brother Charles and get the other coin," I said.

Brom gave an exaggerated sigh and leaned back in his chair. "We're not going all the way to Sylvane for a *coin*. We're finding the island and the Stones."

"We *need* all three coins," I told him. "They are essential to getting the Stones."

Another exaggerated sigh from Brom told me he couldn't care less about the coins nor their potential importance. I continued, "This one ..." I held up Jami's lucky coin. "Won't get us shit if we don't have the other two." My blood boiled. Brom didn't seem to understand the direness of the situation. He appeared to think we'd be able to go into the cave, smash our way through any shields or spells, and break open the chest or whatever held the Stones and be on our merry way. Magic never worked that way. If you didn't go about it the right way, it would backfire and leave you suffering, or worse.

"Then find a way to get the other two fucking coins without me sailing my ship all the way to Sylvane. You promised me those Stones, and if I don't have them in my hand soon, I know a siren queen who would *love* to have you."

"And you don't think she'd be dragging you down right beside me?" I hissed, raising a finger, and getting into his personal space as I leaned across the desk, one hand braced upon it. "Harboring Finn and me while trying to find the Stones under her nose? She will rip you limb from limb and eat your heart like she does all her other prey." I could see the reflection of my eyes in his, and the fire that burned in them. If he wanted to try and take me down, I'd bring him down with me.

He sniffed and curled his lip. "Get me those coins." After nodding to Callum, he stood and retreated into his bed chamber.

Callum escorted me out of the office, but I had no desire to remain there any longer anyway.

Back in my room, Nix chatted with Marley. Finn and Jared had left.

"Any luck?" Nix asked as I joined them on the bed, nuzzling into Nix's side.

I sighed. "Maybe. Who knows with Brom, though. Where did Finn go?" I didn't ask about Jared, not particularly caring where he'd gone.

"He said he needed a nap to clear his mind," Marley said. "He's trying to remember if Jami ever said anything more about his lucky coin." She held her hand out and I dropped the coin into it. "He never mentioned anything to me, other than his mother gave it to him."

Closing my eyes, I let Nix's warmth seep into me and comfort me as we'd always done in the past. It didn't feel the same without Viv on my other side, it was as if I was missing a piece of my soul.

"I don't think Jami knew anything about the coin being important, other than thinking it might bring him luck," Marley said as she studied the coin. "He would have kept it somewhere safer than his pocket if he'd known. Though, if I'd known, I would have wagered for it whenever we made our bets." She smirked as she flipped the coin in the air and caught it.

The edge of a migraine was creeping up in the back of my brain. It was only a matter of time before it took over and became a true hindrance. Maybe Finn had the right idea with a nap.

I stifled a yawn and said, "I'm following Finn's lead and getting some rest in hopes something will come to me in my sleep.

Nix relaxed beside me, settling in as well.

"I'll go ask around the ship. Maybe someone who was close with Jami's brother, Roland, will have some insight," Marley said. The bed creaked as she left, and the soft click of the door told me when she was gone.

"Sleep well, Princess," Nix said.

I huffed a laugh.

Finn

I was not used to spending a lot of time belowdecks. It did nothing to help me forget I was on the open ocean, and when the waves got bad, I was thrown back to that day I lost half my crew.

This day was no different. I lay in my hammock, eyes closed, as I tried to deep breathe my way through a particularly rough panic attack. A few other men were napping around me, but none paid me much mind.

"Uncle Callum said not to bother Finn," a voice whispered, and I recognized it as one of the twins. Either Atticus, who they all called Atty, or Leo.

"Well, Uncle Callum's busy right now," Tabby responded in a hushed voice.

I kept my eyes closed until something prodded my side.

With one eye open, I found Tabby, Leo, and Atty standing beside my hammock with wide eyes. Groaning, I opened both eyes and sat up slowly.

"What do you want?" I asked, bracing myself on the hammock so it wouldn't flip as I moved into a sitting position.

Leo and Atty moved behind Tabby.

"You're our older brother," Tabby said matter-of-factly and lifted her chin. "We wanted to meet you."

I ran my tongue over my teeth, trying to think of what in the world I could say to these kids that wouldn't scare or scar them for life.

"I'm Tabitha, and this is Leo and Atticus," she introduced them.

"I know," I said. "And I'm Finn."

"We know," they said in unison. I think it was the first time I'd heard the twins talk.

"Okay, then," I drawled. "You've met me."

"Do you want to play a game?" Leo asked, poking his head out from behind Tabby.

I stretched my neck, hearing a small *pop.* "Not particularly." The dejected look on Leo's face had me quickly adding, "But I'll play."

God, Finn, maybe you have gone soft, I thought to myself.

We played a matching game with a pack of cards up on the main deck. A few of the crew cheered on Tabby as they went about their daily chores. It made me consider whether growing up on a pirate ship was really such a bad thing. At first, I felt sorry for the kids, growing up surrounded by pirates. But now I realized, they had more protection and family than most kids their age.

"Didn't I tell you to leave him be?" Callum said as he came up behind the twins. Their shoulders went up to their ears as they giggled and hopped up, running away. Tabby followed them, laughing as she went. "Sorry if they were bothering you."

I shrugged. "Not particularly. They're good kids, it seems."

"They are," Callum said, pride clear on his face as he grinned and turned to watch them run up the stairs to join their father at the helm.

I hadn't noticed him up there and wondered what he thought of Tabby and the twins spending time with the son he'd excommunicated.

It was a bit of a struggle to get back to my feet after sitting cross-legged for so long, and I swore I heard Marley laughing from somewhere nearby.

Before I could return belowdecks to relax in my hammock, Brom came up behind me and tapped my shoulder.

"Come chat with me," he said, motioning over his shoulder toward his office. "We can have a drink."

We sat in silence for a solid five minutes, sipping our drinks, before Brom finally spoke.

"What is it that made you change your ways for her?" Brom asked, staring down into his glass.

"Huh?" I lifted my head to watch him more closely.

"Vivianne. The girl," Brom grunted.

I gripped my glass, the coolness calming me slightly. "I'm not talking about her with you." I took another sip of my whiskey.

Brom laughed. "That's just it. She's so important to you, you won't even let your old man in on her secret."

I rolled my eyes. "There's no secret."

Brom tapped his nails against his glass. "There must be some secret if she's captured the infamous Captain Finn's heart and turned him *soft.*"

I released a low growl from deep in my chest. My inner lion threatening to come out. "If you think I've gone *soft*, I'll be happy to prove you wrong."

Brom laughed again. "You think you can pretend I don't see through it all, but no matter how much we both hate it, you are *my* son. You are exactly like me, and I can call all your bluffs."

Heat rushed to my face. "I'm nothing like you," I snapped. "I wouldn't leave my child fatherless, or the mother to suffer the last of her days all alone."

Brom finally stopped laughing. His brows dipped and he lowered his glass to the desktop.

"Your mother was the love of my life, and I never wanted a child. Say what you want, but you were better off without me in your life."

I cocked my head. "If you never wanted a child, why do you have three living on this ship with you?"

"Their mother died giving birth to the twins and I had no choice but to take them with me. Callum raised them, I'll take no credit for that. I've tried once or twice to find a home on land for them, but they're attached to Callum and the rest of the crew."

"Hmm," I mused. It sounded to me like Brom may have a soft spot for his younger children. I couldn't bring myself to care, after years of shoving away any kind of association with the man, he was practically a stranger to me. "Do any of them have the shifter genes?"

Brom scowled. "None have shown it yet, but I'm sure at least one of them will."

"Is that how their mother died as well?" I asked more quietly, thinking of how my mother had died from bearing a shifter child when she was only human herself.

"No." Brom shook his head. "She was a shifter. I wouldn't make that same mistake twice. I'm not a monster."

111

"Contrary to what I've always believed," I said, almost joking, but there was truth to it. I *had* always considered him a monster. What other kind of man would abandon his son and dying wife the way he had?

The day my mother died was a vivid memory for me, and I cursed my father's name that day, over and over, blaming him for abandoning us. If only he had stayed, maybe he would have been able to save her.

Of course, I hadn't known at the time that it had been my fault she'd died. Since she had such little magic, she never should have been able to bear a shifter child, and yet she had. I essentially sucked the life out of her.

Brom cleared his throat. "Believe what you want. It won't affect me one way or another." He leaned farther back in his chair, the back of it touching the wall behind him. "Tell me one thing and I'll drop the topic for good. Is Vivianne your Leona?"

I had no way of knowing whether Brom had truly cared for my mother as much as he claimed to. And I had no reason to tell him the truth of my feelings for Viv. Yet something pressed me not to lie to him. Something in me yearned for this moment with my father, whether I considered him that or not.

"No. Viv is more than that. I will stay by her side so long as she will have me, whether she chooses to join me at sea, or return to her home in Thalassia."

"That's an awfully grand statement to make for someone you met only a month ago," Brom said, steepling his fingers under his chin.

"How long did it take for you to know Leona was *your* one?" I countered.

Brom lifted his chin. "A few days."

112

I chugged the contents of my glass and placed it back on his desk. "We're done here." Shoving my chair back, I stood and strode to the door.

"I'll do what I can to make sure you get her back safely," Brom called after me.

I didn't bother responding. I'd said more than I wanted to him, and I couldn't trust he'd keep his word. But warmth spread through my chest that I blamed on the whiskey, even though I knew better.

I bumped into Lia as I headed back belowdecks to my hammock.

"Going somewhere?" I asked her and she rolled her eyes.

"I'm looking for Marley. Earlier she said she would ask around to see if anyone who had been close with Roland knew anything more about the coins," she explained.

"She can't go far." We went down the stairs together, spotting Marley in her hammock. Lia walked over and leaned against the side of the ship beside Marley.

There were a few other men in their hammocks and some sitting in a corner, playing a game of cards.

"Any luck?" Lia asked Marley.

Joining them, I nudged Marley's hammock with my knee, making it sway. She scowled at me.

"Nothing," she said to Lia. "Turns out not everyone on this ship is happy with Brom's decision to work with you two."

I snorted. "They can get over it."

"They don't like the risk of having you on board, and I don't blame them." Marley kicked one foot over the other. "If the siren queen catches wind that you're on this ship, she'll take it down."

"Well, we don't have much choice now, do we?" Lia said. "As Finn said, they can get over it. I'll see if I can find someone to talk to me."

She turned to leave, when one of Brom's men, Terry, stood from his hammock, blocking her path.

"You don't belong on this ship," he said, his voice low and threatening as he stared Lia down.

"What the fuck did you just say?" I growled. Marley was right about people being disgruntled, but I didn't think they'd have the audacity to say anything in front of *me*.

"It doesn't bother me, Finn," Lia said, flipping her hair as she turned and walked around Terry. I waited until she was up the stairs and out of earshot before I turned back to Terry.

"Don't ever talk to her like that again." I glared at him, and my lips pulled back in a snarl.

"We wouldn't even be out here, searching for some imaginary island, if it weren't for you and that bitch," he snapped.

Before I could react, his fist connected with my jaw and blood dripped down onto the deck. It made me feel more alive than I had in weeks.

Laughing, I ran at him, wrapping both arms around his middle and tackling him to the ground. He tried pommeling my side, but I barely felt anything. Too much adrenaline coursed through me.

I swung my fist, reveling in the feeling of my skin splitting as it collided with his cheekbone. Strike after strike left more blood leaking from both of us.

People egged us on, but I hardly needed encouragement.

"That's enough," Callum's voice boomed in the space. Neither of us stopped until we were pulled away from each

other by the crew. Callum pushed Terry farther away from me and said, "Get out of here."

"I had it handled," I said, wiping blood from my chin with the bottom of my tunic.

"You were losing control, and I don't need them seeing that." Callum jerked his head to the stairs where Tabby and the twins sat wide-eyed as they watched the scene below them. As soon as I made eye contact, they scurried up the stairs and out of sight. Callum strode after them.

My entire body burned with the need to shift, and so I stopped fighting it. The shift came over me, reminding me why I was someone to be feared.

A roar ripped from my throat, and it echoed in the space around me. Anyone who had lingered belowdecks slapped their hands over their ears and ran for the stairs, scrambling to get away.

I laughed and it came out as a low rumbling sound. Shaking out my mane, I stretched my neck and let all the bones pop into place as my shift was completed.

"Always with the dramatics," Marley chided from her hammock. It swung slowly as she pushed a foot off the nearby wall.

Digging my claws into the soft wood beneath me, I whipped my tail back and forth. It felt *so good* to be back in my lion form. I wasn't used to going such long stretches without shifting. I could only imagine how Lia was feeling, since she couldn't shift even if she wanted to.

"*Please* rip someone's arm off," Marley teased. "It would really spice things up around here."

I ignored her and curled up on the floor, ready to take a nap while my body healed.

"Seems like I missed out on a good old-fashioned brawl." Nix's voice came from near the stairs.

"Indeed, you did," Marley said. Her hammock creaked beneath her.

I let out a warning growl, hoping they'd get the hint and fuck off, but they continued their chat. From how close their voices were, I assumed Nix had joined Marley on her hammock or sat on the one beside it. I didn't bother opening my eyes to find out. The magic of my shifted form was already healing my injuries from the fight. It was almost like being drunk, as my head spun, and warmth spread to all my extremities. Even with Marley and Nix's chatter, I managed to fall asleep.

Jami

"If Esme truly wants to help us get out of here, maybe she'll be able to get me a minute alone with Roland. He may have information that is vital to finding the Stones," I said, not caring anymore if Humer heard us. He was half out of his mind anyway; they'd never believe a word he said.

Viv lay on her back and stared at the ceiling. Her feet were propped up against the wall and her arms were stretched out on either side of her.

She opened her mouth to respond when the door to our room opened and Raf strolled in.

"You," Raf said, pointing to Humer. "You're coming with me."

Brows furrowed, I asked, "Not all of us?"

Instead of a verbal response, Raf pointed her electric prod at me in warning, and yanked Humer to his feet by his arm.

Humer left the room without complaint.

"Fuck," I breathed. "Think he'll spill everything for the siren queen?"

Viv righted herself, leaning her back against the wall and crossed her arms over her chest.

"He hasn't talked coherently for more than a minute or two since we arrived here. I doubt whatever he tells her will make any more sense than what he's told us," she said.

"I hope you're right. There's no way he'll let us know when he gets back. We'll be lucky if he *doesn't* come back."

"If only," Viv muttered.

~

Hours later when Humer finally returned, he curled in on himself in the corner. It wasn't until after the guards left that he began muttering to himself, "Don't tell her, don't tell her."

"Don't tell her what?" I tried asking, knowing it was most likely useless.

"Don't tell her, don't tell her, don't tell her ..." He continued as if he hadn't heard me.

I groaned. "If I have to listen to this all day and night ..."

"I will happily take him out," Viv said. "Just say the word." A fire seemed to burn in her gaze as she stared at him across the small space.

I couldn't imagine what was going through her head, but for what he'd done to her, I knew Humer would deserve whatever pain she might inflict on him.

Bending my knees, I put my elbows on them and leaned my head back against the wall. "If he didn't provide useful snippets every now and then, I'd say go for it. But we should probably keep him alive, at least until we retrieve the Stones."

Viv scoffed.

"She can't find the Stones. *I* need the Stones," Humer said, but his eyes were still glazed as if he was lost in his own mind. "To finish my work."

"You've lost your mind, old man," I said, trying not to become too frustrated with his ramblings. "Your work has been done for a long time. I thought spending half your life in prison would have made that stick."

Humer's eyes lifted and his gaze locked on Viv. "My work is never done." His lips lifted in a creepy grin that had me wanting to punch him again for daring to look at Viv that way. But, like always, Humer lost his thread of thought and drifted away, his eyes turning to the ceiling and muttering nonsense.

~

I picked at my stale food that night, not interested in eating as my stomach roiled from all the things that could go wrong with our escape. If Esme couldn't get us the window we needed, we'd be stuck down here until the siren queen decided to dispose of us.

It was the worst kind of feeling—being stuck down here unable to escape or change our fate without an outsider's help.

I couldn't even talk to my own brother to find out what the hell was going on and why he hadn't sold me out. Our short conversation in front of the siren queen had only brought up more questions for me.

"Your mind is reeling; I can feel the steam coming out of your ears from over here," Viv said, setting down her empty plate beside the door from where she sat to the right of it.

I leaned over, remaining seated, to set down my almost full plate on top of hers and leaned against the wall.

"If Esme can't get us all out of here, you need to leave us behind," I said. Viv's eyes widened and her jaw tightened. "I know you said you wouldn't leave me here, but one of us should

make it out alive. And I'm not saying don't let Esme try her way first, that's fine. But if it all goes to shit, *you need to leave.*"

Viv scooted closer to me. "It won't all go to shit, and I won't be leaving you behind. Don't ask me again because my answer won't change."

I groaned. "Then I guess we need to make sure Esme's plan goes off without a hitch." I'd find a way to talk with Roland again and have him help us if that's what it took.

Over the next two days, Esme wasn't with Raf when she came to take us on our bathroom breaks or to shower. I feared she'd been caught scheming and executed.

I'd had enough of waiting around. "You know," I started, an idea forming in my mind. "We've never checked to see if the door is locked, we've just *assumed.*" I stared at the door from where we sat, trying to remember if I'd ever heard the *click* of a lock.

"What are you talking about?" Viv asked.

"It's not like if we got out of here, we could actually *leave,* besides you, of course. But that means maybe they don't care enough to lock the door. They assume we'll stay put because where else would we go?"

Viv sighed. "You're trying to get us killed, aren't you?"

I chuckled. "Come on." I pushed to my feet and tried the door handle. "Low and behold," I said as it turned and the door opened.

Shaking her head, Viv stood and walked into the hall.

"You hold down the fort," I said to Humer, as if he would listen. He watched us from his corner but didn't move.

"Hallway is clear," Viv said. "But you better hurry up. I'm pinning this all on you if we're caught." Her voice was teasing but I heard the underlying fear.

In the hall, I avoided looking out any of the windows into the ocean. Each time I did, my stomach flipped, and I almost lost my breakfast.

We passed the bathroom and showers and came to a fork in the hall. I knew to the right was where we'd met with the siren queen, so I chose to go straight. It was the direction Roland had gone when we'd left the siren queen's room together a few days ago.

"Are we going to knock on every door hoping Roland opens one, and not one of the sirens?" Viv asked, keeping her voice low.

I held up my hand as I heard voices ahead and we stopped. There was a door to my right, but there was no telling what it led to. It could be the siren queen's bedroom for all we knew.

"Isn't there anyone else you could send?" one of the voice's said, sounding closer as she spoke. We couldn't wait much longer, or they'd turn the corner and find us.

Praying to the gods, I went for the door and opened it, pulling Viv into the room behind me. It was dark at first, but a ball of light flickered on at the back of the room, illuminating the space.

It was a closet filled with cleaning supplies. Nothing that could be useful to us, though.

"What now?" Viv whispered.

"Now we check the next room," I said. "Roland's room is in this hall."

"After you." Viv waved her hand in front of her. "I'll let you be the one to check the rooms. At least then I can run if you're wrong."

"You have such little faith in me." I put a hand to my chest, feigning being wounded. "Just wait. I'll find Roland."

The next door I checked was a bathroom. The third door was locked.

"This is it, I bet," I said. "Of course it's locked." I debated knocking, but if it wasn't Roland's room and someone else answered ...

"I'll do it," Viv offered, surprising me. "I'm the one with a built-in weapon." She lifted her hand and showed me her claws.

"Together," I said, raising my fist to knock. Viv nodded and I knocked as we braced ourselves. Viv stepped to the side so she wouldn't be immediately visible and could catch them off guard if it wasn't Roland. I stood far enough back I wouldn't be in reaching distance of whoever opened the door.

The lock clicked and the door creaked open enough for a face to appear. Roland's face. I released a huff of relief.

"James?"

I cringed at the name.

"We need to talk." I pushed past him and Viv followed me in, closing the door behind her. Roland didn't protest, but he crossed his arms and his features were tense.

"You shouldn't be out and about like this. If you're caught—"

"I know what will happen, but if we want to get off this gods-forsaken vessel, then I need to talk with you."

Roland tilted his head. "I'm listening."

"I have so many questions, but I don't have time for them," I said. "You lied for me and gave me your coin, which I guess is important somehow, so I assume you'll be willing to help Viv and I escape?"

He jerked his head in a nod. "The coin is your way to finding the island. Each of our coins disables one of the wards,

except for the final ward on the chest itself, but for some reason I don't remember ever learning how to deal with that one."

With Humer's obsession with the three coins, it made sense they played such an important role in uncovering the Stones.

"We can worry about that later," I said. "Esme is going to help us get out of here, but she needs a distraction. She said finding the island would give the siren queen a reason to bring the vessel close enough to the surface that I'd be able to survive the depth of the ocean."

"What do you need me to do?"

"You need to lie to the queen. Tell her you sense the island nearby and we need to move closer to the surface so you can know for sure," I explained. "Then we'll be able to escape and get your coin to Lia, who has mine."

"Lia?" He cocked an eyebrow.

I bristled. I refused to tell him about her. Just because he was agreeing to help us didn't mean he deserved to know anything about the woman I loved. I'd protect her from my brothers.

"Once we have all three, we can get the Stones and take down the queen. We won't leave you down here with her." Just because my brother had been horrible to me when we were younger, didn't mean I thought he deserved whatever the siren queen had in store for him.

"Don't worry about me. I can take care of myself."

"So, you'll do it?"

"I know it's not enough to make up for the years of pain Charles and I inflicted on you, but it's a step in the right direction. I'll do whatever you need me to." Roland reached his hand out as if he were going to put it on my arm, or shoulder,

but I moved out of reach and his hand curled as he returned it to his side.

My eyes narrowed in suspicion. I had to trust him, because otherwise we'd never make it out of this place, but every instinct in me screamed not to.

Lifting my chin with a newfound confidence, I said, "We have to get back to our room, but Esme will follow your lead once you're both ready."

"I'll walk you back to your room and clear the path if anyone comes along," Roland offered. "It wouldn't do for you to be executed before escaping."

Roland led the way, only having to deflect one siren from crossing our path, and we made it safely back to our room. He didn't linger once we were inside, not wanting to raise any red flags if Raf came to check on us.

"He's your brother," Humer said. "He looks like you."

It hadn't been a question, so I had no intention of answering.

"Three brothers, three, three, three," Humer chanted.

I groaned. "If only we could have stayed away longer."

Viv patted my knee. "We'll be out of here before you know it."

She was right. It was finally real. Roland would be able to spur our escape, and we'd be back with our friends in no time. The hope that gripped me was almost painful.

We're coming, Lia, I thought, hoping she might somehow sense my thoughts as I sent them out into the universe.

When I woke the next morning, Viv was gone.

Nix

Lia was still sleeping when I snuck out of our room. The sun had yet to rise, and the ocean was calm. It seemed like no one was awake, but I noticed Harlan up in the crow's nest.

Taking a deep breath, I strolled over to the railing and stretched my arms over my head. A soft hum filled the air, and I stiffened as I recognized it as a siren song. I peered over the railing and caught sight of a head of black hair bobbing on the surface, her black eyes piercing me as I locked my gaze on her.

"Finally," she said, moving in close to the ship so I had to look down at her. "I've been waiting for someone to notice me. I was tempted to pull out the full song and lure in a pirate to fetch one of you."

"What are you talking about?" I asked, gripping the rail tightly enough to get a splinter.

The siren glanced around before continuing. "I know where your friends are being held. Jami and Vivianne."

My breathing faltered. "Are you threatening to harm them?"

She shook her head. "No. I want to *help* them. But I need your help."

I narrowed my eyes. "How can I trust you?"

"I'm risking everything to talk to you," the siren hissed. "Find a way to trust me, because otherwise, your friends are dead."

I realized she was right. Whether I wanted to trust her or not, Jami and Viv's lives may very well rest in her hands. If there was a way to save them without handing over control of the seas to the siren queen, then I would take it.

Sighing, I leaned further over the railing. "Fine. Tell me why you're here."

The siren nodded, her gaze seeming to brighten, though her eyes remained black. "A mermaid named Bree came to me and another siren." She paused, almost as if emotion were taking hold. "You may have seen Davine's corpse washed up on the beach."

I knew exactly who she was talking about. I hadn't known the siren's name at the time, but she'd been a warning to us to stay out of the water. The mention of Bree brought a swell of grief and pressure built behind my eyes. "We've both lost people we care about," I said. "Get to the point."

"I want to help you end the siren queen's reign," she said. "And that starts with me helping your friends escape."

My breath hitched, and I wasn't sure I dared to exhale or else I might wake from a fever dream and find none of this to be real.

"The queen has them with her in her underwater vessel as she searches for the Azurean Stones. I have a plan to get them out, but it involves leading her to a decoy island where she thinks the Stones are hidden," she paused, giving me a knowing look.

"What do you mean?" I asked, unsure if she was indicating that she knew the map was a fake, and I wasn't about to reveal that.

126

"She's on a wild goose chase right now, and there is no way for me to get the humans out without the pressure of being so far beneath the surface killing them. We need to draw the siren queen to a shallower location and have a plan to distract her and all her guards so I can help your friends escape. Finding the Azurean Stones would be the proper distraction."

"And you believe she will do this for the decoy island? That she won't send someone ahead to investigate *before* surfacing?" I asked.

"I have someone who can convince her to get close enough to the surface," she said, bobbing with the waves.

I ground my jaw. This was probably our only chance of getting them back safely without needing the stones. Sighing, I said, "What do you need me to do?"

"You need to change course, so you'll be close enough to help them escape. Not so close that the siren queen will be suspicious, though."

Shaking my head, I said, "We need to find the real island before she does. We can't risk going off course." As I said it, though, I realized we weren't even sure if we were *on* course.

"I understand your concerns, but we don't have time to debate this. We will arrive at the decoy island in a few days' time and I will have to act. If you want your friends to survive, then you will agree to this. Trust me when I say that I have no interest in the Stones, other than to ensure they don't fall into the queen's hands. All I want is for my life to go back to the way it was before the queen decided she wanted to paint a target on all the sirens' backs and kill any of us who didn't agree with her unending reign."

"I have to talk to Lia about this. She'll make the final decision."

"I've already been gone from the vessel for too long; I need an answer *now*. I'm supposed to be scouting for the island, though I already know exactly where it is."

I considered it all for a minute. If this siren was telling the truth, then Jami and Viv would be back, safe with us, in a few days. If she wasn't ... then what? We might lose a day or two of searching for the island no one could seem to find anyway. It didn't seem like much of a loss in the grand scheme. And, if Viv and Jami were safe once more, then Lia and Finn would have no reason to want to give the Azurean Stones to the siren queen. Instead, we could use them against her and make the sea, our home, safe for all again.

"Okay. We'll do as you ask." It wasn't hard to make the decision, knowing all the benefits that would come out of it.

"Sail northwest, and in four days' time, your friends will be returned to you. I will only need you to enter the water so I may mind speak with you to pinpoint your location on the day of the escape."

"Very well," I said, inclining my head to her. "Thank you," I added, even if she was tricking me somehow. "Thank you for helping us."

She disappeared beneath the surface of the water, her tail flipping out once before she was gone. I watched for a while, to see if she would appear again, but she didn't.

The hollow sound of footsteps coming across the deck made me turn to find Marley walking toward me.

"Did you hear any of that?" I asked.

"All of it," she said. "So, what now?"

I sighed. "Now we convince Captain Brom to head Northwest instead of Northeast."

"You're not going to tell Lia and Finn?"

128

"I feel like I should, but I also don't want to get their hopes up."

"You don't think the siren will be successful?"

I didn't have an answer for that. I prayed to Neros that the siren was successful, but I wasn't going to be naïve in thinking that nothing would go wrong.

"Maybe we should keep this to ourselves," Marley suggested. "For now. Finn and Lia would only want to be more proactive, and it could throw off the siren's plan."

"Mmm," I mused. "You're probably right. We can tell them Harlan saw fog rolling in from the Northwest and that maybe we should head that direction for a few days."

"Harlan?" Marley raised a brow.

I pointed to the man sitting in the crow's nest. "Harlan," I repeated. "I'll inform him in case anyone questions him about it. No doubt he already saw the siren anyway. We have a bit of an understanding, I think."

"Good luck with that." She smirked.

"Are you sure you're okay with keeping this secret from Finn? I know it probably pains you as much as it pains me to keep anything from Lia."

"I have plenty of secrets from Finn," Marley said with a shrug. "What he doesn't know won't hurt him."

I considered that for a second, realizing maybe I didn't know Marley as well as I hoped. "All right, then," I murmured. "I'm going to talk with Harlan first, and then I'll wake Lia if she hasn't woken already. You mind telling Finn about the change in course?"

Marley saluted me and turned on her heel, heading for the stairs. Before she reached them, she turned back to me and called out, "Oh, and don't think I forgot about the fact that I won our bet." She winked and slipped into the shadows.

129

My pulse jumped and I watched her as I placed a hand against the mast, preparing to climb up to the crow's nest.

I will never figure her out, I thought, shaking my head as I climbed.

Viv

Raf marched behind me with her trusty prod in hand. Esme walked beside me, her face impassive. They'd come to our room this morning before Humer or Jami had woken and silently ordered me to join them.

They hadn't told me where we were going, but there was only one possible destination: the siren queen's chamber.

I had no idea what she wanted from me, considering I had no information on the Azurean Stones or the island where they were hidden. So, I assumed it was something else. Something worse.

"After you," Esme said as she opened the door to reveal the siren queen sitting behind her table once more. Roland stood at the back of the room, his hands behind his back as he stared up at the glass ceiling. He didn't acknowledge my entrance.

"Vivianne, how lovely to see you this morning." She grinned, baring all her pointed teeth. "Please, have a seat." Her head inclined toward the chair that had been placed opposite her at the table. It would leave me only a couple feet from her. Much too close for my comfort. But I did as I was told.

As I sat, I said, "Good morning." Being so close to her, the stench of rotting seaweed was almost too much to bear, but I did my best to not react.

The siren queen studied me too closely, and my skin prickled from the attention.

"Would you like some breakfast?" she asked, snapping her fingers before I could respond. Trays of food were brought out and set on the table by two men, meaning they must be mermen, since all sirens were women. My lips curled at the thought of them betraying their own people for this monster.

"Thank you," I said, trying to hide my reaction to her minions. I waited for her to help herself first, both out of feigned respect and to ensure it wasn't poisoned.

Since I hadn't had any fresh fruit and vegetables since being below the surface, I went for those first. They were delicious and I probably ate way more than I should have, but I couldn't stop myself.

I'd been so distracted by my own plate, I nearly threw up my entire meal when I looked up and noticed what had been placed in front of the siren queen. My hand flew to my mouth, and I averted my gaze.

"Squeamish?" the siren queen drawled, stabbing her fork into the human heart before her. "I'd think you'd have a stronger stomach, considering you've killed more than one of my sirens."

Forcing myself to meet her gaze, I stared into the depths of her pitch-black eyes.

"Now." The siren queen paused, taking a bite from the heart, and chewing it slowly as if she thought it might torture me more. It did. "I learned something quite interesting yesterday that I'd like you to confirm for me."

My fork clattered against my plate as it slipped from my grip. I cleared my throat and nodded for the siren queen to go on as terror gripped me and words escaped me.

"Marcus Humer has clearly lost his mind, so I'm hesitant to believe anything he says without fact checking it. Though, he does have quite some interesting information floating around in that mind of his." She tapped her nails on the top of the table. "Tell me, Vivianne, is it true he used to perform experiments on you and other shifters?" The gleam in her eyes told me nothing good would come of this line of questioning, but I also couldn't lie. She already knew the truth.

"Y-yes," I said, my voice shaking.

"Interesting." She ceased her tapping and clasped her hands as she leaned in toward me. "What an asset he could be if he could *continue* his experiments. Sirens, as you know, similar to a shifter, can only bear children with humans or mermen. But if we could create a new, *stronger* species of siren ..." She trailed off, but I knew exactly what she was thinking.

What better way to ensure she never lost the Azurean Stones? Even if someone powerful enough could go against her, she'd have an unstoppable army standing in their way.

The siren queen jerked her head up. "Raf, fetch Humer for me." Raf bowed to her and left the room.

My blood turned to ice and I couldn't move. *No no no no no.*

"Please don't do this." I figured I had nothing to lose. The siren queen already hated me, begging couldn't make it any worse.

The siren queen laughed. "Oh, it's funny you think I care about you past your usefulness to me. Humer can carve you up if he sees fit, and I won't so much as blink."

133

My heart raced, and my vision narrowed. Every nerve in me felt as if it were on fire and the slightest touch would make me combust. I gripped the edge of the table, trying to keep myself in the moment.

This can't be happening, this isn't real, I thought.

Oh, this is very real Vivianne, Humer's voice responded in my mind. I couldn't be sure if it was my own version of him, or if I'd finally lost it.

The siren queen's tentacles moved under the table, two of them wrapping around my ankles and pinning me in place.

"In case you try to run," she warned.

I wanted to throw up. The sliminess of her tentacles cooled my skin, but the rubbery feel moving against me had me clawing to get out of my own body.

Raf returned with Humer, and the smile he wore told me he knew exactly what was about to happen. I wasn't sure whether to be relieved or not that he currently seemed lucid.

"My Vivianne," he purred. "I've waited so long for this moment."

Raf kept her hold on him.

The siren queen looked at him with a gleam in her eyes. "First, I want to—"

"Do you see that?" Roland's voice captured everyone's attention. I'd forgotten he stood at the back of the room. He pointed up toward the ceiling, where nothing but ocean and fish could be seen.

"No," the siren queen said flatly.

Roland hurried over to the table and pulled the map out of his back pocket, unfurling it on the table.

"You wouldn't," he said, and I almost choked on the lump clogging my throat.

134

Rage flashed in the siren queen's eyes, but she focused on the map.

"Only those who were there the day the wards were created can see it, but there is a ripple there." He pointed up to the ceiling again before facing the map once more. "I think we're close. We should get closer to the surface so I can be sure."

Fuck. I realized this was it. This was our chance to escape if the siren queen listened to him. My gaze briefly flicked to Esme, and I could see the anticipation in her rigid stance. Roland was moving up the escape plan to save me from Humer's knife.

The siren queen pursed her lips and stared at the map.

"Fine," she snapped. "Esme, take them back to their room. We will continue this later. Raf, inform the captain that we will be ascending."

Esme gripped my arm, pulling me up from the chair and toward the door, pushing Humer ahead of us.

"If you're wrong, or lying to me," I heard the siren queen hissing behind us. "I will ensure you suffer."

We hurried down the hall, back to where Jami waited in our room. My heart raced at the thought of escaping, but terror still gripped me from the prospect of being tortured again.

"I hope you're all ready," Esme murmured.

The door to our room slammed against the wall.

"Quickly," Esme huffed from where she stood in the doorway, Viv and Humer behind her. "Everyone's eyes are on the island."

I was already on my feet and in another second, we were leaving our prison behind.

"Don't tell her, don't tell her, don't tell her," Humer muttered repeatedly.

I groaned. "If ever there was a time to shut up, now is the time," I said, and by some miracle, his chatter stopped.

"They won't keep the queen distracted long," Esme said, glancing back at us as we hurried down the hall. "She'll figure out Roland is lying."

We all moved a bit faster. At the end of the hall, there was a giant glass window that looked out into the ocean. Nausea washed over me and I stopped in my tracks. Everyone else kept moving, leaving me behind, until Viv noticed I was missing and turned back.

"We don't have time for this, Jami. I know it's hard, I know," Viv pleaded with me, placing her hands on my

136

shoulders. "This is our only chance to get out of here. Lia and Finn are waiting for us."

She released me, and I took one step, then another, slowly moving toward the wide expanse of ocean. Pressure and lightheadedness descended on my mind at the same time. Breathing became harder, but I kept putting one foot in front of the other.

A hard yank on my arm brought me back to full focus. Viv gripped my arm, pulling me away from the window toward a large metal door with a locking wheel in the center. Esme turned the wheel and it creaked, echoing down the hall.

"A little help here," she grunted.

Viv and I both moved at once, but a loud shout made us stop.

"Esme!" Raf bellowed down the hall. We turned to see her running toward us at full speed, her electric prod firm in her grip. "What the fuck do you think you're doing?"

"Shit." Esme stopped her efforts to open the door and turned to face Raf.

"I'll take care of her," Viv said. "You help Esme with the door." She gave me a push toward Esme. Viv's nails extended into claws and Raf narrowed her eyes as she approached.

I rushed to help Esme finish opening the door. As soon as we had it open enough for him to fit, Humer ran through, but Esme and I turned back to help Viv with Raf.

They were still in a standoff.

"You're helping them escape?" Raf asked, anger flashing in her eyes.

Esme held her chin high. "Yes. The siren queen's reign has run its course and nature demands she step down and fade away peacefully so the next regent may take her place. Whoever that may be."

Raf took a single step forward. "You have no right to go against her, no matter the situation. She is our *queen.*"

"If you truly believe that, then you are a lost cause." Esme moved her hand to her chest, holding it there.

Raf snarled and lunged, thrusting out the electric prod, aiming straight for Esme, but Viv and I moved at the same time. Her claws struck true, lodging themselves in Raf's shoulder and chest.

Raf's prod had also stayed its course and slammed into my hip when I'd jumped in front of Esme. The shock it sent through me had my teeth and brain rattling. I blacked out for a few seconds and came to on my knees with Viv and Esme on either side of me.

"You seem to enjoy being shocked," Esme said. "Always quick to take those hits for yourself."

Swallowing the lump in my throat, I managed to smirk. Esme left us for a minute, dragging Raf's body into a nearby closet. I wasn't sure if she was dead, or had passed out from blood loss, but I didn't ask. Apparently, I'd missed that part while I'd blacked out.

Humer waited patiently behind the door, in a capsule-like room. Esme shut the door once we were all inside.

"This is the hard part," she said, pointing to where water slowly trickled in from the ceiling.

"You mean dealing with your psycho siren friend wasn't hard enough?" Viv said, though she'd made it seem easy taking her down. Raf's blood still stained her hands and I noticed they were fisted and shaking at her sides.

"That was an unfortunate turn of events, but nothing that will stop our departure," Esme said. "We're at a shallow enough depth that the pressure won't kill you two." Her gaze flicked from me to Humer. "But this room won't open until it is

138

entirely filled with water, so I hope you can swim. Stay near the top and, as soon as the ceiling opens, Viv and I will get the two of you to the surface as fast as possible."

As if I wasn't freaked out enough at the thought of being submerged, I had to worry about not running out of air before someone could save us.

"Don't worry." Viv nudged my shoulder. "I won't let you drown," she teased, though it wasn't very comforting.

"Also, Roland kick-started this plan before your friends had much time to start heading this direction, so there's no telling how near they are. We may have to travel a bit more of a distance than I originally thought." Esme bit her lip.

"Here's hoping no one notices our absence or Raf knocked out in the closet before we're far enough away they won't catch up," Viv said, letting out a long breath.

The water had already risen above my knees. It was cold enough to make my skin tingle and begin to go numb. If the lack of air didn't kill me, the frigid water might.

Viv took my hand, and I jerked my head to face her, my brows raising.

"We can do this," she said, as if she were talking to herself as much as me.

I squeezed her hand and it stopped shaking. "We can do this," I repeated. I imagined Lia and Finn waiting for us, beckoning us onward and the anxiety clenching my chest eased. "Wait." I turned back to the door we'd come through. "Where's Roland? Isn't he coming with us?"

Esme shook her head. "The siren queen is keeping him by her side. I tried to come up with an excuse to take him away for a few minutes, but there was nothing that would have worked without sparking suspicion in the queen."

"I can't leave him here with her," I said, even though I knew there was no turning back.

"He knew he'd be forced to stay," Esme explained. "He told me to tell you this is his way of making up for all the torture he and Charles put you through when you were younger."

I closed my eyes. The water had reached my shoulders and Viv's chin.

"Don't let go of me," Viv warned, tightening her grip on my hand. "Lia will send me back down here if I come back without you."

I feigned a smile. The water continued to rise, and we swam to keep above the surface. Esme and Viv shifted, ready to move as soon as the top opened.

My eyes automatically closed as the water reached them and I forced them back open, even though they burned from the salt water. It took a few more seconds before the ceiling above us opened like a hatch.

Viv tugged me out of the enclosed space, into the open ocean, and panic struck along with a flashback.

"Where is Jamison?" My father's voice sent relief flooding through me. Roland and Charles stepped aside so I could be seen crouched on the ground, my hands covering my head. They'd been about to throw me into that tub in the forest. I never understood why there'd been an abandoned clawfoot tub out in the middle of nowhere, but it certainly helped Roland and Charles torment me better.

"We're leaving," my father said. "There's a boat waiting for us in the harbor. Our lives are about to change." His gaze burned into me as I stared up at him. It almost felt like he was angry with me for some reason.

140

"Boys!" My mother called to us from the outskirts of the woods. "Our carriage is here!"

"Where are we going?" I asked, finally standing and wiping the dirt from my clothes.

No one answered me and I followed them back through the trees to our house.

There was a strange man sitting in the carriage with my mother when we arrived. He had a black cloak on with the hood up, but his piercing, cold, blue eyes were what had me curling into my mother's side.

"I apologize for the last-minute notice. I'm sure you understand the urgency of the situation," the stranger said.

"My father told me this day may one day come. I'll admit, I had hoped it would be in my lifetime, considering the ... benefits." My father's eyes gleamed as he mentioned the so-called benefits of our strange trip.

"Ah, yes. You will be rewarded for your sacrifice," the man said, nodding.

My mother squeezed me tighter, and I closed my eyes, letting the rocking of the carriage distract me.

I gasped and water rushed into my mouth, making me choke and jerk in Viv's grip. We broke through the surface, and I tried to take a lungful of air in, but instead coughed and spluttered.

"You're not supposed to try breathing underwater," she said.

I cringed. Thankfully, the water wasn't unbearably cold. We were still closer to Asmara than Sylvane, otherwise I'd catch hypothermia within a few hours.

Humer and Esme bobbed a few feet away from us.

"We need to keep moving," Esme said. "Your friends should be in this direction, so long as they listened to me."

"You okay, Jami?" Viv asked.

I hadn't been able to stop coughing, but it was starting to subside. My lungs burned and my throat was raw, but I was alive.

The flashback I'd had was something I'd long forgotten. It made sense that the man who had been in that carriage with us had been a mage. I'd have to try to remember more from that trip because it might unlock some of the mystery behind my family's link with the Azurean Stones.

We started moving again, Viv and Esme towing Humer and I on their backs through the water at speeds I knew they could double if they didn't have dead weight with them. It was faster than I'd have been able to swim on my own.

"What will you do once we're back with our people?" Viv asked Esme.

Esme continued as if she hadn't heard Viv for a few beats longer than usual.

"I've no choice but to return to the siren queen," she said.

"But you'll be killed," Viv pointed out the obvious.

"I chose this path knowing the outcome for myself. I appreciate your concern, but there is no alternative."

Neither of us argued with her, because she was right. There was nowhere for her to hide in the ocean where the siren queen wouldn't find her.

After a few hours, I imagined Viv and Esme were tired of swimming. Even if they were used to it from spending their lives in the ocean, they didn't normally have to lug along an extra 200 pounds with them. Although, I doubted Humer weighed nearly that much, even soaking wet.

"Viv!" A familiar voice had relief rushing through me. *Nix.*

"Viv, over here!" Nix appeared above the waves, her arms above her head as she flagged us down.

"Oh, thank Neros," Viv murmured. I had my doubts that the goddess of the sea had anything to do with Nix's arrival, but I didn't say anything to the contrary. I was too distracted by the prospect we might be close to getting out of the damned ocean.

"How did you know we'd be early?" Esme asked as Nix approached us.

"I've been checking a few times a day. I figured it was worth the risk of being spotted in the ocean to save these two," she said, jerking her head toward Viv and me.

Esme flashed a toothy smile. It was strange seeing her in her true siren form. My instincts told me to get as far from her as possible, but it was much too late for that.

"Is the ship close?" Esme asked.

Nix nodded. "I had to be sure this wasn't a trap before leading you to them," she said.

Smart, I thought.

"I shall leave you to carry this human," Esme said, handing Humer over to Nix like a sack of potatoes. He remained silent, though he seemed quite aware as he observed his new life preserver.

"Why is he here?" Nix asked, scowling at Humer, though she kept him above the surface.

"We might need him. He has valuable information about the Azurean Stones," I explained.

"You should go," Esme interjected. "I'll start back and intercept anyone who may have noticed we were missing, but I can only slow them down."

Pity and grief welled in my chest knowing Esme was headed back for her own execution.

"Thank you for all you've done," I said.

Her eyes flicked to me, and she gave me a curt nod before slipping beneath the surface.

"She's right. We need to go," Nix said. "We're only a half hour from the ship."

I groaned inwardly. I'd hoped we were much closer. I hooked my arms over Viv's shoulders once more and we began the last leg of our trek to the ship.

Finn

"Finn!" Marley called as she bounded down the stairs.

I jolted up in my hammock, nearly causing it to dump me onto the floor.

"Finn," Marley said, almost breathless as she grinned at me. "Come quick. They're back."

Already on my feet, I followed Marley. "Who's back?" I asked as we walked. Instead of answering, she winked and took the stairs two at a time.

"Marley," I snapped, but she had already disappeared out the door. I pushed through it and nearly fell to my knees. Nix was helping Viv onto the ship, Jami right behind her.

Her golden eyes appeared dull from exhaustion, her brown hair was sopping wet, and she was as beautiful as ever.

For a moment, I assumed I was hallucinating, but when Viv's eyes met mine and she smiled, I knew it was real.

I crossed the deck and had her in my arms in seconds. Her arms wrapped around my neck and her feet lifted from the deck. The front of me soaked through from the water dripping off her, but I didn't care.

"You're here," I breathed. "You're *really* here."

She chuckled. "Been dreaming of me, have you?" she teased. I lowered her back to her feet and looked down into her eyes. "Because I've been dreaming of seeing you again too."

Someone nudged my arm.

"Out of the way, she was mine first," Lia said, worming her way into our embrace and wrapping her arms around Viv.

Viv laughed and I released her.

"You're safe," Lia said.

Looking over their heads, I locked eyes with Jami. Swerving around the women, he pulled me into a hug.

"I don't care that your enemies are watching," he said, and I could feel him shaking. "It's good to be back above water."

I hugged him back.

"We need to get moving, now," Nix interrupted our reunion. "The siren queen won't be far behind, and we need to reach the island and get the Stones before she finds us."

That caused everyone around us to spring into action.

"What's going on?" I asked. "How did you escape?" I turned my gaze back to Viv.

"What is the meaning of this?" Brom's voice boomed over us all, stopping everyone in their tracks. "You've escaped the siren queen?"

We turned to him as he came down the stairs onto the main deck. Each step he took was slow and deliberate, as if he were aiming to intimidate. He always had to be the center of attention.

I put an arm around Viv, tensing as Brom neared us. The last time he'd seen her, he'd been using her to keep me in line. I could feel my lion itching to come out, but I had control over it, for now.

A path cleared in the group surrounding us, allowing Brom to pass through.

"It seems we have a lot to discuss," Brom said, pointedly casting a glance at each of us and the newcomers. He looked at Humer last, tilting his head to the side. "Who is this?"

Jami spoke first. "Marcus Humer. He has valuable information on the Azurean Stones. When he's lucid anyway." He rolled his eyes and Viv's body shook with laughter.

Surprised by her reaction, I glanced down at her. I'd been so worried that she'd been suffering having to be held captive with Humer while under the siren queen's thumb, and yet, here she was *laughing*. It made me smile.

Viv's tilted her head and rested it against my shoulder.

"He has his moments," she said, and Jami smirked at her.

Jealousy bloomed in my chest. I was happy she'd had Jami to comfort her while they'd been captives, but I'd rather it had been *me*. I wanted to be the one she laughed with like that.

Cool it, Finn, I chided myself. *You're the one she's holding onto now.* My arm tightened around her at that thought and she smiled up at me.

"I'll be interested to talk with him," Brom said. "Take him to my office," he commanded Callum, who was never far from his side with the twins and Tabby. The kids were nowhere to be seen now, though. "The rest of you help our newcomers settle in. We're on even more of deadline now, so don't fuck around."

Lia chatted with Viv animatedly about her excursion to the Asmaran library, and Jami settled in beside her. I took that moment to step away and catch my breath.

In a burst of flames, a letter appeared hovering in the air before me. I grabbed it before the breeze could catch it and rip

it away. A few of the deckhands glanced my way, surprised by the flames, but everyone else was distracted, so I read it to myself.

Finn –

Keep an eye to the sky. A piece of the puzzle is on its way.

Please tell Jamison that I am sorry. I never would have used him for the warding spell if I'd known the cost it would exact on him and his magic.

Good luck.
Jocelyn

I ground my jaw, trying not to scream. Jami's mother had admitted to draining Jami of his magic for her own purposes, effectively stealing his chances of ever shifting. *He* was *a shifter ... all this time, he could have been flying.*

My eyes found Jami in the crowd. He smiled with his arm wrapped around Lia's waist, her hand on his chest.

"What does that mean?" Nix's voice made me jump and I found her standing directly behind me, having read the letter over my shoulder.

"Goddess above, Nix. You're going to give me a heart attack," I grumbled. I crumpled up the paper and shoved it in my pocket.

She moved to stand beside me rather than behind me.

"A piece of the puzzle ..." she mused. "Could be anything."

"Maybe we're nearing the island?" I suggested.

148

Nix scrunched her nose. "I doubt that's what she meant. Though we are getting close. I can feel it." She breathed in deep as if she could scent the island somehow. Maybe she had a sense for kraken's or fog. I wouldn't put it past her.

"I guess we'll find out," I said.

Lia, Jami, and Viv approached us, and I pulled Viv back into my arms, pressing a kiss to her temple.

"This will never get old," I said.

She laughed. "I hope it never does."

"We should talk in my room," Lia said, her hand entwined with Jami's. It seemed none of us could stand to separate now that we'd been reunited.

We all met in Lia's room, even Jared. I positioned myself between Viv and Jared because I could tell she wasn't comfortable with him around. If he even looked at her wrong, I'd be sure to repay every ounce of harm he'd caused Viv tenfold.

"Why is *he* here?" Viv asked, her eyes narrowing at Jared. "I thought we'd seen the last of him before the prison exploded."

Lia curled her lip and said, "He followed us to Asmara and wanted to help find you all. With some persuasion, we let him aboard, but Finn's been keeping an eye on him."

Jared cleared his throat. "As I'm sure you know from your time spent with my brother, he has valuable knowledge about the Azurean Stones and how to find them. I only wanted to share what knowledge I had learned from him over the years so I might help in some way," he said, speaking fast, as if he was worried we might not let him finish.

"Why are you here *now*?" Viv asked, crossing her arms. Her jaw ticked and I put an arm around her to try and help ease whatever emotion was taking hold.

"I asked him to talk with us," Lia said. "Now that we're all reunited, I want to put together everything we've all learned so we might stand a better chance at finding the damned Stones."

Viv leaned her weight into me, no less on edge, but conceding for the moment it seemed.

It turned out that Viv and Jami had learned much of the same information from Humer that we'd learned up here on the surface. It irked me that Brom had taken Humer into his room for questioning without us; Brom could glean valuable information he might withhold.

"My brother may have lost his mind, but he still has a lot swirling around up there. Most of it has to do with his work, which included trying to find those Stones," Jared said. "It's no surprise even in his mindless babbling that he'd reveal so much information to you."

"Is there a reason he didn't want the siren queen to know?" Viv asked. "After being questioned by her he kept repeating, '*don't tell her, don't tell her.*'"

Jared shook his head. "Probably because he wants the Stones for himself. Or his younger, sane self, did. It's probably ingrained in him to keep as much hidden from anyone else seeking them as he can."

"But not me," Viv pointed out, stiffening against me. I stroked her arm slowly, trying to put her at ease.

"No. You were always his favorite, and I think he trusts you with the information for some reason, even if you're seeking the Stones yourself. He may for some twisted reason believe you're helping *him.*" Jared had good enough sense to appear unnerved by that.

Viv pulled away from me and walked toward the door. "I need a second."

I followed her, and she stopped, as if waiting for me, before going to sit on the steps leading up to the quarter deck. Sitting beside her, I leaned my elbows on the step behind me and stared up at the cloudy sky. There was no hint of blue to be seen today.

"I feel like I've let you down," I said, closing my eyes for a few seconds as the acknowledgement gripped me.

Viv put a hand on my knee.

"What are you talking about?" she asked, turning to me. "You haven't let me down. You've been scouring the seas to find the Azurean Stones so you could save Jami and me. That's not letting me down."

Shaking my head, I took her hand in mine and kissed it lightly. "That's not what I'm talking about. I tortured and killed a siren to try to find you. She had your voice ..." Nausea welled in my gut and almost had me running for the side of the ship, but Viv's grip on me kept me from losing my breakfast. "In my nightmares, you were the one I tortured."

Her grip on me tightened. "Finn, it's okay."

I shook my head again. "I didn't come with you to the prison, I didn't protect you, I didn't ..."

"Can't you see? I don't care about all that. I care that you're *here. Now.*" Viv crushed her lips against mine. I wound my arms around her, pulling her close and inhaling her as if she were the air I breathed.

"I love you, Viv," I said when we finally broke apart. "And I don't want to lose you again."

Viv grinned. "You don't just *think* you're falling in love with me?" she teased, recalling our moment back in Asmara.

I took both of her hands in mine. "There is no doubt in my mind that I love you. If I die tomorrow, know that there is

no one in this world I would rather spend my last moments with than you, my sea goddess."

She rolled her eyes and grinned. "Then I guess I'm safe to reveal that I love you, too, Captain."

I put my hand to my heart. "Oh, goddess, you know what that does to me." I bent my head, pressing a kiss to her lower jaw and felt her tremble beneath me.

Someone dropped down suddenly on the step behind us, making us jolt away from one another as we turned to find the culprit.

An all-too familiar man smirked at us and all the anticipation in me fizzled out.

"Charles," I drawled. "To what do we owe the displeasure?"

"I'm here to help you all save the ocean, apparently," he said. "But first, I'd like to speak with my brother."

Viv

Charles resembled Jami more than Roland. Though they didn't have the same hair color, or eyes, all their other features were almost identical.

"What do you know?" Jami asked. He had his hands fisted at his sides, clearly on edge around his brother as we all stood in Lia's room once more.

"Our three coins hold the power to retrieve the Stones," Charles said.

"As we've surmised," Finn grumbled. I leaned into him, trying to soothe his worries. Both he and Jami clearly didn't trust Charles, and for good reason.

Charles ignored that comment and continued. "The island is shrouded in a fog enchanted to turn any ship away. Roland's coin is spelled so he may direct a ship through without being redirected by the fog. It will also give the holder of it a sense of direction leading to the island."

"I have Roland's coin," Jami said, flipping the coin over his knuckles. "He dropped it into my pocket on the siren queen's ship."

Charles nodded, but I noticed his brows pinch and sadness crossing his features.

"Next, there is a kraken who guards the cave entrance. We will have to find our own way to deal with the monster, for there is no magical way to be rid of it," Charles said. "Then, my coin grants access to the cave. There is a simple ward blocking the entrance which the holder of the coin can pass through and dissolve the ward entirely."

"Convenient you hold that piece of the puzzle," Finn mused.

Charles sighed. "I'll tell you again if I must, but I am only here to help. The siren queen's actions have affected *everyone*, even Sylvane."

"I'm sure," Finn said. "Go on, please."

"Fine. Jami's coin is the key to the chest. You must place all three into their slots on the front of the chest, but Jami's must go last. Once the coins are in place, the chest will open and allow the necklace holding all three of the Stones to be removed. The mage crafted the necklace so it must be worn for the Stones to be used," Charles finished.

"So, technically *Jami* has the final piece to the puzzle, then," Marley chimed in. "Charles and Jami can fight it out as to who gets to retrieve the Stones." Her eyes lit up as if she'd enjoy seeing that fight.

I rolled my eyes but couldn't keep from smiling.

"You don't want the honor, Marley?" Nix teased, nudging Marley with her elbow.

"I'm guessing the necklace is much too gaudy for my tastes." Marley nudged Nix back.

"There is something else you should all know before a decision is made on who will retrieve the Stones," Charles said. "The Stones will absorb the user's magic for themselves, making them even more powerful. Mother said that if used quickly enough, the user may survive."

We collectively seemed to stop breathing as silence fell over us all.

"So, we're risking *death* if we use these Stones?" Marley spoke first.

Finn shook his head. "There's no telling how long we'll need to use the Stones. What happens if whoever wields them *dies* before the siren queen is taken care of? Does someone else have to pick them up and take over?"

Charles sucked his bottom lip into his mouth, nodding his head as if considering the questions.

"If you know the name of the siren queen, you can command the Stones to end her life by absorbing all her magic. But you need her name to accomplish that feat. Otherwise, you will have to use their power to find another way to kill her. It may be as quick as a flick of the wrist, but there's no telling how the Stones will react to whoever wields them and what power they hold."

"Are these Stones not all powerful? If they can give the siren queen the ability to control the entire ocean, why can't I simply wield them and kill her with a lightning strike or something of the like?" Lia asked.

"You're not wielding them," Jami said, but Charles spoke before Lia could respond to that.

"They may be powerful enough for that, but Mother said they have been in disuse for so long, there's no record of how powerful they truly are."

"So, all of this," Lia threw her arms in the air. "Has been based on a guess? The threat of the siren queen, the threat of the *Stones,* may all be nothing? Viv and Jami being taken, for nothing? And we have to decide who may *die* for this?"

Charles held her gaze. "Yes," he said simply.

"I need a moment," she said, striding out of the room. Jami followed her, so I stayed put. She didn't need us both overwhelming her when she was clearly already at her wit's end.

"I'm going to make sure Jami doesn't make things worse," Nix said, leaving the room with Marley close behind her.

"You can go now, too," Finn said to Charles. "We need time to process. Feel free to claim a hammock belowdecks."

Charles hesitated but wound up leaving the room as well.

Finn groaned, "This is all fucked up."

Something nagged at the back of my mind, and I rubbed the heel of my palm against my forehead, trying to remember what it was.

"Humer said some kind of name ..." I said, somewhat recalling him talking about the siren queen along with something that sounded like a name, but I'd been thinking he was speaking nonsense at the time and hadn't paid attention.

"The siren queen's name?" Finn asked.

I nodded. "I can't remember." Rising from the bed, I strode out of the room, not waiting to see if Finn followed because I knew he would. Captain Brom's room wasn't far and, since no one stood outside the door I walked in without knocking.

Callum put his arm out, surprise widening his eyes.

"Captain Brom is busy with Humer right now," he said, though I could clearly see Humer sitting in front of Brom's desk while Brom sat on the corner of it.

"I need a moment alone with him," I demanded. "With Humer."

Humer's back straightened as he turned at the sound of my voice.

"There she is. I knew she'd come." He turned back to Brom partially and pointed to me. "A loyal test subject."

"Watch your fucking mouth." Finn didn't surprise me as he stepped up to my side. I held my hand out, halting him from approaching Humer. Though his words reflected the anger brewing inside me, I needed to present a calm front to get Brom to leave me alone with Humer.

"A minute is all I ask." I moved to stand beside Humer, as much as it pained me to be so close to him.

Brom eyed me curiously but didn't argue. "A minute," he said, rising from the corner of his desk and leaving the room, Callum behind him.

I took his place on the corner of the desk, facing Humer and close enough our knees almost touched. I shuddered.

"Vivianne, dear, I've been wondering what became of you," Humer said, his gaze flicking from me to Finn. "Is this—"

"I have a question for you." I cut him off. "What is the siren queen's name?"

He tapped his chin and hummed. "Three items, three locks, three brothers."

"No. The siren queen. What. Is. Her. Name?" I repeated, hoping to bring him back from his spiral.

His taps turned to knocks on the arm of the chair. "Don't tell her. Don't tell her."

"You know her name; you've said it. What is it?" I asked, the heat in me rising. If only I could remember what he'd said.

Humer tilted his head to the side and pursed his lips as if he might be thinking about what I'd asked.

"Tell me," I pleaded.

"What are you doing out, Vivianne?" Humer's eyes locked onto mine as if noticing me for the first time again, and his nostrils flared. "You should be resting."

I wanted to scream as I realized he'd slipped into a memory.

"The. Siren. Queen's. Name." I punctuated each word, hoping one might strike a chord within him. I placed my palms on the arms of his chair, leaning toward him. Being in such close proximity had every nerve within me firing and my entire body was buzzing, yelling at me to get away.

Humer smirked and I lost whatever grip I had on my temper. My hands wrapped around his neck.

"Tell me her name!"

I barely registered the light touch on my shoulder as I squeezed, and Humer's smirk turned to a silent laugh as he choked.

"Viv." Finn's voice made me flinch, but I didn't let up. He placed a hand on either of my forearms and pried me away from Humer. "This isn't you."

Jerking my arms from his grasp, I whirled toward him. "How do you know?" I stared at him for a few seconds, his brow furrowing, before I stormed out of the room.

The night was cool, and the sea breeze whipped around me, seeming as volatile as my temper. I could still feel Humer's skin against mine ... His heartbeat thrumming against my hands as they'd closed around his neck. A bit longer and I could have been rid of him forever.

Nix waited for me by the rail off to the right. Almost everyone else on board had gone belowdecks for the night.

I leaned beside her, letting my head hang as I stared down at the pitch-black ocean roiling beneath us. The waves were taunting me. *Slip beneath the surface, let go of everything.*

"We can still use the Stones against her, even without her name," Nix said, leaning her elbows on the railing as she faced the opposite direction. "The name might make things a bit smoother, but that's why we gathered an army. We always knew there'd be a fight in the end."

Hot, angry tears leaked down my cheeks.

"Not now," Nix said, and I glanced over at her and realized she wasn't talking to me. Finn stood at the edge of my vision. I turned my gaze back to the sea.

It didn't stop him, though, and he walked to my other side, leaning his forearms on the rail as I had, and clasped his hands in front of him.

"It wasn't my place to step in," he said. "Humer deserves every bit of your wrath."

I scoffed.

"Viv." Finn's voice was low and made my body heat as he used a finger to turn my face toward his. "Don't close yourself off."

My eyes shuttered closed and I took a deep breath, the scent of the salty air cleansing my mind and soul.

Opening my eyes I leaned over, resting my head on his shoulder.

"Thank you for stopping me," I said. "I have enough blood on my hands, I don't need his tainting me too."

Finn's arm came around my shoulders.

"I wouldn't mind taking that burden for you," he said in a teasing tone. "Say the word and I will take care of him."

I smiled despite the morbidity of it all.

"Never thought I'd see the day when you settled down, Finnian," Charles said, walking up and taking the spot Nix had vacated. I hadn't noticed her leave and I assumed she hadn't gone far in case I needed her.

Finn grimaced and turned to face Charles.

"What a delight it is to have you on board." Finn's voice was thick with sarcasm.

I stepped up beside him and put a hand on his shoulder.

"Jealous, Charlie?" I asked, giving him a once over as I did. "Not everyone can snag themselves a mermaid, though your brother did all right for himself, too."

Charles didn't so much as flinch.

"I'm truly happy for you and Jami both," he said to Finn. "I'm not here to cause turmoil or strife."

"I'm not convinced of that yet," Finn said, his muscles tensing. I rubbed a hand down his arm, taking his hand in mine.

"We should rest. It's been a long day," I said, tugging Finn away from the railing. "Goodnight, Charles."

He nodded to us.

Lia

Standing at the back of the ship and watching the wake behind us, I wondered how in the world we were going to take down the siren queen. If the Stones weren't what we thought, if they turned out to be useless, how would we ever defeat her?

Warm, familiar arms wrapped around me from behind, and Jami rested his chin on my shoulder. Some of the tension in me dissolved and was replaced with a wholly different kind of tension as heat pooled in my lower gut.

"No matter what happens, we're going to find a way to win this fight. With or without the Stones," Jami said, pressing a kiss to my neck.

I latched onto his arms, holding him in place as I leaned back in his embrace.

"I missed you so much." My voice was thick with emotion, and the spray of the sea coated me as if tears streamed down my face, though I was sure actual tears weren't far behind.

He kissed my jaw. "I missed you, too."

"I feel like everything is falling apart, and like we're not going to win this war," I whispered, hoping to keep my words between us. I didn't want anyone else to know I was having doubts.

Moving around so he faced me while his arms were still around me, Jami looked me in the eyes, and said, "If anyone can win this war, it's you. I know how determined you are, and how much this means to you. You will find a way, and we are all here to help you. You're not alone."

I leaned my forehead against his chest and soaked in his warmth. "I love you."

"I love you, too, Lia." He pressed a kiss to the top of my head.

I lifted a finger and traced the tattoo peeking out of his tunic where it was unlaced. The edge of the mountain, and an eagle's wing.

"Charles said it might *not* all be for nothing," I said, pulling back and looking up at Jami. "Which means we still have a chance."

Jami shook his head. "Does this mean you're back on the hunt for the Stones?" He grinned and twisted my hair around his finger.

"I never said I was giving up on the Stones, I just needed a minute to worry and doubt and now I'm ready to save the world," I teased. "Just as soon as I show you something."

His brow creased. "What is it?"

I withdrew from his arms and pulled him by his hand down the stairs, back to the main deck, and toward my room.

"It's super important, and I know you'll agree." I turned back and winked at him, and he finally caught on.

"Oh yes, I definitely agree." His face lit up and I wanted to stop and kiss him right there, but I resisted the urge.

"Lia!" Hearing Viv's voice, after going so long of wondering if I'd ever see her again, had me stopping in my tracks, all thoughts of alone time with Jami forgotten.

162

"Viv, what is it?" I turned and walked to where she stood next to the side of the ship. We weren't bothering hiding anymore, since the siren queen was no doubt already on the hunt for us after Viv and Jami's escape.

"We were about to play a round of cards, to get everyone's mind off of the siren queen for a few minutes." When I got close enough, she took my hand which wasn't still entwined with Jami's. "Join us?"

I released Jami and wrapped my arms around Viv. She laughed in surprise.

"Cards sound wonderful," I said, hugging her tight. I couldn't imagine life without her, and what I would have done had we not gotten her and Jami back.

"Finn's gone to get Marley and Nix, maybe even Charles depending on Finn's mood." She rolled her eyes and laughed. "Come on." She tugged my hand and led me to a table which had been set up for us.

The entire game, I kept watching her and swearing to myself that I'd never let harm befall her again. The way Finn always was in contact with her somehow, whether with his arm around her, or their shoulders touching, I assumed he was thinking the same thing.

The only thing distracting me from my thoughts was Jami beside me, and I think I freaked him out a little with my staring at him. I kept thinking I'd blink, and he'd be gone, all of this a dream. But everyone remained, and we enjoyed ourselves for the first time in too long.

The next day everyone was on edge. The siren queen could find us at any time, and the weather seemed to be stirring up something daunting for us as well.

"A storm is coming," Brom declared in the afternoon, before walking up the stairs to the helm and remaining there.

Turning to the horizon, I watched the clouds rolling in. The sky was angry, and we were in the direct path of its rampage.

"Prepare for a rough night!" Brom called out from above. "Tie down everything you don't want to lose." I could have sworn he was smirking, as if the thought of sailing through the storm brought him joy rather than fear.

"Lia," Viv said, her hand grazing my elbow. "Are you all right?"

I nodded. "Mmhmm. Just tired."

"Why don't you try to get some rest before the storm rolls in?" she suggested, waving a hand toward our room. "It's moving slow. You could get in a few hours, at least."

Instead of arguing with her and saying there was no way I'd be able to sleep with the insane amount of worry, fear, and general processing of information swirling around my mind, I headed for the room. Jami was still with Finn, probably helping prepare for the storm, and I hadn't seen Nix in a few hours, so I had the room to myself. It was strange. Since Jami and Viv had joined us, I hadn't been in the room alone.

I sat on the bed and kicked off my boots. Curling my legs up underneath me, I sat back against the wall and pulled a pillow to my chest. The ship rocked slowly, but I knew it wouldn't last. The storm would kick up the waves soon and ruin the steady rhythm we'd settled into.

There was a mirror across the room, over the small wardrobe, and I caught a glimpse of myself. *Some princess,* I scoffed at my reflection.

"Your people are suffering every second that you waste up here," I said to the girl in the mirror. "The siren queen will

break through those defenses unless you find the Stones and end this once and for all."

I pursed my lips, pretending that the girl in the mirror might respond of her own accord, but of course, she remained quiet.

"You tried to condemn them all to her reign. A princess wouldn't do that. A princess wouldn't lose herself to grief and anger ..." Tears welled in my eyes. I leaned my head back, staring at the ceiling. "Your mother was right about you after all. A princess would put her kingdom above all else. Above friends, family, love ..."

"I'm going to stop you right there."

I screamed, not expecting a response, and thought for half a second I'd gone crazy, and my reflection had finally talked back.

Marley rolled out from underneath the bed and hopped to her feet.

"What the fuck?!" I yelled, gripping my pillow tighter.

She rubbed her hand over her hair and shrugged.

"I didn't think anyone would come in here, and it's impossible to get any time alone on this ship. It's actually pretty spacious under there," she explained.

"Why not lay on *top* of the bed?"

She craned her neck, cracking it. "Small spaces help me think better. You'll be glad to know I've thought of a plan to deal with the kraken."

"Great." My breathing was returning to normal.

"But, back to what you were saying before." She frowned. "I think you're being too hard on yourself, and I don't say that lightly. Yeah, maybe a princess shouldn't risk her entire kingdom's well-being to save her best friend and lover, but also, what's the point of living if not to do stupid shit sometimes?"

"I appreciate the sentiment, but I don't think that's a great excuse for what I almost did," I pointed out.

Marley sat down on the bed, leaning back on her elbows, and looked up at me.

"Cole and I used to do stupid shit together all the time. It made life more enjoyable, and certainly more memorable."

My heart ached for her loss and mine. Bree had died that night with Cole, and we'd barely had time to mourn properly before moving on because of this trouble with the siren queen.

"You don't talk about him much," I said. Marley had seemed to be unaffected at the time when Cole had died.

"I don't like to think about the people I've lost. Instead, I focus on the people I still have. Finn thinks I'm heartless, or soulless, or maybe both. I like to think I'm a badass. Either way, there's no point dwelling on those we can't bring back."

It was true, she did sound a bit heartless sometimes, but she also had a point.

"I think that as long as everything works out in the end, and the siren queen is defeated, then you didn't fail your people, or let them down," she said.

"Well, thank you for that. I don't know if I truly believe it, but it does make me feel slightly better." I put the pillow to the side and rested my elbows on my knees. "Now tell me your plan for the kraken."

~

Marley and I requested Brom meet us in his room before the storm hit. Viv, Jami, Finn, Charles, and Nix all joined us. Viv and I took the two seats in front of Brom's desk while he

sat behind it; Jami and Finn stood behind us, and Charles and Nix remained closer to the door.

I let Marley explain her plan from where she sat perched on the corner of Brom's desk.

"The kraken will be drawn in by the ship entering the cove," Marley explained. "And once it has begun it's attack, we recreate what Viv and Nix did to the *Leona.*"

I noticed Finn's jaw tick and I wondered if he still harbored some resentment toward them for that.

"Put all of the gunpowder belowdecks, create a long trail of it for whomever remains on board to light, and then they hightail it over the side into the water while the kraken is blown to bits along with the ship."

No one said anything for a few seconds as everyone processed.

"How will we get off the island without a ship?" Nix leaned against the wall at the back of the room with Callum.

"Assuming the Stones are as powerful as we've been led to believe, then whoever wields them should be able to solve that problem," Marley said. "But as a failsafe, we'll unload enough provisions onto the island before venturing into the cove to last us long enough for one of us to bring back another ship."

"The siren queen will kill us all before anyone arrives to save our sorry asses," Charles pointed out.

"Then you better hope the Stones hold enough power to transport us all back to Asmara before she can arrive," I said. It wasn't entirely unheard of for a witch or mage to be able to transport themselves across far distances, so long as they were powerful enough. I had to imagine the Stones would hold that kind of power if the siren queen believed them strong enough to gain control of the ocean.

"It's the only way," Brom said, taking a long swig of whiskey from his glass. "But I'll be the one to do it."

I stared at Brom, shocked by his response. I thought it was going to take a lot more convincing to let us blow up his ship.

"Of course." I nodded. "As soon as the ship blows, taking the kraken down with it, we need to move. The siren queen, if she didn't already know where we were, would be alerted by a disruption that large."

Viv shifted beside me in her chair. "But who will go into the cave?" she asked.

"I will," Finn, Jami, Charles, and I all spoke at the same time.

"My family protected the Stones all this time, I'll be the one to rediscover them," Charles said.

Jami rolled his eyes. "*Our* family," he corrected. "As you said, my coin must be placed last in the chest, so I think I'll be the one to retrieve them. Besides, I don't trust you."

Charles threw up his hands. "I flew halfway across the ocean to help you and your friends!"

"I'm the princess of Thalassia, who were the original owners of the Stones," I reminded them. "I'll be the one to retrieve them."

Finn was the only one who stayed out of the argument.

"I guess that means I'll be the one staying behind with you, Brom," Viv said, recapturing my attention as Jami and Charles continued to argue.

"You will not!" I grabbed her hand. "You should be on shore, with Finn."

Viv cocked her head to the side. "I'm not going to ask anyone else to risk their lives for our plan. And if you plan on

going into the cave as soon as the ship blows, then you can't be a mile away in the water."

I tried to come up with some reasonable excuse to keep her out of harm's way, but I couldn't. She had a valid point.

"I can do this," she said, smiling. "You worry too much about me."

Sighing, I nodded. "You're right. I know you can do it."

"Well, I'm glad that's settled," Brom said, sarcastically.

Jami

When we left Brom's cabin, rain pelted the deck and had everyone on edge. While I thought we'd reconvene in the room we'd all been sharing, Lia, Viv, and Nix walked straight into the rain.

They each held their arms wide and turned their faces to the sky while the rest of us remained covered in the stairwell.

"Guess I should have expected they might enjoy the rain," Finn commented beside me, grinning as he watched them.

"I'm not going out in that," Marley said. She crossed her arms, leaned against the side of the stairwell, and propped her foot against the wall.

Brom came up behind us and paused beside Finn.

"Your mother used to be the same way whenever it rained," he said. "Claimed it helped clear her mind."

Finn's smile disappeared and Brom continued out onto the deck and toward the stairs leading to the helm. He'd remain up there until the storm passed, I assumed.

"I don't mind a little rain." I left the safety of the stairwell and stepped into the downpour. It immediately soaked me through, so there was no point turning back. I caught Lia in my

170

arms as she twirled in the rain. She laughed and draped her arms over my shoulders.

"Does it help ease the ache?" I asked, smoothing her hair to the side of her face.

She shook her head. "It makes it worse, actually, but it feels nice at the same time ... If that makes sense? Like every muscle in me is aching to shift, but the rain soothes the pain, though it also causes it?"

"You'll be back in the water soon." I kissed the top of her head. "And the siren queen will never be able to tear us apart again."

We moved together across the deck in a dance. There were other people around us, trying to keep the sails steady and ensuring we stayed on course, but none of them paid us any mind.

"Have you thought about what will become of us after all of this?" Lia asked, her voice almost drowned out by the storm.

My arms tightened on her, and I kept us dancing amidst the raindrops.

"I honestly haven't been able to think about much past defeating the siren queen. It's been all-consuming since being beneath the ocean with her ..." My eyes closed, and my throat constricted from the memory of being trapped down there. Lia's fingers trailed over my cheek and down to my chest. We'd stopped our dance.

"Viv told me about the electric prod one of the sirens had," she said.

I laughed, and Lia's eyes widened in surprise. "The shocks were nothing. I would gladly take those over being parted from you again."

171

Her smile didn't reach her eyes. "I was so worried about the both of you. I would have done anything to get you back. *Anything.* And I'm ashamed of that."

Brows furrowed, I took her hands in mine, removing her arms from around me and steering her to the stairs so we could sit. Rain still pelted us, but it didn't bother me.

Once we sat, I didn't need to prompt Lia to explain.

"As soon as the siren queen had taken you and Viv, Finn and I decided we would go after the Azurean Stones," she explained.

I nodded. "I figured you would."

"But not to use them against her," she said, taking her hands from mine to cover her face. "We planned on trading them for you and Viv."

I put my elbow on my knee and propped my chin on my fist as I considered her words.

"You were going to *give* the siren queen the Stones?" I asked, as if she hadn't made it clear enough already, but my brain was having trouble processing. We'd been working so hard on keeping them out of her hands, it made no sense she would have handed them over.

Lia sighed and inclined her head. "If it was the only way we could get you both back safely, then yes, we were going to give her the Stones."

I pressed my fist against my mouth, trying to figure out what to say.

"But then the siren helped you escape, and now you're here, and we don't have to consider that anymore," Lia continued. "I wished on the stars every night for another option, and one was given to us."

It wasn't that I was upset with Lia for caring for Viv and me so much that she was willing to risk the entire ocean for us ... Well, actually, that was exactly it.

"I love you, Lia," I started, sucking my bottom lip between my teeth, and letting it out slowly. "You and Finn. Fuck, I'm sorry." I dropped my head into my hands. "I don't want you to put me above your kingdom."

Lia's hands wrapped around my wrists.

"I could have not told you, but I thought you should know. It's been eating at me, and I can't sleep knowing the harm I would have caused ..."

I lifted my head and looked at her. I couldn't tell if it was tears or raindrops trailing down her cheeks, but I wiped them away anyway.

"I'm glad you told me. I don't ever want you to think you can't tell me anything, and this doesn't change anything between us. Do you hear me?" I slipped my hands into hers and laced our fingers. I wouldn't say it aloud, but it *did* change things. Because I knew I'd do the same for her, and we both had other people relying on us. It wasn't right ... but we'd cross that bridge when we came to it. "Promise me you won't let me come between you and your duties to your kingdom again? Okay? I know how much being their princess means to you."

"I promise." She leaned her forehead against mine.

Splashing footsteps had me turning to find Charles approaching.

"Sorry to interrupt, but can we talk privately for a minute Jami?" Charles seemed unsure for the first time in his life.

I glanced at Lia, who nodded at me. "Okay." I followed Charles to the side of the ship where no one would bother us. Everyone else was too busy hiding from the rain or keeping the ship on course.

"I've been waiting years to say this because I wanted to say it in person." Charles picked at the bottom of his jacket. "I'm sorry for all the pain Roland and I caused you."

"You mean, for trying to kill me time and again?" I crossed my arms over my chest and looked out to the water. "Because that's how I remember it. Fighting for my life any time either of you came near."

Charles braced himself with his hand on the side of the ship and put his other hand on my shoulder. "We never wanted to kill you."

I scoffed. "That's comforting."

"Jami, please. We were dumb kids back then, and I'd like to start over now. I'd like a chance to be a real brother to you." The plea in his voice had me doubting myself. I'd been so set on hating Charles and Roland my whole life, it seemed like a betrayal to forgive them now. But maybe it wouldn't be so bad to have brothers who actually cared about me.

"I don't need you or Roland. I never did. Finn's been there for me through it all, even while you and Roland tormented me." I flashed back to the day Finn invited me home with him for the first time. The calm, warm meal we'd shared with his mother. *Leona.* She'd been more of a mother to me than mine.

Charles took his hand from my shoulder and ran it through his wet hair. "I don't know what to say besides I'm sorry."

"If you want to be a brother to me, then fine. I won't try to stop you. But I am also not going out of my way to change my life to make room for you. I truly hope that maybe one day we can be *real* brothers, as you put it. But I won't get my hopes up."

The rain did nothing to cool me down as my nerves heated my skin and made my ears ring.

Charles flipped his coin over his knuckles absentmindedly as he stared at the roiling ocean.

"Can I see your coin?" I asked, not sure why, but I had the urge to hold all three. Pulling mine and Roland's from my pocket, I held my hand out to Charles, and he dropped his on top of the other two.

A strange sensation came over me and I was thrown back in time to a memory I'd long forgotten.

The mage stood in front of me and beside us sat a large chest filled with gold.

"This is where I'll be putting the Stones," he said. "The gold is here to insure if you ever need to take the Stones and hide them elsewhere, you'll have the means to do it."

I stared up at him, confusion warring with fear in my mind. Mother and Father were gone, and I wasn't sure why they'd left me alone with the mage.

"Your hand." The mage took my hand before I could lift it. Mine was much smaller than his, and he easily opened my fist so my palm was revealed. "This will only hurt a moment."

I cried out as he slid a knife from his pocket. Though I tried to squirm away, he held my hand tight.

Blood oozed from the clean cut he'd made by pressing the knife against my palm. He pulled me by my hand toward the chest, pressing my bloodied palm against its exterior and held me there.

A tugging sensation started in my legs and moved all the way up to my head. My cut pulsed, and my energy seemed to sap out of me.

When he released me, I nearly collapsed from exhaustion, but somehow managed to stay standing. My palm

stung and I wrapped my other hand around it, trying to dull the pain.

"You are the only one who will know it is your blood that binds the ward on this chest. Without your blood, this chest will never open. Even if someone has all three coins, and makes it this far, they will be blasted back by the ward."

"What's happening to me?" I asked, more concerned with the strange emptiness I felt inside.

The mage knelt in front of me. "You made a great sacrifice today. Your magic is tied to this island and all the wards. It will fuel it for many years, until the day you die. You will find someone else to take your place by then, so that no one will ever find these Stones."

I snapped back into the present. Charles hadn't noticed anything amiss, so I assumed my flashback hadn't lasted more than a few seconds.

My magic ... I had magic, or should have had the mage not stolen it from me. My parents had offered me as the ward's power source so they could collect the money that came from helping the mage hide the stones. There was no way I would have chosen to give up my magic for that, so they'd taken it from me and hidden the truth.

My limbs tingled and my stomach roiled as I considered the possibility that I could have been a shifter just like my brothers. I felt sick.

I had to keep this to myself because it would be my leverage to ensure I was the one who went into that cave and retrieved the Stones. No one could get them without me.

"Are you all right?" Charles asked, reaching out as if to touch my shoulder, but then shoving his hand in his pocket instead. "You look a little queasy."

I cleared my throat and stepped away from him. "Fine. I need some rest is all. I'll talk to you later."

Legs shaking as I crossed the deck, aiming for the stairs leading down to the bunks, I knew I needed to process what I'd just seen.

"Jami." Lia caught up with me. "My room is currently occupied, mind if I join you down below for a while?" She wrapped her hand around mine and leaned into me. Her smile soothed my nerves and was a welcome distraction.

"Of course not."

A loud bang followed by a few smaller crashes came from below and we ran to the closet where the noises came from to find quite the surprise.

Nix

After spending a few minutes in the rain with my sisters, I decided it was more painful than comforting to remain in the storm. So, I headed belowdecks.

"It's awfully wet out there," Marley commented as she followed me down the stairs, shaking off the rainwater from crossing the main deck.

I stopped at the bottom of the stairs and turned back, coming face to face with her. Her lips quirked up in the corner.

"You are so ..." I took a deep breath.

"What?" she asked, accentuating her 't'. Amusement lit up her gaze.

Looking to the side, I tried to gather myself and push down the frustration and utter *need* to touch her. But I failed.

My hands came up on either side of her face, tangling in her short hair at the sides of her head. Water dripped from me onto the few remaining dry spots of her clothes. She only hesitated a second before her arms wound around my waist and pulled me against her and our lips collided.

It was much more chaotic and messier than any other kiss I'd had, and it seemed fitting.

178

Turning slowly, Marley pushed me against the closet door beside the stairs and fumbled with the handle.

"Inside," she commanded before kissing me again and we stumbled backward into the closet. The door shut behind us and darkness enveloped us. A *snick* told me she'd locked the door.

My hat flipped off my head, and I wondered if Marley had done that purposefully as my braid fell over my shoulder.

Marley's lips trailed down my neck to my collarbone. My head fell back against a shelf, knocking something off and making a *thud*. A small moan escaped me.

Unaffected by the disturbance, Marley's fingertips edged my shirt up, but her eyes met mine before going any further.

"Tell me if you don't want this," she said, almost gasping, clearly as breathless as I was.

A small laugh bubbled out of me. If only she knew how long I'd *yearned* for this. "I want this," I said. "Don't stop."

Marley kissed me again, slipped my shirt over my head, and let it drop to the floor to join whatever other mess we'd created. Her knee came up between my legs, and I ground against it.

Her hand slipped down the front of my leggings as she lowered her knee, and her fingers replaced the pressure against my clit. A single finger slipped inside me, teasing and slow.

"Is that all you've got?" I asked, breathless as I ran my hands beneath her shirt, and pulled her a little closer.

A second finger joined the first inside me and her thumb traced circles as the others began their pumping motion. My grip on Marley's waist tightened before I scraped my nails up and down her back trying to ease the tension building inside me.

Her tongue flicked my nipple, and I looked down as she sucked it into her mouth. Right as I thought I was about to crash

over the edge, the shelf behind me gave out, sending me and the shelf's contents crashing to the floor. I'd had a firm enough grip on Marley that I brought her down with me, and I burst out laughing.

"Are you all right?" she asked, smoothing the hairs that had broken free of my braid off of my sweaty face.

"Fine," I said, gripping her chin and kissing her before she could worry anymore. "Perfect."

"It's not how I imagined this going." She laughed, shifting her weight so it wasn't wholly on me.

"You mean, you've imagined this moment for us?" I asked, brows rising and heart soaring at the hope that I hadn't been the only one pining.

Footsteps pounded down the steps and I knew we only had seconds before someone was banging on the door to find out what had happened.

Leaning over from where I sat, I grabbed my shirt from beneath the cleaning supplies and other containers that had fallen on it. Marley helped me back into it and even replaced my hat on my head, tucking my braid up underneath, even though I had no reason to hide it anymore.

"Next time, I'll make sure you finish," she said, winking before she hopped to her feet and unlocked the door. It opened almost immediately to Jami and Lia, both wearing curious faces.

"Why am I not surprised?" Jami said as he met Marley's gaze and then found mine.

Marley helped me to my feet.

"I feel like there are better places ..." Jami started as we exited the closet.

"You've had your own quarters for years now, to make things easier for you. When you share a bunk room with twenty

other people, you get creative when it comes to finding privacy," Marley said.

"Hm," he mused. "I guess." He eyed me curiously for a second.

"Nix," an older, male voice surprised me, and I stopped short beside a barrel as we entered the crew's quarters. Harlan sat in the corner, half concealed by the barrel, a piece of parchment spread over his lap. He'd hardly spoken to me before, so I hadn't recognized his voice right away.

"What are you doing down there? Shouldn't you be in the crow's nest?" I asked, leaning on the barrel, and peering down at him. Marley moved to stand beside me, while Jami and Lia sat on a nearby hammock.

Harlan grunted and struggled to stand. I offered him a hand, helping him to his feet. He placed the parchment on the barrel, and I realized it was a copy of the map of Jami's family's island that I'd drawn and must have left up in the crow's nest.

"I found this and couldn't help but take a look." He pointed a long, knobbed finger at the island and tapped it a few times. "I've been to this island, a long, long time ago. Back before you were born, I'd bet."

I didn't remind him that I was a mermaid and hundreds of years old, so that was impossible.

He continued. "I know where it is. We're not too far off, but we'll need to change course a bit if this is where we're headed."

Lia and Jami had joined us by the barrel and were standing behind me.

"We need to tell Captain Brom," Lia said. "Will you come with us?" she asked Harlan.

He stretched his back, wincing. "I will. Gimme a second to recover from sitting on the floor."

I turned to Lia and Jami. "You two go, we'll meet you there."

"Who is this nice, young lady?" Harlan asked, jerking his chin toward Marley as he continued his stretches.

For some reason, my face grew hot and butterflies erupted in my stomach as if he'd caught us.

"Erm, this is Marley, she's one of Finn's crew," I said quickly. I rubbed the back of my neck. "Marley, this is Harlan, he sits in the crow's nest."

Harlan burst out laughing, surprising us both.

"That's not my name!" He managed to get out amidst his raucous laughter. "Name's Barrow."

Damn it, I should have known.

"Harlan suited you better," I said, laughing with him.

Marley bumped me with her shoulder and smirked at me. "Come on, let's take *Barrow* to the captain," she teased.

I'd never live this down.

Finn

Nix and Lia had both left Viv to stand in the rain alone. I walked toward her as she moved to the side of the ship. Right before she reached the side, a wave rocked the ship and knocked her off balance, sending her careening backward.

I lurched forward, catching her and setting her back on her feet.

"Careful. I wouldn't want you falling overboard, or else I'd be obligated to follow and save you," I said.

She turned to face me, my hands still on her waist.

"If that happened, *I'd* be the one saving *you*," she pointed out.

I lifted my shoulder and smirked. "Maybe."

Lightning flashed to my left.

"We should get undercover before the full storm hits," I said, taking Viv's hand.

"Lia and Jami went belowdecks, which means Lia's room is open." Viv raised a brow with a devilish grin.

"It *was* ours, first," I reminded her. We'd stayed in that room when Brom had taken us as collateral for his children. Though it had truly been safer for them on land while he'd

183

traveled to Asmara, he'd had ulterior motives for keeping us on board back then.

Viv tugged on my hand and without further discussion, we tucked into Lia's room, locking the door behind us. Turning on me, Viv pushed me back against the door and I let out a snarl, pulling her to me.

"Sorry, did you expect to be the one in charge, Captain?" she teased, her fingers trailing down my chest.

"You know what it does to me when you call me that." My voice turned rough and low, my inner lion closer to the surface in my aroused state.

"I know," she whispered, smirking. She grasped the hem of my shirt. A question entered her gaze and she hesitated. In answer, I kissed her fiercely.

Our movements became jerky and desperate as we each rushed to remove our clothes and join together. The distance had done nothing to tame the feelings I held for her. I wanted all of her here, now, and forever.

Dropping her last article of clothing onto the floor, Viv bared herself to me. I afforded myself one long glance at her before kissing her slowly, guiding her back toward the bed.

Her bare skin against mine drove me crazy with need, but I would take my time with her. This might be our last chance to be together before we fought the siren queen, and I couldn't say what would come after that.

She fell onto the bed, propping herself on her elbows as I followed her down, kissing between her breasts and creating a line of kisses down her stomach to her most sensitive parts. A small moan escaped her as my tongue traced that same path in reverse.

Her hands fisted in my hair, and she pushed me back down, making me chuckle.

184

"Don't worry," I told her. "Whatever you wish, I shall give you." I dipped my head back between her thighs and my tongue circled her clit as I drove two fingers inside her.

Viv's back arched and her hips moved up, matching the movements of my tongue. I trailed my free hand up her abdomen and around to her back, removing my fingers from inside her, and flipping her onto her stomach. A small gasp escaped her, but she turned her head and met my gaze before bracing herself.

I stood at the base of the bed and lifted her hips to line up the tip of my hardened cock with her entrance and eased myself inside. I moved torturously slow at first.

"Finn," Viv moaned.

I slammed back into her and kept a rigorous pace. Viv's body tightened around me, and as I was about to finish, I pulled out and flipped Viv once more.

"Captain," she breathed, smirking up at me as she backed up fully onto the bed, and I followed on my hands and knees.

I kissed her hard enough to bruise and she scraped her nails down my back as I entered her once more and we finished one after the other. Thunder muffled Viv's scream of pleasure.

Lying beside Viv, I pulled her against me. Sweat beaded on my brow, and I absentmindedly wiped it. She curled against my side and fell asleep with my arm around her.

I laid awake, thinking over everything Charles had told us about the coins and the Stones. One of us would have to give up our magic to get to the Stones, and I wasn't going to stand aside and let someone else take that on themselves. Lia needed her magic to lead her people. Without being able to shift into her mer form, she wouldn't be able to be the princess of Thalassia.

Not that I would have accepted Viv as an option, but she was already going to be helping Brom with the kraken, so I didn't need to worry about her trying to go for the Stones. Jami didn't have any magic to give, meaning the Stones would likely kill him, so there was no chance I was letting him go in that cave. And I didn't trust anyone else to retrieve the Stones.

Viv wrapped her arm over me and pressed her lips to my shoulder.

"Something's eating at you," she murmured.

I turned in her arms and kissed the top of her head.

"It doesn't seem real, having you back," I said, keeping the rest of my thoughts to myself.

Her bangs had fallen over her eye, and she tilted her head so they moved aside.

"Well, it's real." She kissed me sweetly. Having her back felt like a dream, and yet I knew we were about to live through a nightmare. Facing the kraken, finding the Stones, and taking on the siren queen may very well be the end of our story.

Viv's hand against my cheek pulled me out of my thoughts once more.

"Stay with me, Captain," she said.

I pressed my forehead against hers and let out a long, slow breath. Was I really considering giving up my magic to get the Stones? There had to be another way to kill the siren queen. But we didn't have time to figure that out. The Stones were the only surefire way we could kill her without losing more of our own people.

Three loud knocks on the door had me pulling up the sheet to cover Viv out of instinct, and then I remembered we'd locked the door.

"I wouldn't interrupt if it wasn't important," Jami called through the door. "Meet us in Captain Brom's room."

I sighed and met Viv's gaze. Her hand cupped my cheek.

"We'll have more moments like this after, I promise," she said, kissing me once more.

Once we were both dressed, we headed for Brom's room. Jami, Lia, Nix, and Marley were already there, waiting for us. No one sat, not even Brom.

"We know—well, Barrow knows where the island is," Jami announced. "And once we're close enough, I'll be able to sense it."

Brom cocked his head to the side. "*Sense?* As in some witchy shit?"

Jami rolled his eyes and dug his hand into his pocket, pulling out one of the coins.

"This coin was spelled to lead the holder to the island where the Stones are hidden. So, yes, I'll be able to sense it."

Brom shrugged. "Just checking. Wanted to be sure we're not following another hunch." He cast a glance at Lia. "Barrow can join me at the helm, and once this storm passes, I'll have you up there as well."

"No, I need to be up there *now,*" Jami demanded. Lia put her hand on his bicep, her features tense.

My eyes widened in surprise. This wasn't like Jami. He usually was much calmer and less irritable under pressure.

"Fine," Brom snapped. "Let's go." He clomped out of the room, his boots squelching. The rain had thoroughly soaked him while he'd been at the helm.

Jami followed Brom from the room, but Lia remained behind.

"I'll go with them," I said, nodding at Viv before leaving.

The deck outside was slick from the rain and I almost slipped as I headed for the stairs leading to the upper deck.

Sheets of rain made it difficult to see, but I knew the layout of this boat as if it were my own. Most ships were alike in that way.

The stairs creaked beneath my weight, and I was reminded of all the times I navigated my own ship through storms much like this one. Nostalgia washed over me and a sense of ease. For the first time since my ship had been destroyed, I felt no anxiety or fear being aboard this ship.

"You'll want to turn a few notches to the west," Barrow yelled over the storm's clamor.

Brom adjusted the helm, turning it as Barrow directed. Jami stood beside him, his arms crossed, and hands clenched.

I walked up on the left side of the helm, opposite Jami, while Brom stood between us, hands gripping either side of the helm.

We'd changed course originally when Nix claimed that she'd seen fog that could have possibly been from the mysterious island to the east. Of course, now I knew that was all a lie to get us closer to Jami and Viv's location. It irked me that Nix and Marley had kept the secret, but I couldn't stay mad since it resulted in Viv and Jami's safe return.

Water dripped down my hair and into my eyes, and I had to keep blinking to clear them.

Jami would hardly look at me, seeming almost determined to ignore my presence. I walked over to him, pulling him aside.

"What's going on?" I asked.

"Nothing," he said too quickly.

"It's not nothing. Tell me," I demanded, keeping a firm grip on his arm.

We hit a large swell and the ship rocked, throwing us both sprawling onto the deck.

"Man overboard!" someone yelled from below.

We climbed over one another to get back on our feet, running to the side to try and see who'd gone over.

"I've got them!" Nix, who had appeared on my right, dove over the side into the water.

"Where the hell did she come from?" I asked Jami.

"Beats me. She's probably been there the whole time hiding behind a barrel or some shit. I can't keep up with her."

Her head popped up above the water a few seconds later, a blonde head of hair being dragged beside her.

Jack, I thought, shaking my head.

"He hasn't quite gotten his sea legs yet," Brom said from where he'd come up on my other side. "This will teach him to be more careful. He won't always have mermaids around to save his ass."

"He's still a child," I reminded him.

Brom scoffed. "So are Tabby and the twins, yet I've never had to fish them out of the ocean."

"You—"

"Finn, it's not the time." Jami gave me a knowing look and I swallowed the rest of my words. I could tell off Brom another time. Gods knew he gave me plenty of opportunities.

A group of men were hauling Nix and Jack back onto the ship. The worst of the storm seemed to have passed. The rain was lighter and the clouds less doom and gloom.

"You should get some rest," Jami said, drawing my attention back to him. "We'll reach the island soon."

I tilted my head. "You're so sure?"

He nodded and walked away from me, back to where Brom stood at the helm.

As much as I wanted to talk to Jami about what had been bothering him before, I had something else I needed to do. I had a good feeling I knew exactly what was eating at Jami, and it

was the same thing eating at me. We both thought we would be the ones to get the Stones in the cave. We both wanted to be the ones to make the ultimate sacrifice, though for Jami, it would much more likely mean death rather than a simple loss of magic. I needed to ensure Jami wouldn't be able to get near those Stones.

I wound down the two sets of stairs to get belowdecks and found my target.

"Charles," I said, making him lift his head from his pillow on his hammock.

"I heard Barrow and Jami are leading the way," he said. He dropped his head back down and stared at the ceiling as I approached. "We must be close."

"Do you remember the island? Do you remember exactly where the Stones are?" I asked, skipping over the frivolities of small talk.

"Vaguely. I remember a lot of walking and then taking a small boat to a cave, but I don't remember if I went in or not. I think Roland and I may have stayed outside with our mother while Jami went in with the mage and our father."

"Do you think you can bring me there while everyone else is distracted by the kraken?"

Charles' gaze flicked to meet mine. "You won't be the one to retrieve the Stones."

"I'm sure as hell not letting Jami risk his life for this," I said. "I'll do it to ensure it isn't him."

Charles swung his legs to the side and planted them on the floor. "Let me be the one to retrieve them. It's the least I can do to make up for all the horrible things I did to him ..."

I shook my head. "I can't. I'll be blunt and say I don't trust you, and this mission is too important."

190

Charles huffed. "I figured as much. I understand why you don't trust me, but that won't stop me from trying to take on this burden."

"We'll go together, then." I would overpower him in the end and ensure I retrieved the Stones, but he didn't need to know that.

"Fine. I'll take you to them once we're off the ship. Someone will need to keep Jami distracted, because he'll be expecting everyone to go after the Stones."

"Marley will do it." She cared about him almost as much as I did, even if she'd never admit it and I knew she'd also want to keep him alive. "Jami said we'll arrive at the island by morning, so I should go talk with her now."

"No need," Marley said as she dropped down from a nearby hammock hanging high enough I couldn't see who had occupied it.

"Gods, Marley," I gasped, clutching the front of my tunic. "You're going to be the death of me."

She lifted her shoulder and leaned against the hammock's post.

"I'm game. I'll keep Jami distracted while the two of you go off to save the world."

"We're not exactly saving the world," Charles said.

"Don't sell yourself short. The siren queen taking over the entire ocean would mean controlling the trade markets, controlling the inhabitants of the ocean, and anyone who tried to sail it. Even if the kings don't believe this affects them, it *will.*" Marley spoke so casually it was almost as if she didn't care too much herself, but she was just stating facts.

Footsteps alerted us to someone coming down the stairs and we all turned to look. Lia strode toward us.

"Nix told me you were talking about who would be retrieving the Stones, so I came down here to inform you it will be me," she said, crossing her arms and lifting her chin.

I shook my head. "How did Nix ... You know what, I'm not even going to ask. No. You're not involved in this. You will be staying as far from those Stones as possible, along with Viv."

Lia moved closer, raising her finger and poking me in the chest. "You can't tell me what to do, *Captain.* I think my title holds a bit more authority than yours."

I laughed. "Sorry, *princess,* but you won't be changing my mind."

She dropped her hands to her sides and smiled sweetly. "We'll see about that."

My gaze flicked to movement on the stairs as Viv came down them. She wore her best *don't fuck with me* face and it made me want to take her back to bed.

"What, did Nix tell you too?" Marley asked, hanging her head over the side of the hammock.

Viv looked up at her, unsmiling. "I have eyes. I saw Lia coming down here, and assumed it was something I should be in on. Of course, everyone thinks I'm too fragile to handle any of this." Her gaze swept over us, and guilt clenched my chest.

"We don't think you're too fragile," Lia tried to say, but it came out too high and was clearly a lie. "I mean, you just escaped the siren queen after spending a week trapped in a room with the man who held you captive for two years. I'm sorry for trying to protect you from this." Lia pressed her hand against her chest and reached out for Viv's.

"I don't need your protection. I can handle this. I'm the one who's going to help Brom take care of the kraken." Her gaze fell to the floor, and she dropped Lia's hand, her throat

bobbing. "Because you all think it's going to keep me out of the way. I'm so stupid." Her hand flew to her mouth.

Moving into her space, I put a hand on her shoulder and a crooked finger under her chin to make her look at me.

"If I lost you to the stupid Azurean Stones, I'd use them to ravage this entire world for daring to take you from me. So, yes, I'd rather you help Brom blow up his ship than come to that cave with us." The intense burning building in my gut at the thought of losing Viv was almost all consuming. I managed to keep my inner lion at bay, but barely.

"And you think I don't feel the same way about you? Or Lia?" Viv's gaze flicked between me and Lia. "Losing either of you would destroy me. I can't fathom ..." She jerked her chin from my grasp.

"That's why I will do it," Charles said. "No one cares whether I live or die, let me risk myself for this."

"Don't be so self-deprecating," Marley drawled. "Someone cares. Just not us. Let him do it. He's got enough magic he probably won't die."

I turned to look at Lia and she gave me a slight nod. It killed me to lie to Viv, but I needed to keep her safe.

"Fine," I said. "Charles can do it."

"If you think you can handle it," Lia said, swinging her head to look at Charles.

"Easy peasy," Marley commented, hopping down from the hammock. "I need food."

Turning on her heel, she strolled up the stairs and out of sight. Lia linked her arm with Viv's and steered her away and up the stairs too.

"Lia's kind of scary," Charles said, though he smiled at where she'd stood. "I understand what Jami sees in her."

"You're damn right, she's scary. Stay away from her," I warned. I wouldn't put it past Charles to try and steal her away from Jami, not that she'd let him think he could succeed.

We parted ways with our plan in place. As soon as we reached the island and evacuated the ship, Charles and I would sneak away to head for the Stones. So long as everything went as planned, the kraken would be dead, or at the very least distracted, by the time we had to take the small boat over to the cave and we'd be able to get the Stones before anyone else could try. Jami, Lia, and Viv would all be kept safe and sound.

A part of me worried for Viv since she would be on the ship when the kraken attacked it, but I knew she'd be able to get away as soon as the fuse for the gunpowder bomb we'd created was lit. Everything would be fine and by the end of the day, the siren queen would be dead and we'd be free to move on with our lives.

Gods willing ...

Viv

The long boat bobbed in the water as the last group loaded onto it. As Jami had predicted, we'd come across the island not long after the sun rose. He'd been the only one to see it since it was shrouded in fog for the rest of us without the magic of the coin. Once we'd passed a certain threshold, though, the fog had cleared, and the island came into view.

Finn strode over to me, pressed his forehead against mine, and closed his eyes. I kept mine open to memorize his every feature, just in case.

"You'll be waiting for me on the beach, right?" I asked.

"Finn! Time to go," Jami called from beside the rope leading to the longboat.

"I'll see you soon," Finn said. He kissed me one last time before climbing down into the longboat. I didn't take my eyes off them until they were nearly at the beach.

A hand clamped onto my shoulder, and I turned to Brom. "I'm counting on you," he said. "Let's take care of this kraken so we can get back to our people."

I'd never expected Brom to agree to this plan. A ship to a pirate captain was almost as sacred as a child. Sometimes it *was*

as sacred as that. But he'd seemed different the past few days. Not as arrogant, maybe.

He headed for the helm, preparing to steer the ship into the heart of the inlet where the kraken resided. All the gunpowder had been moved to the center of the ship belowdecks, ready to be set alight. I checked our gunpowder trail to insure it hadn't been broken while everyone left, but it was still an unbroken line all the way to the barrels. Brom would light our makeshift fuse, staying long enough to ensure it made it down the stairs, and then he'd jump overboard where I'd be waiting in the water to bring him to shore.

We were counting on the kraken being too distracted by taking down the ship to worry about me, but there was a chance things would go wrong.

"It won't be long now," Brom called down to me. The ship was entering the kraken's territory. We had to wait until the last possible second to set off our explosion. This was our only shot at killing the kraken, and Charles wouldn't be able to get in and out of the cave safely if it survived. It was bound to protect the cave.

Once we were past the rock walls bordering the inlet's opening, Brom stood beside me.

He cleared his throat and stared straight ahead. "If anything goes wrong, I need you to leave me behind."

I whipped my head to the side to look at him. "Nothing will wrong," I said. "I won't be leaving you behind."

Brom laughed. "I've lived a good, long life. If things go off without a hitch and I survive this, then so be it. However, if I'm not in the water with you ten seconds after lighting that fuse, *leave me.*"

This was a side of Brom I never thought I'd see. A self-sacrificing man.

196

"I can't go to that beach without you," I argued. "Your men—"

"My men know their captain would choose to go down with his ship if push came to shove. They won't blame you."

"But—" The entire ship rocked, sending Brom and I sprawling across the deck. My back slammed against the side of the ship, jarring me.

The wood beneath us creaked and I gasped as a giant, mast-sized tentacle shot into the air directly over my head.

"Go, Vivianne!" Brom yelled as he crawled toward the stairs where the gunpowder trail began. "Don't look back."

I tried to push myself to my feet, but the ship rocked again, slamming me back against the side. Groaning, I braced myself as it happened once more. The giant tentacle wrapped itself around the mast overhead, snapping it in two. The top half fell into the water, causing a giant splash that washed water up onto the deck and soaked me.

"I won't light this until you are off the ship!" Brom said. "Finn would never forgive me." I thought I heard amusement in his tone.

"Just light it!" I called back. "I can't move." I panted from the exertion of trying to stand as the ship continued to rock vigorously.

"Get. Up. Vivianne." Brom ground the words out, any hint of amusement gone. "Don't make me come over there."

Steeling myself, I sat up and grabbed a hold of the rail. My arms ached as the ship swayed in the opposite direction and my body threatened to roll with it. The kraken had the entire ship in its grip. It was the perfect time to light the gunpowder.

I pulled myself to my feet with every ounce of strength I could muster.

"Light it," I cried out.

Brom lit the fuse, and it sputtered out after a few seconds, barely making it to the stairs.

He lit it again with the same results.

"It's damp," Brom said. The splash from the mast falling into the water had soaked the entire deck. Tentacles were beginning to crush the sides of the ship. "I must go down there. Goodbye, Vivianne."

Before I could protest, Brom stumbled down the stairs. I couldn't wait to find out if he succeeded, because otherwise, I'd be blown to bits along with the ship, and hopefully, the kraken.

With one last burst of energy, I hauled myself over the side of the ship and plummeted into the water. I shifted immediately upon hitting the water and swam as fast as I could toward shore, not looking back until I thought it was safe.

When I looked back, I could see the kraken in all its glory. A massive, bulbous body attached to the giant tentacles I had seen from the ship. I hardly had any time to take in the sight before the ship exploded and a blast of water caught me and ripped me away from the scene. Debris blew past, scratching me.

Tumbling head over tail through the water, I tried to stop myself, but the current from the explosion was too strong. Something hard struck me, and everything went black.

Finn

My heart nagged at me to turn back. I didn't want to leave the beach behind without knowing if Viv made it off that ship safely. But I had to do this while she wasn't there to stop me.

Lia led the way while Charles and I followed close on her heels. She kept trying to convince us that she should be the one to retrieve the Stones, but there were so many reasons why I knew she shouldn't. We'd objected when she first joined us on our trek for the Stones, but neither of us dared hold her back. I'd seen what she was capable of when she was on a mission.

The path we trudged on clearly hadn't been tread in quite some time, as it was non-existent. The only evidence it had ever been a path before had been Charles's word that he'd walked it when he was younger with his parents.

I kept a close eye on Charles because I still didn't trust him.

"Why are you so keen on this? You've never cared about Jami's wellbeing before," I muttered, my irritation almost palpable in the humid air. I snuck a glance at Charles, whose face remained impassive.

"Roland and I were cruel to Jami when we were young, I'll admit it," Charles said.

Lia laughed but didn't turn back. "From what Jami told me, *cruel* is an understatement."

Charles sighed. "I deserve that. You're right."

"So, what changed?" she asked.

"After Jami left, we thought life would be better, but we realized how much we truly missed him. Our mother made a comment about how we'd run him off, and we realized that maybe we'd been too harsh on him." A twig cracked somewhere far off to our right, but we kept moving, and Charles continued talking. "It wasn't as if our lives had been easy, either. Jami received all the attention and praise before our parents came into money. After ... things changed for all of us, and Roland and I saw our opportunity to take out all our pent-up jealousy and anger on Jami while our parents were distracted by their new responsibilities."

"Sounds like a load of crap," I said. "Jami has always been the outcast of the family, even before your parents were paid off for hiding the Stones."

"I'm not going to fight with you or try to defend myself. I deserve every bit of anger you or Jami throw my way. Just know that I deeply regret the past and I'd change it all if I could."

I harrumphed.

Lia pushed a leafy branch aside, holding it a few seconds longer than necessary so it wouldn't smack Charles in the face. I kind of hoped she'd let it go.

"Thank you," he said.

Lia shrugged and ducked beneath the next branch.

When we shoved our way through a particularly stubborn bit of foliage, we came back to the inlet which we'd

need to cross to get to the cave. Hopefully the kraken was well enough distracted at that point he wouldn't come for us.

A longboat was tied to a small post sticking out of the ground where our path ended.

"This is it," Charles said.

Lia climbed into the boat first, followed by Charles and me. Charles rowed with the only set of oars. It was blissfully quiet as we made our way to the small beach before the cave.

A large enough opening for two people to walk through side-by-side loomed after a small stretch of sand. On either side of the opening, sheer rock extended on either side, and up higher than the tallest mast of the ship we'd been stuck on for the past few weeks.

"There it is," Charles said when we approached it on foot, as if we hadn't already guessed as much. He pressed his hand against the invisible barrier and it shimmered as it held firm.

We all stood gaping at it, as if we'd never seen a cave before. My heart raced as I realized that it was *real*. Inside that cave, the Stones were waiting to be used.

Lia held two coins in her hand, staring down at them. Jami's and Roland's. She was only missing Charles's coin.

"Give me the coins, Lia," Charles said, holding out his hand toward her.

Shaking her head, she stood her ground.

"I am the princess of Thalassia, *I* will retrieve the Stones and take down the siren queen," she demanded. Charles started to object, but she put her hand up to stop him. "You both have your reasons for wanting to be the ones to do this, but please, let me do this for my people."

Charles inclined his head and stepped away from the cave entrance, holding out his coin to her.

I tried to beat her to it, but she snatched it before I could.

"Lia, think about this," I said. "The Stones will drain your magic. You *need* your magic to lead your people and keep them safe. Let me be the one to use the Stones so you won't need to worry about losing your ability to *be* Thalassia's princess."

Shaking her head, she stepped backward into the cave. A small ripple-like shimmer washed over her and for a second, there seemed to be a barrier between her and us. It dissipated almost instantly.

"We can come with you," I said, reaching out. My hand passed over where the barrier had been without any push back. "Let us come with you."

"No, rejoin the others. Make sure everyone is ready once I get the Stones. I'll find a way to get us all back to Asmara so we can ready the army for the siren queen." She turned and ran deeper into the cave.

"Damn it," I hissed, turning back to the water. I stared at Brom's ship. The plan should be in action to take down the kraken. I could see tentacles slithering up the sides. But I could also still see someone on board.

I ran to the edge of the small beach. "They should be getting off the ship any second," I said, staring intently at the figure when I noticed another figure. "Why aren't they jumping? Why isn't the ship exploding? Something is wrong."

"Go. I'll keep an ear out for Lia in case she needs help." Charles pointed to the long boat.

"But—"

"Go."

I didn't wait for him to tell me again. Hopping onto the boat, I started back toward the beach. It had been a short trek to

the cave, but now I felt as if I was moving at a snail's pace as I watched the kraken envelop the ship. The ship rocked with the kraken's weight, and the figures fell out of sight.

No, no, no. Where is she?

I scanned the water, hoping I'd missed them jumping ship and I'd see them on their way to shore, but there was no sign of either of them.

Waves lapped at the sides of my boat from the kraken's movements, threatening to overturn me. A lone figure, who I was close enough now to see was Viv, threw herself over the side of the ship, straight down into the water. I could see the ripple from where she shifted, and I knew she was currently swimming as fast as she could away from the ship. So, I rowed toward the beach.

The explosion created a massive boom that reverberated through the inlet and left my ears ringing. Chunks of the boat were sent flying through the air, narrowly missing me. I could do nothing but watch as the waves from the explosion toppled my long boat and dumped me into the ocean.

Debris littered the water and I grabbed onto a piece of wood that kept me afloat as I made my way toward shore.

Viv still hadn't surfaced, though she should have already made it to the beach. I spotted Nix wading into the water, and she waved me down, pointing to a spot nearer to me.

"I think she was hit!" Nix shouted to me.

I dove beneath the water, keeping my eyes peeled for any sign of Viv. The explosion had kicked up a lot of sand and seaweed that made it difficult to see much at all. Resurfacing, I swam closer to where Nix thought Viv was and dove down once more. I spotted her lying on the bottom, unconscious.

Thankfully, she was in her mer form and wasn't struggling to breathe underwater, even unconscious. It took me a

few seconds to reach her, scoop her into my arms, and kick off from the sand to make it to the surface.

Nix arrived as I resurfaced with Viv in my arms, and she took Viv so I could swim back to shore. Nix's tail was much more powerful than my legs when it came to swimming, so she had no trouble getting Viv back to shore.

Laying Viv on the dry sand, Nix knelt beside her, and I on the other side. Blood seeped from a gash on her forehead where something had struck her.

I trailed a finger under her chin, inspecting her to insure she had no more wounds. Her eyes opened, and she smiled up at me. Relief flooded me and I kissed her.

When I pulled back, she shifted and sat up.

I put a hand at her back. "Careful. You shouldn't move too quickly. You might have a concussion."

She waved off my warning. "I need to tell you ..." She bit her lip and wrapped her arms around her knees as she pulled them to her chest. "Brom didn't make it. He had to stay behind to set off the explosion. Our fuse didn't work."

I closed my eyes. I'd guessed as much when I'd seen her go over by herself, but I hadn't anticipated the pain I'd feel hearing the truth.

"I tried to wait for him, but he made me leave him behind," she explained, tears trailing down her cheeks.

My last one-on-one conversation with Brom flashed in my mind. He'd promised he'd help me get Viv back safely from the siren queen. And now he'd risked his own life to ensure she made it off that ship alive. Maybe it wasn't enough to forgive him for a lifetime of indifference and rejection, but it left me confused and ... grateful.

I pulled Viv into my arms.

204

"Where's Lia?" she asked, scanning the beach when she pulled away from me.

I glanced at Nix at the same time she looked at me.

"Where is she?" Viv demanded, pushing herself to her feet. "She said she'd let Charles go into the cave ..."

Nix and I scrambled up beside her and Nix stepped in front of her.

"I promised I wouldn't let you follow them," she said. "I love you, Viv, but I can't disobey Lia."

Her brows rose and her jaw dropped in disbelief, her eyes flicking to me. "Lia put you up to this?"

"I'm sorry," Nix said.

"I'm so stupid. Of *course* Lia would go for the Stones. She feels obligated as the princess. And you." She turned on me, poking me in the chest with her index finger. "You let her go!"

I rubbed the back of my neck. "Not exactly."

"You ..." Viv looked between Nix and me, and I knew she could read the guilt written on our faces. "You went with her! You were going to leave me here ..." She dropped her head into her hands. "I took for granted that you'd let Charles be the one to risk himself for this. You *let* me believe he'd be the one to retrieve and use the Stones."

"I came as soon as I realized something had gone wrong on the ship. I wouldn't have left if I'd known you'd need me," I tried to explain. "I argued against Lia going in, but she took the coin from Charles before I could, and ..." I stopped, scanning the beach. "Nix, where is Jami?"

Nix sucked air between her teeth and scrunched her nose. "He went after them a few minutes ago. Marley and I tried to keep him here ..."

"Shit. He's going after Lia." I started for the path, and Viv kept pace with me.

"I'm coming with you. If it's not too late to save my best friend and sister, I won't give up this chance."

I would never let Viv take Lia's place, but I wasn't about to tell her that. I'd take Lia's place before I let Viv anywhere near those Stones.

"I know the way," I said, taking her hand. She squeezed it, letting me know she'd put aside her anger and we were in this together. Or so I hoped. I kissed her temple and we headed for the cave.

Jami

The mage had told me that if someone other than me tried to open the chest, it would blast them away. I didn't know exactly what that meant, but it couldn't be good.

I shoved through the undergrowth of the forest, fighting against every branch that dared block my path. I had to make it in time to stop them. My brain told me I was too late, but I couldn't give up.

What if Finn went in? I thought, and then a worse thought ... *what if it's Lia?*

I pushed myself harder. When I'd left the beach, Viv hadn't appeared yet, and the kraken was taking down the ship. I didn't know if she'd made it off the ship ... I couldn't worry about that. *One thing at a time, Jami.*

A boom echoed behind me. The ship had exploded. Shaking my head, I ignored it. There was nothing I could do about what was happening back at the beach. All I could focus on was reaching Lia in time.

I stopped as I reached the end of the path and saw the cave opposite a stretch of water. My stomach flipped as I watched Charles pacing, alone, in front of the cave. *Who went in ... Finn or Lia? Or both?*

207

I shook my head and dove into the water.

"You're not supposed to be here, little brother," Charles said when I walked up on the beach, dripping wet.

"My blood is needed to open that chest! No one else can do it. Holding all three coins triggered the memory, and I didn't want to tell any of you because I knew you'd fight me and find a way to use my blood to open the chest without me present."

Charles' face changed, his mouth opening and his eyes slowly widening as realization dawned on him. He glanced back at the cave. "Lia."

"No," I gasped and ran past Charles into the cave. The barrier had already been broken by Lia passing through with Charles's coin.

Without a care for my own safety, I ran through the cave. My feet slipped on water that pooled on the floor, dripping from the stalactites hanging above me. It didn't matter. I ran faster, my chest heaving. If Lia tried to open the chest ...

I'd get there in time.

"Lia!" I yelled out, hoping she'd hear me. I had no idea how deep this cave was. "Please, Lia."

The cave opened wider, and there was another turn up ahead. I took it without slowing, scraping my shoulder against the rocks jutting from the wall.

Lia came into view, kneeling in front of a small golden chest.

"Lia!" I cried out, but it was as if she couldn't hear me. She didn't react. "Lia, stop!" I tried again, but she continued placing the final coin into its slot on the front of the chest.

Finally, she turned toward me as I entered the cavern. An explosion-like blast emanated out from where the chest sat, throwing Lia across the cavern, and knocking me off my feet.

Slamming into the ground, I rolled against the cave wall, and it knocked the breath from my lungs.

"Lia," I gasped out.

She coughed somewhere to my right, and I thanked the stars she was alive.

Gathering my strength, I pushed myself to my feet and stumbled toward where I'd last seen her.

Lia groaned and I turned to find her crumpled against the cavern wall. Blood trickled down her forehead, and her eyes were clenched shut. I ran to her.

"I'm here," I said, checking her for any serious injuries.

Tears trailed down her cheeks and her lower lip quivered as she opened her eyes and met my gaze.

"I couldn't let anyone else do it, I'm sorry," she said, her voice hoarse. "It had to be me."

I wrapped my arms around her and pulled her close. Her entire body shook with sobs.

"I'm sorry," she repeated, over and over.

I couldn't find it in me to respond, so I just held her. A slight humming sound came from the chest, and it seemed to whisper to me, drawing me in.

"I should have told you the truth." I brushed my thumb over the cut on her head. "My blood is needed to open the chest. My magic sealed it, and my magic is needed to open it."

Lia shook and I realized she was laughing.

"You don't have any magic left to give it," she said. "That's why it had to be me. If it took any more of yours ..." She trailed off.

"This is *my* problem to fix, Lia. *My* family created this seal, and now I have to break it." I gripped her hand, squeezing it too tight, but I couldn't bring myself to let go.

She sat up, blinking slowly. "I think I have a concussion." She squinted and dragged a hand down the side of her face. I helped her to her feet and we went to the chest together, kneeling in front of it.

"Open it, and I'll take the stones," she said.

"What if it takes your magic and your ability to shift? Did you think of that? Of not being able to shift anymore? I've never been able to, it wouldn't matter for me," I argued.

"At least you'll be okay," she said, her voice diminished and quiet. Two words I'd never have used to describe her before.

The coins were still in place in the chest. We had to open it no matter what, and we didn't have time for the back and forth. So, I took a rock from the floor and dragged it across my palm. It was much more painful than the knife the mage had used in my memory.

I pressed my hand to the chest and waited.

A *click* broke the silence. As the chest opened slowly, blue light leaked out until it was wide open. The light faded to reveal a silver collar-like necklace with three blue Stones set into it resting atop a pile of gold. Each stone was the size of my thumb nail, and I couldn't imagine how three such small Stones could have caused so much turmoil.

"We did it," Lia murmured.

"So, you did," a voice came from behind us, and we both turned as Jared stalked out from the shadows with Humer.

I jumped to my feet, but Jared pulled out a pistol and pointed it at me.

"Back down, *pirate,*"Jared hissed. "Make any other moves and I'll put a bullet through your head."

I slowly put my hands up and knelt back down beside Lia.

Lia's hands inched toward the chest. Jared cocked the gun and took a few steps closer.

"Same goes for you, *princess*. Don't make me kill your boyfriend."

Lia's lips parted as if she were about to speak, but then her eyes flicked to me and she snapped her mouth shut, her jaw flexing.

"I'll be taking that necklace," Jared said. He moved toward the chest, veering toward the back of it to avoid coming in reach of Lia or myself and keeping the gun aimed at me.

"You don't know what you're doing," Lia said through clenched teeth. "The siren queen will kill us all."

"That's your problem. My brother and I simply want to finish his work, and then he can die peacefully." Jared smiled at Humer who had remained where he was on the other side of the cavern.

"Your brother has lost his mind! How do you think he'll be able to do *anything?*" I asked.

"The Stones will restore his mind while he possesses them." Jared took the necklace and kicked the chest shut before walking back to his brother.

There was nothing Lia or I could do now, even if we wanted to risk my life. The Stones would give them more power than anyone else.

"Put it on," Jared said, urging Humer to take the necklace. When he put it on, it was almost as if a veil had lifted, and Humer's eyes widened in surprise.

"You've done it, Jared," Humer said, a smile stretching across his face. Jared lowered his weapon and holstered it at his side. "Our work can finally be completed."

"How did you get past Charles?" I asked. Fear clutched my chest as I thought of Charles alone outside of the cave.

"After taking the long way around the island, giving your friends plenty of time to arrive, we waited until Charles was distracted by the ship's explosion and slipped inside. It was all too easy," Humer explained.

This meant they'd been inside before me, and I'd probably run past them in my haste to get to Lia.

"You lied to us the entire time," Lia growled. "From when Viv and I met you in the prison to when you asked to help save Viv and Jami."

Jared laughed. "Of course, *I lied.* You'd have never helped me if I'd simply asked. I needed you to think I was against my brother. Not his partner. I fed you enough information to get you to trust me, and now ..."

"Now we get to change the world," Humer finished.

Viv

Anger and grief roiled inside me as if the ocean had claimed and controlled me, but I didn't have time to deal with that. We moved as fast as we could through the overgrown forest. I knew we were too late. I knew Lia had already gone into the cave to retrieve the Stones. It didn't stop me though.

There was a spot where it looked like there should have been a longboat on the shore as we came to the inlet leading toward the cave. I could see a small beach at the mouth of the cave where Charles stood by himself. My heart dropped and my jaw tensed. That meant Lia had gone inside.

"We'll have to swim since I lost the boat," Finn said.

I was still upset with him, but I understood why he'd gone with Lia. He'd meant to save Jami from trying to get the Stones, which I would have done for Lia. It didn't mean I had to forgive him right away though. I'd make him work a *little* harder for that.

Slipping into the water, I shifted and swam with Finn at my side until we reached the beach, and I shifted once more. Charles greeted us.

"Lia's still inside," he said.

Without any more preamble, I headed into the cave.
Finn caught up with me and his hand closed around mine, but
he didn't force me to stop, he kept walking with me.

"I'm coming with you," he said.

My breath caught in surprise as my gaze met his.

"You were going to risk yourself to use the Stones," I
said matter-of-factly. If Lia hadn't gotten to them yet, there was a
chance he might try to take them so she wouldn't have to.

He dropped his head to his chest. "I was trying to keep
everyone I love safe."

I swallowed, realizing how much this decision had
weighed on him. Whatever happened, I wouldn't blame him for
the outcome. This had been an impossible decision, and
someone had to do it.

We hurried through the cave, and voices became clear
as we approached where the Stones must have been kept.

"Is that—" I started, recognizing one of the voices and
terror clutched my heart.

"What the fuck," Finn murmured as we both started
running.

The cave opened wider, and I stopped. Lia and Jami
knelt on the floor before the open chest. Blood dripped down
Lia's face, but she seemed okay otherwise. There were no
Azurean Stones in sight. Until I turned to the right.

"Oh," Humer said, a smile spreading on his face.
"Vivianne, how lovely you've chosen to join us."

I glanced back at Lia, and she mouthed *run*. But I stayed
put. I wouldn't leave her here with that monster.

Humer moved toward me, and I put up a hand as I
faced him. My jaw dropped as I noticed the necklace he wore:
three bright blue stones gleamed from the settings that rested

214

against his chest. It explained the clarity in his eyes, and the lack of strange mumbling.

"Vivianne, dear, we've waited so long for this moment," he said, but he had stopped his advance. "I'll be taking you with me."

"The fuck you will," Finn growled, stepping in front of me. "You won't be leaving this cave alive."

My gaze caught on the gun holstered at Finn's side. It might not do anything against Humer while he wielded the Stones but ...

I took a chance. Grabbing the gun, I cocked it and pressed it against my own temple.

"Viv no!" Lia cried out, making Finn turn back to me, his gaze widening in horror.

Jared rolled his eyes and Humer laughed.

"You wouldn't, Vivianne," Humer said, reaching out a hand to me. "Hand it over."

"You want me so badly?" I asked, setting my jaw and steeling my gaze. "Bring all of us back to Asmara and help us defeat the siren queen. Then I'll *willingly* allow you to finish your *experiments.*" I spat the last word. No matter how my stomach churned with the thought of letting him work on me, I would do whatever it took to keep everyone here alive. "Or else I'll kill myself here and now and you'll have to start all over. Something tells me you don't have the time for that."

Humer pursed his lips as if considering my offer.

"Let her," Jared snapped. "We don't need her."

Humer whirled on him. "Do you realize how long it took to get everything just right? The Stones can only do so much. I don't have the time to find a new specimen as perfect as Vivianne. The Stones will kill me before then."

"Good riddance," Finn said.

Humer turned back to face us. "Don't test me, lion boy."

"Don't do this, Viv," Finn said to me. "We can find another way."

As much as I wanted to trust that we would, there was no other possibility I could see at the moment, and I wouldn't risk losing this chance to have the upper hand.

"Let me use the Stones on you *first,*" Humer amended. "Then I will bring all your friends back to Asmara and let them kill themselves trying to fight the sirens there."

"You can use the Stones on me *after* you return us all to Asmara and then you will help us defeat the sirens. The Stones are the only way we can win against the siren queen." I remained firm.

"So little faith in yourselves. Fine." Humer rolled his eyes. "I will get everyone back to Asmara first." He held out his hand and flexed his fingers. "Gun, please."

"No." I stepped back. "This is the only thing I have to ensure you do as I say."

"You test my patience, Vivianne." He flicked his fingers at Lia and Jami. "Get up. We're leaving. *Now.*"

I didn't dare move, afraid if I gave them a single opening, they'd get the gun from me, and I'd lose any advantage I thought I had.

"Walk," Humer said to Lia and Jami. They obeyed his command, leading the way out of the cave. "With me, Vivianne." He held his arm out, expecting me to walk with him.

My entire being revolted against the idea, but I had little choice.

"Go," I said to Finn. "I'll be okay."

The set of his jaw and the steel in his gaze told me he wouldn't leave my side.

I bit my lip and closed my eyes, trying to will my strength to remain as I pressed the gun to my temple, the cool metal warming from the extended contact.

"Please, Finn."

"*Please, Finn,*" Humer mocked. "Go, now, or I'll make her kill you. Do as I say, Vivianne." His voice became more entrancing and before I understood what was happening, I took the gun from my temple and pointed it at Finn.

Humer laughed and Jared yelled at him.

"If you can do that, why agree to her demands at all?" Jared asked.

Humer gave an exaggerated sigh. "Human will is fickle, brother. The second it takes for her to decide to pull the trigger would be faster than I could command her not to."

Finn backed away from me. "Only because I won't let my death be on your conscience," he said.

Tears welled in my eyes, but they wouldn't fall. Whether it was Humer or myself that held them at bay, I couldn't be sure.

"You can leave him be," Humer said and the invisible pressure that had held my arm in place before, released, and I was able to drop the gun. "I won't make you keep threatening yourself in order to uphold our deal," he said once Jared had followed Finn.

"Why? You are far more powerful right now than any of us," I said, sniffling as the snot that came along with tears dripped from my nose.

Humer's brows lowered and he gave me a serious look. "You are precious to me, Vivianne. I won't let anything happen to you."

I craned my neck as disgust slithered its way through my body, leaving me tense and nauseous. Hearing him speak lucidly brought back way too many horrible memories.

Humer linked his arm with mine and pulled me away from the cavern. I walked on instinct so I wouldn't be dragged, but the entire walk passed in a blur.

It was almost as if Humer were hauling me back into his underground bunker, about to restart his experiments and force me to watch him perform them on others who would never see the light of day again. But this time would be different. This time I was ready and no matter what happened, I'd come out whole and stronger on the other side. I would not allow him to break me again.

Nix

Brom's people were restless, and I had to be the one to tell them that their captain was dead. I'm sure many of them already assumed the worst, since they'd seen Viv return without him, but now they were all staring at me, waiting for an explanation. An explanation of which I only knew half.

I'd never been great at public speaking, but I cleared my throat, preparing myself. Before I uttered a word, Marley stepped up and started talking.

"Brom didn't make it off the ship before it blew," she said matter-of-factly. "Viv waited as long as she could, but something went wrong, and Brom told her to leave him. So, she did. Your captain went down with his ship."

A beat of silence passed before Callum stepped up.

"As he would have wanted," he said.

"Where's Dad?" Tabby appeared from behind Callum, taking his hand and tugging on it. Atty and Leo stepped up on his other side. "Why isn't he back?"

Callum crouched down to be face to face with her and the twins. I turned away from them, unable to watch their lives being upended.

"Thank you," I told Marley. I walked toward the path our friends had taken at the edge of the beach.

Marley kept pace with me, her hands in her pockets.

"Pirates are used to dealing with loss and change. They'll be fine," she said.

I peeked over at her. "Are you trying to *comfort* me right now?" I asked, smirking. "Seems very unlike you."

Her nose scrunched and she huffed a laugh. "Trust me, it felt just as strange to say it as it was to hear it."

I brushed my shoulder against hers. "Thanks for the effort."

"Want me to fly over to the cave and check on the others?" she offered.

I shook my head. "I'd rather have you here, if that's okay."

She put her hand to her forehead, saluting me and giving me a wink. "Aye, aye."

I couldn't contain my laughter, despite the grim situation. I'd never been as lighthearted as my sisters, but something about Marley brought it out in me and I could literally *feel* my spirits lifting in her presence.

"Has anyone ever told you you're quite good at comforting people?" I asked, and it was her turn to laugh.

"Never." She wiped an invisible tear from her eye as if the thought was too hilarious. "I've been told I'm heartless, uncaring, unfeeling, soulless, and a whole bunch of other similar adjectives, but never *comforting*."

Taking a seat at the edge of the sand as it turned to greenery, I patted the ground beside me.

We watched the others on the beach for a little while, as they navigated the loss of their captain, and my heart went out to them. Brom may not have been a great person, or someone I

really cared about at all, but I knew what it was like to lose someone. Now, at least, I knew Bree hadn't died for nothing. Her sacrifice had been what pushed the siren, Esme, to help Jami and Viv. Without her, they would still be on the siren queen's vessel at the bottom of the ocean.

"Do you think they'll choose Callum as their new captain?" Marley asked. "He seems the most obvious choice."

From what I'd witnessed on their ship over the past couple weeks, I'd agree that Callum seemed the best option. But that didn't mean there wasn't some other power dynamic we didn't know about going on with the crew.

"We now known Roland is still alive and he was Brom's first mate. So if he somehow escapes the siren queen, then maybe they'll appoint him captain," I suggested. "Though, in the meantime, I'm sure Callum will be chosen."

"Hmm," Marley mused, plucking at the grass between her legs. "I guess it doesn't really matter. Won't affect me one way or another."

The longer our friends were gone, the more antsy I became. I needed a distraction.

"What do I owe you?" I asked Marley, trying to trick my brain into thinking of something, *anything,* other than what was happening in the cave.

"What?"

"Our bet. You won. What do I owe you?" I reminded her. We'd never specified what the winner of our bet would get.

Marley's head tipped back with laughter. "Oh. That." She tapped her chin in deliberation. "I have several things in mind."

Before I could ask what those things might entail, I spotted Humer in the middle of the crew.

"Has Humer been there the whole time?" I asked, realizing I hadn't seen him in a while. Nor his brother Jared. "What is he doing?"

Humer's arms were stretched out and he seemed to be talking to the entire group.

"Probably spewing some of his unintelligible nonsense about the three Stones and the three brothers. I've heard him mumbling it on the ship," Marley said.

Pounding sounded behind us as someone crashed through the forest, and we both turned to see Finn in his lion form running at top speed.

Spots filled my vision, and I grabbed Marley's hand. Something had gone horribly wrong.

Finn

It took every ounce of self-restraint not to shift. My skin felt as if flames were beneath it. I ground my jaw and clenched my fists as tightly as I could to stay in control.

Viv and Humer walked behind me, but I didn't dare look. He held the power, and there was nothing any of us could do to change that until he either died or yielded the Stones to someone else. I couldn't imagine the latter happening.

Please, whatever god or goddess is listening, let Humer die before he can do any harm to Vivianne, I prayed silently. I wasn't the praying type, but now seemed the best time to start.

The cave walls were beginning to suffocate me, and I could have sworn they were closing in on us. It wasn't long, though, before we were out in the open and Lia and Jami stood waiting for us by the water.

Humer stepped out of the shadows of the cave into the sunlight. His skin was so pale I was surprised he didn't turn to ash as soon as the sun hit him, but he didn't seem too affected by it. I couldn't imagine he'd had much time outside in the last twenty years since he'd been imprisoned.

"Brother," Jared warned. "You shouldn't push yourself too much. You need to conserve what little magic you have."

223

No. Let him use it. Let the Stones suck him dry, I thought, narrowing my eyes. I rolled my shoulders trying to ease some of the tension knotted there.

"I need to practice transporting people if I'm to uphold my end of the bargain." Humer looked pointedly at Viv, smiling.

My neck cracked as I craned it, hoping to keep calm. Fear flared in Viv's eyes, and I knew she thought I was losing my hold on my lion. But so long as her life was on the line, I'd do everything in my power to remain non-threatening.

Deep breaths. In and out, I sucked down a lungful of air as if it would do anything to help.

In the blink of an eye, Humer and Viv were standing at the mouth of the cave, and then they weren't. Air left me and my heart dropped into my stomach.

"Where the fuck did they go?" I roared, whirling toward Jared, ready to shift and tear him apart. Before I could, Humer reappeared, alone.

"Where is she?" I asked, pinning him with my gaze.

Humer chuckled. "Safe on the Asmaran beach. Don't worry, I warned her that if she has even moved an inch when I returned, I'd kill you."

I imagined myself clawing the stupid grin off his face.

"Now, I think I can do us all at once," he said, reaching a hand toward Lia and the other toward Jared.

"You promised to return *everyone,*" Lia reminded him. "Not just us."

Sighing, Humer said, "Yes, I know. Do you want me to return you to Asmara now, or not?"

Lia bit her lip and turned to Jami, who nodded. They walked hand and hand toward Humer. Jami took one of Humer's outreached hands, and Jared took the other. Lia held her hand out to me. I didn't move.

"Keep her safe. I'm going to make sure everyone else gets off this island safely before I come," I said. As much as it pained me to remain behind, I wouldn't leave the rest of our people. Brom's people were our people now, despite their ire toward us, and I'd make sure they made it back to Asmara.

Lia didn't have a chance to respond before they blinked out of existence. I hesitated a moment, wondering if I should wait to see if Humer returned to this spot first, but then realized I was wasting time.

Diving into the water, I swam across the narrow channel separating the cave and the rest of the island. Once I was back on land, I shifted and ran as fast as I could for the beach.

The immense relief I felt from shifting made me realize how much pain I'd been in while holding myself back. I'd never had to show so much restraint before.

"Captain!" I heard Marley before I saw her. She and Nix sat at the edge of the forest where it turned to sand. They both stood as I shifted back and ran up to them.

I breathed heavily, unable to catch my breath from my all-out sprint.

"What's wrong?" Nix asked, her eyes flicking behind me to the forest as if she expected someone to be chasing me.

Taking one last deep breath, I'd recovered enough to say, "Humer has the Stones."

Amidst their gasps and questions, I spotted Humer among the others gathered on the beach, and the entire group of them started converging toward him.

"Come on, I'll explain when we're back in Asmara." I ushered them to the rest of the group. "Hold my hand," I commanded Marley.

"This is a first," she quipped, but did as I said. Nix took her other hand.

When we reached the closest of the crew, I put my hand on their shoulder, and once everyone was connected in some way, the world disappeared.

Before I could comprehend the non-existence of myself, we landed on the Asmaran beach, alive and well. The noise from everyone talking around us was almost deafening. Everyone sounded confused. It had all happened so fast ...

Humer was much closer to us now than he had been on the other beach.

Marley's lip curled as he approached. "Take one more step, I dare you," she ground out.

"Marley, no," I said, putting my hand on her shoulder and pulling her behind me.

"Oh, I wasn't coming for you," Humer said, shaking his head with laughter. "You're simply in my way."

Striding past us, Humer found his true target standing at the edge of the water with Lia. *Viv.* Relief washed over me at the sight of her. But this was far from over.

"What. The. Fuck." Marley glared at me, awaiting my explanation.

"Lia opened the chest and Humer got the Stones. I don't know all the details. All I know is Viv made a deal with him that he would return everyone to Asmara and help us defeat the siren queen ..." I trailed off as I watched Humer reach out to Viv and take her hand. The pure rage that flowed through me had me moving without thinking.

Nix grabbed my arm and held me back.

"In exchange for what?" she asked. When I didn't answer, her grip tightened, and she pulled me to her side. "In. Exchange. For. What. Finn." Her teeth were bared and her nails dug into my arm.

226

"She would allow him to finish his experiment on her with the Stones. Otherwise, she threatened to kill herself so he couldn't use her." The words fell like stones between us and had nausea swirling low in my gut.

Nix released me.

"What do we do?" Marley asked.

I stared at Humer and Viv. This was the part where she would hold up her end of the deal and let him use the Stones on her. After everything she had been through to escape him and move on with her life, she was now right back in his clutches and about to be back under his knife.

I would risk my life to save her from that fate.

Turning to Marley, I answered her, "Nothing." There was nothing we could do. It wasn't only my life I would be risking if I tried to stop Humer. It was Viv's, and Lia's.

Marley started to protest, but I interrupted her. "I need you to follow them. Keep hidden but stay nearby in case something goes wrong. If they need your help, don't hesitate to intervene."

Marley nodded and shifted into her hawk form, taking off.

I scanned the beach, noting that Brom's crew were all huddled together. Walking over to them, I found Callum.

"Brom," I started and then shook my head. "My father may not have always been a good man, but I'm still sorry he's gone."

Callum put a hand on my shoulder.

"He would never have admitted it to you, but he was proud of you," he said. "And now, I believe, he'd want his crew and ship to go to you."

Stunned, I gaped at him.

227

"That ship the kraken took down wasn't his only ship," Callum went on. "He has another, docked in Sylvane, that he'd want you to have."

"I couldn't," I said.

"It's yours. You can do what you want with it."

"We'll discuss this later, but right now, you need to take your men and get out of here. Keep Tabby and the twins safe and get to higher ground. There's nothing any of you can do to help us now, anyway."

"Thank you. I'll keep everyone safe, and we will meet up with you once this is all over, Captain." He smirked as he said it and I wanted to punch him for it. But instead, I walked away, because my *real* crew had just arrived.

Lia

Being transported with magic was the worst form of travel. For a brief second, all the world ceased to exist and existential dread set in, before you were deposited somewhere entirely different.

That lingering feeling left a bad taste in my mouth. As soon as we landed on the Asmaran beach with Viv, I sent Jami to the hotel to update Khali. No matter what happened with Humer, we'd need to be ready to fight the siren queen. She could arrive at any time and, even without the Stones, she'd still be a terrifyingly powerful opponent.

"We'll find a way to stop him," I murmured to Viv. Jared was close by but didn't seem keen on eavesdropping. I guess he already had everything he wanted. He had his brother back, even if briefly, and he'd pulled one over on us.

"Don't bother," Viv said. "Focus on the siren queen. If Humer thinks you're trying to do anything against him, he may change his mind about helping us after he finishes with me."

Her throat bobbed and her face was paler than usual. I took her hand and squeezed it.

"I won't let this happen."

Viv met my gaze. "Maybe it won't be so terrible. He's already done all the painful work, now it seems like the Stones are all he needs to finish the job. A little magic to ensure I can bear a cross-bred shifter child without dying." Tears filled her eyes and one slipped down her cheek.

I reached up and wiped it away.

"You're right. It will probably be painless, most magic is," I lied. There was plenty of magic that could cause immense pain but saying that wouldn't help Viv in this situation.

"Maybe this is all happening for a reason," she continued. "Maybe this is what the gods want. For a new era of shifters to emerge."

I stepped in front of Viv. "Is that what you really think? That you were *meant* to suffer for over two years at the hands of that monster simply so the gods could fulfill some twisted form of destiny?"

She shrugged. "I'm doing my best to think of anything that would explain why they'd put me through this again." Her gaze fell to the sand beneath our feet. "I thought they were the reason I was saved from his clutches in the first place, but now I'm right back where I started."

I took her other hand, holding both in mine. "No matter what their plan is, it doesn't matter if it's not something *you* want. Say the word and I will do everything in my power to stop this all from happening. But if you truly want this, then I'll stand back and let it unfold. Unless I see you're in pain. Then nothing will stop me from killing Humer. Not even some stupid stones."

The corner of her mouth lifted slightly.

"Thank you, Lia. I can't say if this is something I want, but I do know the consequences if any of you step in, and I can't bear to lose any of you. So, please refrain from killing Humer until after he has helped us defeat the siren queen."

I sighed. "The Stones will probably finish him off by then anyway."

"And promise to stop Finn from doing anything reckless, too. I know he'll try, but I—" A sob broke her voice, and I pulled her into my arms, hugging her tight. "I can't lose him, Lia."

"I know. I'll do my best." I allowed her a moment to break down, and then I stepped back, resuming my place at her side. I didn't want to raise any red flags for Jared or Humer when he returned. A few minutes later, Brom's entire crew, Finn and Nix among them, appeared on the beach.

"He's coming this way," I told her. "Do you want me to stay?"

"Yes." Her voice wavered.

I stayed by her side. Humer came up to her other side, taking her hand. I cringed on her behalf.

"Are you ready, my Vivianne?" he asked. "Do this and all of your people will live."

"I know the cost of our agreement," she hissed. "I'm ready."

"It should be quick and painless. But then again, I've never done this before, so it could be slow and torturous." He laughed heartily and I wanted to tear his throat out. But I kept my word to Viv and did nothing.

"Are we doing this or not?" she snapped.

I brushed my hand against hers, trying to help in the only way I could by reminding her that she wasn't alone this time.

Humer laughed again. "Let's go somewhere private." He waved a hand to Jared who came jogging over.

"You can use one of our rooms at The Flight Deck Inn,"
I offered. At least I knew Viv would be moderately safe there.
"And I will insure no one interrupts you."

Humer pursed his lips.

"How generous of you," Jared said, his tone skeptical.
"Though, I'd rather use a place of *our* choosing."

Waving his hand at Jared, Humer said, "The place
doesn't matter, and we don't have time to dilly-dally. I can feel
the Stones sapping me of life as we speak. I'll most likely be
dead in the morning."

It was strange to me that he cared so little for his own
life, but then again, his entire life seemed to be his work. I
assumed finishing this experiment with Viv would make him feel
as if he'd fulfilled his life purpose. What a sad thought.

"Lead the way, Princess," Humer said, breaking me out
of my thoughts.

I nodded and headed toward the inn. Finn caught my
eye, and I shook my head at him in warning.

Don't, I mouthed at him, hoping he would understand.

Once we were on the docks of the port, a red hawk
flitted in and out of my vision. Finn had sent Marley to keep an
eye on us. Good. I might need her if things went wrong.

I had no intention of doing anything to stop Humer.
However, if he suddenly dropped dead, I might need someone
to take out Jared while I went for the Stones. There was no part
of me that believed if Jared got his hands on them that he would
agree to help us as his brother had. Jared had no ties to any of
us and would abandon us to our fates in a heartbeat. Unlike
Humer, who had a warped kind of infatuation with Viv.

From the way he acted with her, it was almost as if he
loved her like a daughter, except he wanted to be able to
perform experiments on her anytime he wanted. He walked

with her, hand in hand, even though she clearly loathed him. It made me sick.

"Try anything and I'll blow Viv's brains out." Jared's breath was hot against my ear. I'd been so caught up in my own thoughts I hadn't noticed him come up behind me. "I don't care what my brother says. With the Stones, we can do anything. We don't need your friend."

I bit my tongue. The worst part of this whole thing was that none of us would have the satisfaction of killing Humer because the Stones would do it for us. He would die too easily. Too painlessly. I'd heard about people having their magic absorbed before, and supposedly it was like falling asleep when it finally sapped the last remnants of life from you.

For Jared, though, I'd make sure he died a slow, painful death.

The people in the port moved around us, not seeming to realize what was happening. We looked like nothing more than two pairs heading home for the day. The sun would be going down soon, and this place would transform for the nightlife.

"It's at the top of this hill," I said, needing to fill the silence between us all somehow. The activity of the port faded behind us.

Jami and Khali were in the inn's entryway when we arrived. Both wore confused looks, but Jami had enough wits about him to let us pass without incident.

"I'll head back to the beach, and you can join me once the word has gotten out." Jami spoke to Khali loud enough for everyone to hear. I knew it was only for my benefit, so I'd know where to find him when we were done.

We took the stairs to the third floor and entered the room Nix had shared with another of our sisters, Korra. I chose it over the others because its window faced the water. I might be

able to see some of what was happening down there if I could stay near it. It was also smaller than the others, so we would all be in closer proximity. I'd try to remain closer to Humer than Jared.

No matter what, I'd make sure to get those Stones as soon as Humer died. Jared could have them over my dead body.

Viv

I was strangely calm as I laid down on the bed. Jared stood in the corner with his arms crossed and his gaze pinned on Lia. Lia stood at the foot of the bed, as close as Humer would allow.

The entire walk had felt like a dream. Faces and buildings passed, but if I tried to recall them now, nothing came to mind. I'd resigned myself to the fact that this was happening no matter what. No one could save me from this fate, and maybe that was okay. Maybe, like I'd told Lia, this was what was meant for me. I'd bear this burden and learn to live with it as I had before. Humer would never have control over me again after this. Not only because he'd be dead, but because I wouldn't *let* him.

I closed my eyes.

"Tell me if you feel anything," Humer said as he hovered his hands over my abdomen.

A tingling sensation started in my chest, followed by a tugging that dragged the tingling into my lower abdomen, and toward my pelvis.

"Tingling," I gasped. Whatever he was doing, it was working.

"I think it's working," he said. "All my life has led to this moment."

I had to open my eyes because it sounded as if ...

Tears streamed down Humer's sunken cheeks. His hands hovered over me, his work not yet finished, but we both knew how this would end. *We could have changed the world,* he'd said. And he was right.

If what was happening right now would truly mean I could have children with another shifter, then the world would change. I couldn't be sure if it would be for better or worse.

Humer leaned to the right and caught himself as if he were losing his balance. Lia inched closer, but so did Jared.

Out the window, a red hawk sat on a nearby tree that I knew I could only see from this angle.

"I'm hot, can we open the window?" I dared to ask.

Humer gave Lia a curt nod and she leaned over to crack it open enough that Marley could get in if we needed her. Humer wasn't going to last much longer.

A part of me loathed the fact Humer would die so easily after all the pain he'd caused. Not only to me, but to all those shifters who didn't make it out of his experiments alive. I wished I could give him some justice by making his death as horrific as theirs. Instead, he was gifted with the opportunity to see his life's work completed.

Not necessarily, said a small voice in the back of my mind. He'll never truly know if it worked. And I would find a way to use that against him.

I called on the memory of the pain from when Humer used to do his experiments on me and let that be my guide. Sweat beaded on my brow as I squeezed my eyes shut and winced.

"What's happening?" Lia asked, fear lacing her voice.

236

"I'm not sure." Humer sounded uncertain.

I groaned and clutched at my scars which truly did itch from the magic working beneath them.

"It hurts," I whimpered, though I felt no pain.

Lia's footsteps moving closer to Humer were unmistakable, followed by heavier steps which must have belonged to Jared.

"Stop this," Lia hissed. "It's not working; you're making things worse."

"We must see this through," Humer said.

"Don't touch me," Lia said, and I cracked open an eye to see Jared clutching her upper arm. She tore it from his grasp and they both went back to their respective places.

The magic working beneath my skin actually felt calming, and healing. However, I curled in on myself, trembling as I did my best to fool Humer. Lia's foot tapped against the floor, and I wondered how much it would take for her to intervene. I didn't want to push her to that in case Humer lashed out at her. But then again ... If I could distract Humer and Jared ...

"I changed my mind, Lia!" I gasped out. "The Stones are going to kill me!" I prayed to Neros that Lia would understand what I was trying to do. I thrashed and let out an ear-piercing scream, holding it for longer than necessary.

Humer and Jared both lunged for me to hold me down, and a giant hawk crashed through the window at the same time Lia made a move for the necklace.

Jami

"What's going on?" Khali asked once Lia, Viv, Humer, and Jared were all out of sight.

"I don't know. But Humer has the Stones, and we can't try to interfere with what he's doing. I trust Lia to know what moves to make next. In the meantime, we need to get to the beach."

"I don't like the idea of all this, but I trust Lia, too. If you say she has that under control, then I won't worry about it." Khali's gaze drifted to the stairs, worry creasing her brow despite her words. I understood her hesitance to walk away so easily. It went against my every instinct to do it. What if Lia had wanted me to follow? What if she needed me? What if everything went wrong?

But I wouldn't follow her. She and Viv could both take care of themselves, and I knew that if I followed them, I'd risk putting them in even more danger. So, I went back to the beach.

Walking through the port alone, I paid attention to what was happening around me. There were fewer people in port than usual, and I wondered if they sensed what was about to happen. A full-on assault by the siren queen, despite being confined to the sea, could be deadly even to those on land. She

had more power than any other siren and could do considerable damage.

"Jami." Nix popped up in front of me, making me jump.

"Gods-dammit, Nix," I gasped. "When will you stop doing that?"

She smirked. "When it stops being funny." Her smile dropped and she asked, "Did you pass Lia and Viv?"

"Yes. They are at the inn with Humer and Jared. I assumed I shouldn't interfere." I ran my hand over my jaw, my shoulders slumping.

Nix put a hand on my arm, comforting me in a small way. "Marley followed them. If they need us, I want to be close. So, I'll find whatever tree she's perched in."

"Be careful," I warned.

When I reached the beach, a small kernel of hope sprouted in my chest as I saw how many people were already gathered to help in the coming fight. At least two hundred people waited on the sand, or in the water. There were even some familiar faces.

Our crew, who we'd left behind in Lanteria after our ship had been destroyed, were all gathered around Finn. Despite the circumstances, he beamed at them. Seeing them all together again reminded me of how many we had lost to the siren queen all those weeks ago.

"Jami!" Finn called me. "Did you see her?" His smile faded and his muscles were taut.

I nodded. "They're at the inn. Lia is with them, and Marley and Nix are nearby."

"It kills me not to be there," he said, and I could see the truth of that in his eyes. "I promised her I wouldn't let him hurt her again."

239

I put my hand on his shoulder. "You couldn't have seen this coming. None of us did. Viv knows what she's doing."

Finn shook his head.

"How's everyone else doing?" I asked as I turned to face our crew, putting on a fake smile. "It's so good to see you all."

Garrett stepped forward as chatter broke out. "We've been waiting for the chance to get back at the siren queen for the lives she took. We may not all be able to fight in the water, but we'll all play a role."

"Of course," I said. "Finn will delegate tasks, because we won't be able to be in the water either." At least this time, gods willing, we'd have the Azurean Stones on our side, which should make it a quick fight. If Humer cooperated.

Finn focused his attention on Garrett. "Actually, Garrett, keep watch on the inn and come back and tell me as soon as anything happens. Even if you sense something off. Marley is there as backup. I need you to be my eyes and ears."

"Yes, Captain," he said, before shifting into his hawk form and taking off.

"Everyone else, standby. The siren queen could arrive at any time, and we need to be prepared. If you hear the hint of a song, cover your ears and tell me, Jami, or Khali. Whoever is closest."

A collective, "Yes, Captain," went up around us.

"Is someone already scouting the water?" I asked.

Finn's gaze drifted to the waves. "I sent out some of Lia's sisters. They'll let us know if anything is amiss."

A commotion closer to the water began, and Finn and I pushed through the growing crowd to see what was happening.

"Where did he come from?" someone asked.

"Is he a mermaid?"

"Can't be a siren."

240

Shouldering my way past the last line of people, I gasped.

"Roland." Finn said his name before I could. He kept walking, catching Roland as he fell forward, seemingly exhausted.

Unable to move from the shock, I watched from the edge of the crowd.

"How did you escape the siren queen?" Finn asked.

Roland coughed violently and rasped, "Where's Jami?"

"Answer my question first," Finn demanded. He lost his grip and Roland fell to his knees in the sand. I hurried forward, helping Finn get Roland back on his feet.

"I'm here," I said.

"Captain," someone called from the crowd. "I can hear a song."

Before either of us could react, Roland's arm swung up and agony tore through me, ripping a scream from my lungs. Spots swam in my vision, and I slumped down to the sand, losing consciousness as shouting began in the water.

Finn

"Jami!" someone yelled and a few of our crew members converged on him.

Screams assaulted us from the water.

I stood rooted to my spot, still propping up Roland. One second, I had Roland's arm over my shoulder; the next I was in my lion form, pinning him to the sand with one massive paw, ready to tear his head off.

"Wait, wait, wait!" he cried out, dropping the bloodied knife and putting his hands up to shield himself as if that could stop me.

"He's not going to make it if we keep him here," one of my men, Liam, said.

My claws flexed, digging into Roland's chest and making him cry out.

"The siren queen made me do it!" he said. "Without my coin, I'm not protected from her song anymore."

I growled.

"Finn!" Khali came up beside me. "We need him alive. He got past our scouts somehow and he may know what the siren queen has planned."

242

I turned my head to her, teeth bared. She stared me down, unafraid.

"Let. Him. Go."

I turned back to Roland, snapping my jaws to scare him enough to piss his pants then stepped back. Khali grabbed his arm and pulled him away.

"I'll take care of this," she said, and began asking him questions.

I overheard Roland saying that the siren queen would be waiting on the outskirts of the fight.

Instead of continuing to listen to Khali, I joined my crew who were helping Jami. He was way too pale for my liking. Someone held a rag tight against his upper right pec where he'd been stabbed.

Still in my lion form, I crouched down, they caught on to the fact that I was offering to carry Jami. It was the best option to transport him to a healer.

"I know I said we should get him out of here, but I don't think we should move him," Liam said. "I don't think he'll survive if we do."

Panic speared through me. I shifted back and knelt beside Jami, taking his hand in mine. *Cold.*

"Someone get a healer," I commanded.

"Camila already went to find one."

Camila had always been quicker to the draw than most of the men on my ship. I'd have to remember to thank her for that later when we weren't in imminent danger.

"Lia ..." I trailed off. She needed to know, but if anyone interrupted Humer, he might do something unhinged and make matters far worse.

An eagle flying overhead caught my eye and I whipped around, thinking Roland had made a run for it, but he stood with Khali only a few feet away, watching that same eagle.

It landed beside him, shifting into Charles.

Jumping to my feet, I confronted him.

"Where the fuck have you been?" I'd been so busy with everything else going on, I'd forgotten that he'd been waiting outside the cave for us, and then had conveniently been missing once we'd returned with Humer.

Charles shoved his hand into his pocket and pulled out the three coins.

"Take one," he demanded. "You too, Roland. I'll give mine to Jami."

I crossed my arms and stared at him like he was crazy.

"They're useless now," I said. "Roland already tried and possibly succeeded in killing your brother."

Roland ducked his head, guilt crossing his features.

"Jami is strong, I have faith he'll survive this," Charles said, moving his outstretched hand closer to me. "These will protect their holder from a siren's song. Take one."

I begrudgingly picked up one of the coins, inspecting it before putting it into my own pocket.

Charles dropped another into Roland's hand and then went to Jami, kneeling beside him.

"Jami and Lia came out of that cave first. He gave me the coins and told me to run. So, I headed back to the beach, and when Humer came, I hitched a ride with the rest of you back here and have been biding my time."

"So, you sat by and watched Roland stab Jami?"

"That's why I came, because I knew if Roland were still under the siren queen's compulsion, he'd need his coin back to break that spell so he didn't do anything else."

I hated that I had to trust Charles, because I didn't have the luxury of time to question him further and figure out what he was up to.

"Who's that?" Charles asked, pointing toward the port.

Garrett was flying low and headed straight for us. He shifted as soon as he reached us, and my stomach clenched as I remembered that I'd sent him to keep an eye on Viv.

"What's wrong?" I asked.

At the same time, he said, "I heard a lot of screaming. I think something's going wrong."

Without considering what may happen if I went bursting in there, I ran. I shifted mid-run and watched people scatter to get out of my way. A lion running through the port wasn't exactly a common occurrence. I knew that if anything had truly gone wrong, Marley would have interfered, but that didn't stop me. I kept running and prayed I wouldn't be too late.

Lia

The necklace clasp released too easily, as if it *wanted* to be taken, and time slowed while I stared at it.

This was my duty, not only to the ones we had left behind on the beach, but to my people in Thalassia. I would do this for everyone we had lost, and everyone willing to help us fight the siren queen. My heart ached thinking of how I had almost condemned the people I now fought for to the siren queen's reign.

I fastened the necklace around my own neck before Jared or Humer reacted.

A rush of adrenaline and power flowed through every part of me, lighting me up inside. If I dug down deep, I could feel all different kinds of magic from the previous users of the Stones. Shifter magic, witch magic, and even a mage's magic. I wondered if it was the same mage who had stolen the Stones from Sylvane in the first place.

Give us everything, a whisper floated through my mind.

When I tried to pull on the Stones' magic, it felt like there was a barrier between that magic and mine. They were two separate things, fighting inside me for the upper hand. The

stones seemed to want to guard the magic within them, but I would command it to do my bidding.

"Jared, Humer, back away from Viv," I demanded, and Jared stepped back. Humer stumbled, falling to the floor.

His hair seemed grayer and his wrinkles deeper. The Stones had sucked the life from him, and he was hanging on by a thread.

Marley stood at the foot of the bed, while Nix straddled the now completely open window. I smiled at them.

"I have a fun task for you," I said, biting my lip from the sheer excitement surging through me. Every emotion felt heightened.

"Anything," Nix huffed. I'd never seen her winded before. My gaze flicked to the tree she must have jumped from and was impressed she'd made the leap.

"Bury Humer," I said. "Alive. Though, he won't be alive much longer. So, you better be quick about it. I'd like him to suffer a little."

Marley moved before Nix did, but Nix's brows furrowed.

"Is there a problem?" I asked her.

She shook her head, letting out a hard sigh.

Viv sat up in the bed, seemingly fine now that Humer's control of the magic had ended.

"Unless you want the privilege," I told her, realizing she was the one who most deserved to deliver Humer's fate.

"No." Her gaze shifted to Jared. "He's not the one I want anymore."

I smiled and jerked my head at him. "I'll hold him for you, if you wish."

Jared backed further away, inching for the door, but I transported myself there, blocking it. He sneered at me.

"You're too late, Humer already finished his work," he said.

"No. He didn't," Viv countered. "If he had, I'd know. All I feel is pain."

Give him to us, the whispering came again. *Give him to us.* The whispers became more demanding.

"No," I said aloud, trying to fight off the Stones' influence.

You want power. Give him to us.

I gripped my head, trying to figure out what to do. I could take Jared's power, feed it to the Stones, and in turn become even more powerful myself. I'd need that power to defeat the siren queen, so it only made sense ...

Dropping one hand to my side, I held the other out toward Jared and a slow smile slowly spread across my face.

"Jared Manes, I command you to yield your magic to the Stones." The words came out of my mouth as if I'd known them all along. Slowly, a hazy mist-like stream of magic seeped out of Jared's chest and entered my body through my outstretched palm. The Stones against my collarbone glowed a vibrant blue as they absorbed the magic through me.

Jared crumpled to the floor, dead.

"Lia," Viv snapped. "He was supposed to be *mine.*" There was more than anger in her gaze. *Fear.* Marley and Nix held Humer between them and kept their gazes averted from mine.

They will all fear you, the whisper said.

I cleared my throat, slightly unnerved. "We have more important matters to attend."

In a blink, I transported myself down to the front desk of the inn.

248

"Make sure no one goes upstairs and don't worry about the body that's about to be brought through here," I commanded the front desk woman. She nodded, hardly looking at me.

Satisfied, I transported myself back to the beach, leaving everyone else behind. I couldn't stand their judgment any longer.

People were moving all around me. Shifters were being drug out of the water to be healed, or ... I gulped. Our people were already dying.

In the water, turmoil on the surface indicated fighting beneath. A few familiar heads popped up and I recognized my sisters. I wanted to go to them and help them, but I needed to find the siren queen.

My eyes scanned the beach, and I did a double take as I spotted Jami. A man and woman knelt on either side of him, and a red stain marred the sand beneath him.

Kill them all, the whispers tugged on my anger, stoking it. I pushed it back down.

"No," I gasped, clenching my teeth, and holding the Stones' will at bay. I ran to Jami.

Give us everything ...

I fell to my knees beside the woman on Jami's right.

"What happened?" I asked, breathless from my internal battle.

The man lathered some kind of salve over a wound in Jami's shoulder, but Jami didn't move. His eyes were closed and his breathing shallow.

"He may not make it," the woman said. "You're Lia. I recognize you from Lanteria. I'm Camila, one of Finn's crew."

"I don't care," I snapped, feeling bad almost instantly. "Tell me he'll be okay," I demanded of the man who I assumed

was a healer. Magic stirred in my veins, and I wondered if there was anything I could do to help.

My fingers brushed against the Stones at my neck.

"The wound is healing, but he's already lost so much blood," the man said.

"If he needs blood then *give him blood.*"

Give him blood, the voice in my head echoed.

The Stones' magic heeded my command, and the healer choked as blood flowed from his nose, mouth, and eyes. For a moment, I was horrified. But as I continued to watch, something in me shifted, and I became more fascinated than anything.

"Oh my god," I breathed.

Camila screamed and jumped to her feet.

I watched the blood moving toward Jami, and realized there was no avenue for it to enter his veins and be of use to him. Grabbing my dagger from my side and taking Jami's arm from the sand, I cut into his vein and waited as the blood moved faster, going exactly where I had wanted it to go.

"You killed him." Camila sounded horrified, but I ignored her.

I smoothed Jami's damp hair from his face and leaned down to kiss his forehead.

"Keep watch over him," I told Camila. "I have a siren queen to deal with."

Give us everything ...

Camila opened and closed her mouth several times when I walked past her. Even without a direct command from me, she did as I asked and knelt beside Jami.

"If anything happens to him, or he doesn't survive," I started, turning back to her. "Then you will meet the same fate as the healer." The thrill that gave me almost made me hope she fucked up.

The necklace pulsed against my collarbone, a constant reminder of its presence. I gripped it, letting its power seep into every part of me, and giving myself over to the Stones.

I strolled away. The words *give us everything* ... echoed through my mind.

Viv

I stared at the spot where Lia had been mere seconds before. She wasn't herself, and it had to be because of the Stones.

"Are we still ..." Marley trailed off, gazing down at Humer held between her and Nix. "I mean I'm down if we are, but otherwise." She shrugged.

"Wait," Humer gasped and coughed. "Vivianne." His eyes found me, and he beckoned me toward him.

Hesitantly, I stood and moved closer.

"You must know, the Stones granted me with clarity, and I remembered that you asked me a question ..." He coughed violently and blood spattered onto the front of his shirt. "The siren queen's name is Sereida."

Sereida. That was the name he'd said while we were on the siren queen's vessel. The one I couldn't remember.

"Why are you telling me?" I asked.

"Because I want you to live. Even if I failed. And I made you a promise." He reached out and his fingers grazed my chin, making me jerk back.

I wanted to yell that I had won, that I had lied and made him believe he had failed, even though I knew deep down that

he'd *succeeded.* But I swallowed my gloating. I'd let him die thinking he'd failed. He deserved that and much more.

"Thank you," I said, straightening my back and lifting my chin. "I'll tell Lia."

His eyes widened and fluttered closed. "Don't let her hold onto the Stones too long," he murmured. A few seconds passed, and his chest stopped moving. I double checked his pulse, and he was gone.

"Well, I guess we don't have to bury him alive now," Nix commented.

"We'll let Lia believe you did," I said. "Take him and bury him, then join us at the beach. I have to get to Lia before she goes after the siren queen."

As an afterthought, I added, "I'll distract the woman at the front desk while you two carry the body out. There shouldn't be anyone else down there. Most people staying here right now are with us or Khali, so they'll all be down at the beach already."

Marley and Nix hefted Humer up between them, dragging his feet a little. He honestly looked as if he was unconscious, which would make this easier.

"What about that one?" Marley said, pointing to Jared in the corner.

"We'll deal with him later. Lia only told you to bury Humer, so we'll do that in case she asks about it. The Stones are making her ... different. I don't think we should lie to her or test her patience right now." It was scary to think the Stones could change her so much in such little time. Humer hadn't seemed that different from his younger self, but his younger self had been as callous and self-serving as the Stones now made Lia seem to be.

I feared what we may find when we reached the beach, but I would worry about one thing at a time.

253

At the top of the stairs, I could hear shouting down below. Nearing the bottom, I recognized the second voice.

"Let me up there, or so help me ..." Finn stopped yelling when he saw me.

The front desk woman blocked his path, her arms stretched to either side of the stairwell.

"Lia told me not to let anyone upstairs," she said.

"You're all right," Finn spoke over the front desk woman's head. "Garrett came to me and told me there was screaming and I didn't think, I just came here."

I smiled at him. "I'm fine. Humer and Jared are both dead, and Lia has the Stones, but I'm fine."

"Speaking of which," Marley said as she and Nix made their way awkwardly down the stairs. "Out of the way."

The front desk woman huffed and returned to her desk. I assumed Lia had already warned her that we'd be coming through, since she seemed unbothered by the body being hefted out of her inn.

Finally able to reach me, Finn pulled me into his arms and kissed the top of my head.

"I thought ..."

"I know. I'm fine," I told him again. "It was a ruse to distract Jared and Humer long enough for Lia to get the necklace. And it worked."

He pulled back and looked me over, as if not believing I was truly fine. Once he was seemingly reassured, he took my hand and led me outside.

Marley and Nix were already headed for the woods behind the inn, and we headed for the port.

"The sirens had arrived and were beginning their attack when I left," Finn explained. "No sign of the siren queen yet."

"Well, I need to find Lia. She transported herself to the beach before Humer told me the name of the siren queen. *Sereida.*"

"We'll find her."

"We have to be careful, though. She's a little unstable from the Stones. I don't know how much they've changed her, but from the small amount of time I spent with her ... She is definitely not herself."

"Got it. Find Lia, but don't piss her off." Finn smirked, and I couldn't help but smile back.

We didn't pass nearly as many people on the way to the beach as we had on our way to the inn. There were a few stragglers here and there, but otherwise, the port seemed deserted.

Nearing the beach, it seemed anyone who had been in the port either fled or joined in the fight. People hurried about helping the injured, or simply watching the water.

"If I had to guess, she's probably with Jami," Finn said. "He was with a healer when I left him."

I gasped. "A healer? What happened?"

"Roland stabbed him. His excuse being that the siren queen made him do it, though I'm not entirely sold on that."

Walking across the sand, we dodged people and shifters in their animal forms. Jami came into view, lying by the water, with a woman I didn't recognize.

"Camila," Finn called the name and the woman looked up at us. "Has Lia been here?"

Camila's gaze darkened and she frowned.

"Yes. She murdered the healer and stole his blood ..." Her words came out stilted as if she were fighting back a sob.

Murdering innocents ... That was certainly not Lia.

"It's the Stones," I told Finn. "We need to find her and take them off."

"But the siren queen," he reminded me, as if I could forget.

"I'll give her the name first, and it will be a quick death. She did it to Jared, and he was dead in seconds. But the siren queen needs to be close enough to hear her, so we'll need to find her first."

"Lia went into the water, and I haven't seen her since," Camila said.

"How's Jami?" Finn asked.

"His breathing has evened out, and he seems to be healing faster since Lia did whatever she did ..."

"You can go, I'll look after him," Finn told her.

Camila laughed a mirthless laugh. "I would if I could, but it's in my best interests to stay here and protect him. I was told by Lia that if anything happens to him, or he doesn't survive, I'll meet the same fate as the healer."

Finn swore.

I shook my head. "I'll find her and ensure she doesn't wear those Stones a second longer than necessary. You two take care of Jami, and I'll find Lia."

"Be careful. I love you," Finn said, and the words plucked at my already aching heart.

"I love you, too." I kissed him, taking a few extra seconds of our precious time to soak in his warmth and strength, and then headed for the water.

As soon as I was out deep enough, I shifted and slipped beneath the waves. There was even more chaos happening underwater than there was on shore. Shifters were battling sirens, but there were also shifters who seemed to be on the

opposing side. Shifters who fought for the siren queen, as Veera the bat shifter had.

I scanned the water but couldn't see Lia, so I reached out to her in my mind.

Lia, are you here? I called out to her. There was no response. *The siren queen's name is Sereida. Please let me know if you can hear me.*

Still nothing.

Of course it wasn't going to be that easy.

I gave the fighting a wide berth, trying to stay out of it while I searched for Lia. I imagined that the siren queen wouldn't come in too close, since she knew we had the Stones. She'd want to draw the person with the Stones out and take them on alone. She'd have a better chance of winning that way.

Lia wouldn't be stupid enough to go off on her own, but this wasn't really Lia anymore. I was contending with figuring out the mind of an entirely different person. Those Stones would make this infinitely harder.

Something slammed into my side, sending me careening through the water. When I righted myself, I saw the culprit. A mermaid faced off with me, her bright blue hair flowing behind her as her blue eyes darkened with malice.

What are you doing? I reached out to her in my mind.

I'm doing what needs to be done. The siren queen is going to change this world for the better and make us a species to be feared once more.

My eyes flitted from her to the surface, wondering if I could outrun her until I found Lia. She lunged for me, claws extended and prime to rip into me.

Bracing myself for her attack, I let her think she had the upper hand. Her claws dug into my shoulders, earning a cry from me that was lost to the sea.

There's more to life than being feared. I tried to distract her as I struggled to shove her away from me, but she kept her grip as she pulled one clawed hand free and reeled it back for another strike.

I lashed out, grabbing her wrist before she could get her claws in me again.

I don't want to hurt you, but I will if you make me, I warned her. There were people back on the beach counting on me to ensure Lia took out the siren queen and I wouldn't let this mermaid hold me back.

Releasing her claws from my other shoulder she drifted back, and I almost thought she'd decided to heed my warning. The vacant eyes and the pitying smile spreading over her face told me that nothing would stop her. She'd already accepted her fate.

I darted down as she lunged for me again. Swimming as fast as I could, I headed for the ocean floor. She came after me, as I'd anticipated. I stopped short, pulling back and surprising her as I caught one of her arms and yanked her toward me.

My claws dug into her chest, making her gasp. I'd needed the extra momentum from my move to give me the strength needed to break through her ribs, and it had worked as I knew it would. Bubbles trailed from her mouth and blood seeped from beneath my hand that was primed to rip her heart out.

Do it, she said into my mind.

Even though it wasn't my first time killing a fellow mermaid, I still had a moment's hesitation. I could understand being driven to such desperation that this mermaid had sided with the siren queen, the only one she believed strong enough to keep her safe from the evils she saw in the world. I'd once been in a dark enough place that I may have even been swayed to join

258

her myself. But I was out of that dark place, and now I needed to deal with this mermaid so I could help my friends.

It took all my effort to take her heart out, and as soon as I did, I released her, letting her body float away from me on the current. Staring at her heart in my hand, I had the urge to throw it away from me, but in the water, it wouldn't go very far. I dropped it as I'd done her and let it sink out of sight.

Without another thought for the mermaid or what I'd done, I continued my search for Lia, occasionally calling out to her, but never getting a response.

My body was yanked to the right as if I were caught in a rip current. I let the current take me as far as it could, but then it stopped. This was no natural phenomenon. I was getting close to my target.

Lia, I'm coming, I sent the thought to her, even though I was pretty sure she was blocking her mind so the siren queen couldn't get in her head if they were currently fighting.

I headed in the direction the pull had come from and was soon hit with another, letting it tug me along once more.

The siren queen came into sight first, since she was much bigger than Lia and blocking her. It was her currents I kept getting caught in as she hurled them toward Lia to keep her away.

"Just in time for the fun!" The siren queen used her manipulation of the water around her to draw me in close until she could wrap a tentacle around me. Lia didn't seem phased by my arrival.

I pointed to Lia and then at my own head, hoping she might open her mind to let me in.

Sereida! Her name is Sereida! I screamed inside my own mind. Still, Lia didn't respond or react as if she'd heard. We needed to get above water.

I pointed to the surface, not caring if the siren queen saw. Maybe she'd be intrigued enough to lead the way up there herself.

Lia narrowed her eyes at me.

Trust me, I tried mouthing the words to her. Normally, Lia would have no problem opening her mind to me or following my lead.

Moving her hands as if creating a ball, Lia brought them together and pushed them up, swimming for the surface with a burst of speed. The siren queen, me in tow, also shot upward, as if Lia had captured us within an orb of water.

Once we breached the surface, water cascaded down around us like a waterfall, revealing Lia once more.

"Now we can talk like civilized people," Lia said.

The siren queen scowled and threw her arm forward, shooting a spear-like object straight for Lia. With a wave of her hand, a small jet of water knocked the object aside, and it shattered. It had been an icicle.

"Sereida!" I cried out, not knowing if I would get another chance. Lia and the siren queen both snapped their gazes to me. Lia's brow furrowed in confusion, while the siren queen shook with rage. Another tentacle slapped over my mouth.

"Where did you hear that?" she hissed, her face mere inches from mine. Her black eyes widened, and she bared almost all her pointed teeth that could tear my flesh from my bones.

"Sereida," Lia said the name, and the siren queen whipped her head back toward her. "Release Vivianne and do not try to escape."

The tentacles that covered my mouth and wound around my waist slipped away and I dropped into the water. I swam

over to Lia, though I kept some space between us. I didn't entirely trust her either.

"End this, Lia," I said.

"It could be fun, having the siren queen, *Queen Sereida,* at my disposal." Lia tapped her finger against her chin as she studied the siren queen. "Call off your sirens."

"I must go underwater to do that," the siren queen said through gritted teeth. She was fighting the influence of the Stones, and I worried she'd be able to break free if Lia didn't finish this quickly.

"Five seconds. Go under the water, call off your sirens, and then come back here. For each second you are late, I'll take a tentacle." Lia giggled and turned to me. "That sounds fun, right?"

The siren queen dipped beneath the water and no more than five seconds later, reemerged.

"Lia, you need to end this now. The longer you use the Stones, the more of your magic they will take," I warned.

Lia sneered at me. "You don't control me. *I* am the princess of the sea."

"Princess of *Thalassia,*" I corrected. "They are waiting for you to finish this fight so they can be free once more. Don't make this harder than it needs to be."

As I'd seen the siren queen do before, Lia lifted herself above us on a wave of her own creation, looking down upon us.

"I have the power to become Queen of the entire ocean. Do you really think I'd give that up so easily?"

My mind raced as I tried to come up with a response. "What about Jami?" If she wouldn't take down the siren queen and finish this for her own people, then maybe she'd need more motivation. The only other thing I could think of was her love for Jami.

"What of him? He can be my king," she said, grinning.

"He won't want that," I argued. "He's waiting for you on the beach, and he's expecting you to do as we planned. Take care of the siren queen and then return the Stones to a safe place."

"You don't know what he'll want!" she yelled, a giant wave forming behind her and crashing down on us.

Neros, help me, I prayed, as the spray settled, and Lia turned her focus back to the siren queen.

In a last-ditch effort, I reached out in my mind to any of my sisters who may be in the water.

If you can hear me, bring Jami out into the water. Lia needs his help.

Jami

Sweat beaded on my forehead as the sun beat down on me. I turned my face from the glare, wincing.

"Jami!" Finn's voice was distinct. "He's waking up."

I tried to clear my throat, but it was so dry I coughed instead, and my eyes flew open.

"What's happening?" I rasped. "Am I dead?"

I assumed I was alive, considering I was on the beach and Finn was hunched over me, but it never hurt to be sure.

"You're alive. Thanks to Lia," Finn said, smiling down at me. There was a crease between his brow though, and his smile seemed forced.

"Where is she?" I asked, propping myself on my elbows. Pain erupted in my shoulder, and I gasped, dropping back onto the sand. It felt as if I'd been stabbed all over again, but this time I remained conscious and couldn't escape the pain.

"She may have saved your life, but you're still healing. The healer put on a salve that will speed the process, but when they took his body, the salve went with him," Camila explained. "I didn't think to grab it, given the circumstances." Her lips were pursed, and her fists clenched in her lap as she knelt beside me.

"Body? What happened to him?" I shook my head. "Never mind. Tell me later. Where is Lia?"

"Somewhere out there," Finn said, indicating the water. "Hopefully taking care of the siren queen once and for all."

I reached out to Finn. "Help me sit up."

He inspected my shoulder and took my hand, putting his other hand behind my back.

"Move slow. We don't want to reopen the wound; it's only barely stopped bleeding thanks to the salve we have no more of," Finn instructed.

I braced myself and waited as Finn helped me sit up. Teeth gritted against the pain, let out a long breath and tried my best to not cry out.

Panting, I dropped my chin to my chest.

"That was too much, we should make him stay here until he's better healed," Camila said.

I met her gaze. "What's gotten into you? Usually you're all about getting back into the action."

She cringed.

A large shadow passed over us and we all looked up, gaping at the dragons soaring overhead. Khali was easy to spot, the smallest but no less fierce of them, leading the group. She swooped down low, grazing the water and sending up spray that made it look as if her dark purple scales were shimmering.

Dipping her long claws into the water, she grabbed hold of something, and when she came back up, I realized she held a siren in her grip. A nearly ear-shattering scream split the air, but it ended abruptly as Khali tore the siren in two and dropped it back to the waves below.

"Shit," Finn breathed, and I nodded in agreement. I knew Khali was strong, but it was on a whole other level seeing her in her dragon form like that.

The other dragons followed her lead, taking sirens from the water and either ripping them apart, or dropping them on shore to be taken care of by our army who couldn't fight in the water.

A leopard shifter ran by us, taking up the latest siren dropped ashore. Once they'd finished her off, they shifted back into their human form, and I recognized Tobias.

"Good to see you again," he said as he walked past us without stopping. He was on a mission, heading away from the water.

"The feeling isn't mutual," I muttered, remembering how buddy-buddy Tobias had been with Lia the last time we'd seen him. Jealousy seemed like an odd emotion to be feeling at a time like this, but it reared its head anyway.

"Jami!" Nix came running over to us, dripping wet and distracting me from my petty thoughts. "Lia needs you."

"What?" Camila jumped to her feet and faced Nix.

Nix looked Camila up and down. "Viv sent out a call for help. Lia needs Jami," Nix explained. "I'll bring him out there."

Camila scoffed. "He can't go in the water, he's still healing. It's almost like Lia *wants* him dead so she can kill me next."

"Cammy," Finn chided. "I understand your fear, but I won't let Lia harm you." He stood and I wished I could do the same, but it was all I could to remain sitting.

"Please, let me take him," Nix said. Her hands were shaking, and I could tell she was afraid for her sisters.

"I'll go. Lia needs me, and I won't let her down," I said. "But I can't stand, so someone is going to have to carry me into the water." As humiliating as that might be, it was necessary, and I wouldn't let it keep me from getting to Lia. If she truly needed my help, then I would do whatever I could to be there for her.

"I'm coming, too," Finn said.

Nix shook her head. "I can't bring you both and no one else is disengaged right now to help. I can only bring Jami."

Finn bit his lip.

"Don't worry, I'll make sure they both come back safe," I tried to reassure him, though I had no idea how I was going to be of any help in the ocean. I wasn't a bad swimmer, but I had no weapons that would give me any kind of advantage against the siren queen, or any siren for that matter. They could overwhelm me in a second. But I had to trust that Viv knew what she was doing by asking for me to go out there.

"Fine." Finn bent down and lifted me, carrying me out into the water. I hissed when the saltwater hit my wound. The pain intensified and then leveled out. Nix followed and once we were deep enough, she shifted. She took my good arm and draped it over her shoulder. I kept the other tucked against my chest, trying not to aggravate my wound.

"I'll keep in contact with my other sisters and hopefully one of them will be able to update you," she told Finn.

We started moving out further into the ocean. Finn remained waist deep in the water, watching us go.

Heads of different shifters popped up around us, shifting back into their human forms.

"What's going on?" Nix asked as we swam by.

"The sirens are retreating," one of them said.

"That's good news," I managed to get out between deep breaths. It was my only option to fight back the searing pain in my shoulder.

"I don't know," Nix murmured. We left everyone behind and moved faster. "If the siren queen has commanded her sirens away, then why does Lia need your help? If she has

the siren queen at her mercy, she should be able to take care of her and be done with it. Something is wrong."

I mulled over her concern in my head. She was right. There was no reason Lia would need my help. She had more power than anyone in the world currently and could control the entire ocean if she pleased.

"Have you talked with Viv again?" I asked, hoping Nix might have gleaned a bit more insight into the situation.

"I told her we were on our way."

I took one arm from around Nix and pressed it to my shoulder, making sure the wrappings remained in place.

"What did she say?" I asked, playing with the edge of one of my bandages.

"Hurry."

Lia

I could see it all now. *Queen of the ocean.* With the siren queen to do my bidding.

"Sereida, I'd like to send the king of Asmara a message," I said. He and the other kings would get what was coming to them for not agreeing to help in this war. I'd make them see how wrong they were when they claimed the siren queen wasn't a threat to them.

"What kind of message?" she asked, a wicked grin replacing her usual scowl. It was all the more menacing with her pointed teeth and black eyes. I wondered if I could pull off that look.

"Lia." Viv's tone was a warning, and I ignored her. She had no idea what this kind of power was like. What it could do. She'd understand once she saw what came of it. Once she realized how freeing it would be for our people. No one could ever turn us away again for being mermaids.

"I know the power you hold over the ocean, a power I can now also harness." Still held aloft by my wave, I moved toward the siren queen and raised her to be level with me. "I'd like for you to send a tidal wave for the port."

"You'd like it destroyed?" the siren queen asked. She didn't have eyebrows, but her forehead wrinkled in surprise.

"Not destroyed, but damaged enough to show King Danforth he was wrong. He should have feared your reach."

"With pleasure."

"Wait!" Viv cried. "There are innocents on the beach that will be killed if you do this!"

I hesitated, something inside me screaming that I couldn't hurt innocent people.

Power comes with a price. Give us everything ... the whispers said.

"Do it, Sereida," I commanded. I turned to watch and groaned in annoyance when I realized that Jami and Nix were headed our way. "Wait."

"Lia!" Jami's voice triggered something in me, and I smiled.

"You're alive," I said, lowering myself back to surface level and looking him over. I met them halfway. "Why are you out here?"

"I was worried about you," Jami said.

"Viv asked you to come, didn't she?" I pinned Viv with my gaze. Annoyance and anger flooded through me. "She thinks you'll be able to stop me, doesn't she?" I threw my head back laughing.

"No," Jami said over my laughter. "She doesn't want me to stop you. She wants me to help you. So here I am, what do you want me to do?"

I studied him, tapping my chin. There really wasn't anything he could do out here.

"I need you to get out of the siren queen's way so she can send a tidal wave for the port," I said, smiling sweetly.

Nix gasped. "What? No!"

269

"I didn't ask for your input, Nix," I snapped.

"What will happen if we don't move? Will you kill me, Lia?" Jami asked. "Is that what you want to do now?"

The image of him half dead on the sand flashed in my mind, and fear coursed through me.

Power has a price, the whispers started again.

Shaking my head, I tried to think clearly. I didn't want to hurt anyone, especially Jami. But I wanted to be queen. I wanted to be all-powerful.

"Lia, this isn't you. You wouldn't harm innocent people or risk the lives of loved ones. You think you're in control because you have the Stones, but they are controlling *you.*" Jami reached out to me and I almost took his hand but then snatched mine back. It was a trick.

"No. I am in control," I said. It was true. Nothing was more powerful than me.

Jami licked his lips and shook his head. "That's what they want you to think. I'll prove it to you. If you still want to send the tidal wave once you take the necklace off, then I'll move aside and let you. You can keep the necklace, just take it off."

Do not listen. Power comes at a price. Give us everything ...

"They want you to kill me so you'll lose your biggest asset," the siren queen said from behind me.

"I said nothing about killing you," Jami said. "I couldn't care less about you or your sirens. I care only for Lia."

His gaze stayed locked on mine, and I could see the truth of his words and the love he held for me.

"I—" I tried speaking but the necklace tightened, and I grabbed at it.

270

Give us everything, the whispers became louder and more insistent.

"Lia, forget about the siren queen, just take it off!" Jami pleaded with me. "It's going to kill you!" Tears shone in his eyes.

Don't give in, the Stones demanded. The necklace was growing hot against my skin.

"This isn't what I wanted," I told them, ignoring everyone who watched around me. "I never wanted any of this."

We need power. Give it to us. The Stones were so hot they were almost burning. I plucked at the necklace, hoping to alleviate the pain, but it burned my hands.

I knew what I needed to do.

Yes, give us everything.

Facing the siren queen, I took a deep breath, blocking the whispers from my mind.

Lifting myself once more on a small wave, I held my head high as I spoke clearly and precisely. "Sereida, queen of the sirens, I command you to yield your magic to the Stones."

She whipped her head back and forth, fighting against the Stones' influence. Fear spiked through me that if anyone were strong enough to fight off the magic of the Stones, it would be her.

Doubling down, I spoke louder. "Sereida, I command you to yield your magic to the Stones."

Her hands clutched her head and her tentacles lashed around her, sending up small waves. "No!" she screamed. "I will not let you defeat me so easily!"

The necklace lifted from my collarbone, pulling forward as if it wanted to be closer to the siren queen. So, I moved my wave closer to her and let myself drop down, placing me face to

face with her. Slipping my hand to my waist, I grabbed my dagger and held it to her throat.

"Do not fight me, Sereida," I hissed. "You have killed thousands of innocents, and it is time *you* paid the price."

A tentacle slithered over my arm, wrapping around it.

"I have searched high and low for those Stones you wear so callously around your neck like a prize." Her black eyes blazed a deep red. "They belong to *me*."

"Yield your magic to the Stones!" I yelled, pressing my dagger harder against her throat, not caring that it drew blood.

A gurgling sound came from her and then, just as with Jared, a misty stream of magic seeped from her, flowing out of her body and into the stones. She screamed in defiance, clawing at herself as if she could capture her magic and put it back, but it was useless. The Stones glowed a vibrant blue, and the whispers died down, as if they were satiated for the moment. I pulled away from her, placing my dagger back into its sheath and watched as the life drained from the siren queen. As soon as all her magic was gone, her body sank to the depths of the ocean.

"You did it," Viv said softly, as if she feared my reaction.

"Now the necklace, Lia," Jami chimed in from behind me.

I stared at the place where the siren queen had disappeared, my chest heaving from the exertion it had taken to make her yield with my power. Or, with the Stones' power. Because it wasn't really mine.

Reaching for the clasp, the whispers rose up again, but I understood what was happening now. Jami was right, they were in control the whole time. They were the ones with the power, not me. And with each additional second I wore the necklace, they would steal more of my magic.

272

The necklace dropped into my hand, and I held it out to Viv. "Take it. I don't trust myself." She swam to me and took it.

"It's not your fault," Viv said. "The Stones are the most powerful objects in the world, no one would have been able to resist them."

"That doesn't change the fact that I almost killed all those innocent people ... That I *did* kill an innocent man to save Jami." Shame pooled in my gut, making me sick to my stomach. I'd almost succumbed to the Azurean Stones; I'd almost let them win.

I couldn't look at Jami. I didn't want to see the disgust, or the disappointment I expected to find in his eyes.

"We should get back to the beach," I said.

No one argued. Nix brought Jami with her, and Viv followed, with me at the back. I half wished a siren would come up and drag me down, killing me in the process, so I wouldn't have to come to grips with the loss of such power and the atrocity I'd committed.

Because it wasn't just disgust with myself, or regret that I felt. I felt hollowed out. Not only was the power from the Stones missing, but some of my own magic as well. I didn't know exactly how much had been taken, but it was enough for me to notice its absence.

I could still shift, I made sure as we swam, going back and forth between my mer form and my human form. But the little magic I used to be able to use in my human form was gone. I could no longer extend my claws or manipulate the water unless I was in my mer form.

Viv must have noticed my strange behavior and dropped back to swim beside me.

"It's going to be all right," she said. "You'll get used to your new limits."

I rubbed at my collarbone where the Stones had left a welt from their intense heat. "At least I'm alive. At least I can still shift." If that had been taken from me, I wasn't sure I'd even want to continue living.

Viv moved closer and touched my shoulder. "You'll grieve for a while, and we'll be by your side every step of the way. But one day, it will seem normal."

I leaned into her touch and closed my eyes. "I know. Thank you, Viv. For not hating me."

She scoffed. "Why would I hate you?"

"Because I ignored you and threatened you." I scrunched my nose.

She laughed. "Oh, that's nothing. I knew it wasn't really you. It was hard to tell how the Stones affected Humer because he'd always been an ass, but with you, it was like you did a one-eighty. It wasn't you at all."

"Shit," Nix said, capturing our attention. The port had come into view.

I gasped. "No."

There was no beach and little left of the docks. Debris floated in the water, and bodies. I retched at the sight of them. Covering my mouth, I turned back, tears blurring my vision.

I did this. I killed them. A sob wracked me.

"Lia," Jami's voice made me turn back to the carnage. Nix still supported him, his arms around her shoulders. "This wasn't you. The siren queen is responsible for all of this. If it wasn't for her, we never would have needed the Azurean Stones. Don't forget that." The weight of his gaze bored into me. He could see right through me. I choked back a sob.

We kept moving forward. Water had flooded the port, and it poured out of buildings as it receded back to the ocean.

274

The siren queen had sent the tidal wave without us knowing. She'd heeded my command before I could stop her. Now that she was dead, the ocean had calmed, but the damage had already been done.

"I did this." It was hard to breathe as we swam past the bodies. "I killed them." My heart pounded and cold crept in, making my movements slow.

The silence around me was confirmation enough that everyone blamed me for this. As they should.

Finn

"Run!" Korra shifted from her mer form as she rose from the water. "Everyone needs to get to higher ground now!"

The sirens had gone, so I had no idea why she was so afraid of this new threat.

"What's going on?" I asked as I ran up to her.

"The siren queen is sending a tidal wave this way. Viv sent the warning, but it may already be too late."

"The siren queen's not dead yet?" That wasn't right. But we didn't have time to figure out what was going on. We needed to get people to safety.

Thankfully, most of the shifters were out of the water, and they helped those who were injured off the beach. Getting to the docks wouldn't be enough, though. We'd need to move even higher. And if the wave was already on its way, there wasn't enough time.

The ground shook and I thought it was the wave, but a roar told me something entirely different. *Dragon.*

I turned and saw a horde of six dragons land on the beach. They all barely fit.

"To the dragons!" someone yelled, and people ran for them. Khali was among the dragons. She lowered her head to

the sand, creating a ramp for people to climb onto her back, and the other dragons followed suit.

It was a magnificent sight. I shifted into my lion form and headed for the docks. Korra was still standing at the top of the stairs leading from the beach to the docks. I nudged her.

"I have to make sure everyone is safe," she said.

But I wasn't going to leave her behind. Nudging her harder, I pushed her away from the stairs.

"I have to ..." Her jaw dropped as she stared out at the water. I swung my head. The wave was here. Korra finally hopped onto my back and let me whisk her away. Unsure if I could outrun the wave, I ran as fast as I could heading for a tall building outside of the port. Hopefully it could withstand the wave.

Crashing down the door, I headed for the stairs and had us on the top floor within seconds. Whoever owned the knife shop must have headed home when the fighting started.

Korra leapt from my back and ran for the window, watching as the wave struck the docks. I shifted and joined her. There was nothing we could do now but watch.

"Lia did this," Korra said, her shoulders tense.

"You said the siren queen—"

"I know what I said." Korra sighed. "Lia is using the Stones to control the siren queen. Not to kill her and end this fight, but for her own gain. She wants to rule the ocean. Nix filled me in. Viv wouldn't give me all the details."

I put my arm around Korra. I understood Viv's need to protect Lia, but also Nix's duty to report exactly what was happening to their sisters.

Though the wave wasn't tall enough to reach the floor we were on, water had made it to the first floor. It covered the entirety of the port, but it had begun to recede.

"It will be all right. Jami and Viv will figure out a way to stop her."

Korra grimaced. "You have so much faith in them, and her."

"As should you. They are *your* sisters," I said.

"Which is why I fear that Lia may be lost to the Stones' power. She's always been ambitious. And she already threatened to give the Stones to the siren queen, why not keep them and use the siren queen instead? She can have everything she wants." Her shoulders slumped and she gripped the windowsill as she leaned against it.

My jaw slackened and I rubbed my brow. "You don't truly believe this is what she wants? Do you?"

She shrugged and I dropped my arm back to my side.

"Lia considered giving the siren queen the Stones because she thought it was the only way to save Viv and Jami. When she saw another way out, she took it. The Stones are in control right now, but that is *not* Lia. She would never do this of her own accord."

Korra kept her mouth shut. There was nothing more I could say to try to convince her, either.

After watching the water for what seemed like hours, something finally changed. Four familiar heads were moving steadily toward what remained of the docks.

"There they are!" I exclaimed, though Korra didn't seem as excited.

"You go, I'll keep watch from up here a while longer," she said.

The water on the first floor was knee deep, and as I went out the doorway and closer to the docks it rose to my waist. Nothing would keep me from getting to Viv, though. My time on Brom's boat had helped me overcome the worst of my

anxiety when it came to being in the water, and assuming the siren queen was dead, I now had no reason to fear it.

I walked for as long as I could, the water shoulder height by the time I stood on the docks.

"Finn!" Viv called to me. "What are you doing out here?"

"I saw you coming and couldn't wait," I said, moving as fast as I could through the water until she was in my arms. "I'm never letting you out of my sight again." I kissed her.

She wrapped her arms around me. "I should be saying the same thing. I was worried you wouldn't escape the wave." Pressing her forehead against mine, she closed her eyes.

"We have company," Lia said, making us both turn our heads to where the water hadn't reached. A royal carriage was headed down the narrow street.

"We need to get rid of the Stones," Nix said. "That's the only reason he's here. He couldn't care less about the port."

Viv held them up between us and I jumped away on instinct.

She laughed. "They don't bite," she said, winking.

A red hawk landed on a piece of nearby debris, and I could have sworn she was laughing too.

"Marley and Nix can take the Stones and hide them somewhere they'll never be found," Lia said. "Don't tell any of us where you put them either."

Nix passed Jami off to Lia, took the necklace from Viv, and disappeared beneath the water. Marley took off into the sky and soon they were both gone.

"I'll talk with him," I offered. I still hadn't forgotten about Phil, the man who had been killed by King Danforth or one of his lackeys, after I'd already extracted the information the king had wanted from him. All this time I'd assumed that man

had gone back to his life, and it had taken Captain Kerrigan's men to tell me otherwise.

"I don't think we'll have much choice but to all be there. He'll want to know what happened with the siren queen," Lia said.

We walked toward where the royal carriage waited. The water tried pulling us in the opposite direction, but it wasn't quite strong enough. I had to help Lia with Jami, but at least he could walk with our support.

One of the footmen opened the carriage door and King Danforth stepped out. He wore plainclothes, but his crown was a dead giveaway for any onlookers.

"You'll forgive us if we don't bow," Lia said. "Our friend has been injured and needs our support to remain standing."

King Danforth rolled his shoulders. "If you present me with the Azurean Stones, then *all* will be forgiven," he said. Someone had clearly been whispering in his ear about our progress, considering the last time we had talked to him he'd had no idea what the magical object was.

"We don't have them," Lia said, lifting her chin in defiance. "They're lost to the ocean, as they should be. No one should wield that much power."

King Danforth narrowed his eyes and clasped his hands behind his back.

"Yet, you did. And survived, might I add. Much to the detriment of my port." He waved a hand over the destruction and then replaced it behind his back. "Give me the Stones, Princess Aurelia."

"She speaks the truth. The Stones are gone," I said. "No one will ever find them or use them again."

"I did not ask you for your input, *Captain.*"

280

I bit my tongue. Picking a fight would do nothing to help our situation.

"Perhaps we should discuss this elsewhere," Lia suggested. "We can come to an agreement on what we will do to help you rebuild, and how you will absolve us of any fault considering you refused to assist in this fight and left your people to die."

King Danforth's eyes widened, and his nostrils flared. "You would dare tell me what I will do? How I will respond to this atrocity. I will punish the lot of you how I see fit."

"The siren queen sent the tidal wave which destroyed your port." Viv stepped in, striding over to the king, and getting in his face. "She could have done it at any time, but thankfully she chose a time when we were somewhat prepared. *Our* people saved your people while you ignored that anything was going on."

I had to restrain myself from smiling as I admired Viv and her courage. Seeing her stand up to the king had me questioning how I had gotten so lucky as to have her love me.

"Ma'am," a guard said as he stepped between the king and Viv. "Please back away."

Viv smirked. "Oh, I'm done here anyway. We all are. Unless the king wants to explain to his people how he knew this fight was coming and did nothing to prepare for or stop it."

King Danforth looked like he was about to argue, so I added, "And if you fight us on this, I will be sure your citizens know how many of their friends and family you've killed in the pursuit of leverage."

"I never—"

I put up my hand. "Don't bother. I know the truth of what became of the men after I delivered them to you." My lip curled in disgust.

His mouth snapped shut and he waved a hand as if to let us pass.

"Thank you," Lia said with a smile.

"This is far from over," King Danforth warned, but none of us turned back as we made our way toward the inn.

𝒩ix

Marley and I walked beneath the moonlight on a beach somewhere on the east coast of Cantalla. We hadn't decided where we'd hide the Stones yet, but I needed a break from the water. There had been no sign of sirens on our way here, and I wondered if maybe they were having some kind of ceremony to decide on a new queen, or if they were simply enjoying their freedom for a while.

"Is there anywhere we could hide the Stones so they'd be safe? I mean, look how hard that mage tried to hide them, and we busted in there and took them like it was nothing," Marley said.

"I don't know. I feel like as long as people know they exist, they'll look for them. I think the original mage who stole them had the right idea in keeping them and passing them down through his family so no one else knew of them and eventually the world forgot about them."

"Well, *someone* spilled the beans, since the siren queen caught wind of them," Marley pointed out.

"True. Probably Jami's parents, or the mage who worked with them. People can only keep secrets for so long. All

truth comes out in the end." I kicked up a whole mound of sand, flattening it when I stepped on it.

"Hm," Marley mused. "Do you have any secrets you've been keeping? Any truths that need to come out?" She nudged my arm, and we stopped walking.

I turned to face her. "I've no idea what you're implying," I teased. "If I did know what you were talking about, though, I'd say my truth has already been revealed. On a ship, in a closet." I leaned in closer. "With your mouth on my ..."

She put her finger to my lips. "Such dirty secrets," she said.

I laughed and took her hands. "We have all the time in the world to create more secrets together, if you want."

"I'd love nothing more." Her mouth pressed against mine and I slipped my tongue between her lips, savoring the taste of her.

Later, as we lay beneath the stars, I thought about the idea of exploring the world with Marley, rather than returning to Thalassia. It didn't seem like such a bad idea.

As if reading my thoughts, she said, "What if we take a break from our lives? Instead of hiding the Stones, we'll keep them with us, like that mage did, and keep them safe for a while. Then, someday, when I'm long gone, you can find somewhere, or someone, to take care of them, and return to your duties in Thalassia."

I hummed as I considered her idea. "You wouldn't miss Finn and Jami?"

"Of course I would. But I can visit them if I want. This isn't about *never* seeing anyone again, but just living our own lives for a while. Separate from our duties or who we were before." Marley turned to her side, using her hands as a pillow, and locked her gaze on mine, awaiting my answer.

Matching her position, I couldn't stop myself from smiling. "I think I like the sound of that. Could this be considered your winnings from our bet?"

Marley leaned in, closing the distance between us, and kissed me. I dug my hands into her hair and pulled her closer, pressing my body flush against hers.

"I have something a little different in mind for my *winnings*. You won't be getting off that easily," she teased, pressing her lips to mine again.

I'd needed this for so long. It was like her body was electric, making every part of me ignite with a frenzied sort of passion, and I couldn't wait to explore every inch of her beneath the light of the stars.

Lia

We learned that most of the bodies we'd seen floating in the water after the tidal wave had been dead *before* the wave. But not all.

Khali, Ryder, and the other dragons had been able to get almost everyone to safety, but there were some who didn't make it in time. Those lives were on me. I'd killed them, no matter what everyone else said.

I'd received a fire message from Nix saying she and Marley would be gone for a while. The letter had said: '*We'll keep searching for a safe space, but for now, there's no point in settling down.*' I knew she meant that there was truly no safe place to put the Stones. Given the widespread knowledge of the Stones's existence, people would be hunting for them. So, Nix and Marley would keep them safe.

It worried me, since I knew how dangerous the Stones could be. But I trusted Nix more than anyone to be able to handle this task. If anyone could resist the power of the necklace, it was her. And, she had Marley to back her up.

The rest of us had settled back into our rooms at the inn, while the shifters who had survived the siren attack joined us. By the fourth morning after, most of them had gone home. The

286

only ones remaining were Finn's crew, Brom's crew, my sisters, Khali, and Ryder. Of course, not all of them were staying at The Flight Deck Inn, but we were all gathered in the dining hall this morning. Our final morning together.

I hovered on the edge of the crowd, and a hand brushed my elbow. Turning, I found Ryder behind me.

"I'm heading out," he said, giving me a sad smile. "It was lovely to see you again."

I let out a huff of air. It had been nice having so many old friends together, but I knew that eventually everyone would have to move on with their lives.

"Thank you for everything," I said. "Where are you headed?" I tried to keep my tone light, but grief weighed it down.

He smirked. "I'm thinking of paying Justine a visit."

My face fell and I shook my head. "Tell me you're joking. She will *hate* that."

Ryder raised his brows. "What makes you think she didn't invite me back? Maybe she misses me."

"Stop it." I shoved his shoulder but couldn't stop myself from laughing. "If you truly go, I need to know how she reacts."

Ryder tilted his head. "I'll keep in touch," he promised. "Take care of yourself, Lia." Brushing my hair over my shoulder, because it had grown long enough to do that again, he took a step away.

"You too."

After he was gone, I made my way to the front of the room and took a seat on top of the bar so I could see everyone. It took a few minutes, but once Finn took his place beside me, everyone seated at the table around the room quieted.

"This is a little weird, being here with you all now," I began.

My sisters were the closest, to my right, and they all looked exhausted. I'd sent a few of them out into the ocean to search for sirens, but they were still nowhere to be found.

"As all of you know by now, the Stones are gone, and we expect you all to spread the word that they were destroyed. The less people looking for them, the better," Finn said from beside me. He stood with his leg propped up on a barstool to my left, looking like a true captain, though I knew his intentions for this meeting.

Viv and Jami sat on the barstools between Finn and I, ready to jump in and speak if Finn or I forgot anything important, or simply lost the will to talk about something. To be honest, it was more for my sake than Finn's.

Finn continued. "If anyone wants a witch to wipe your memories of the Stones, we encourage that; the less we all know the better, but we won't ask that of any of you. King Danforth may have backed off for now, but he'll be back on the warpath soon enough."

I cleared my throat and added, "I've requested my friend, a witch from the Asmaran library, Shannon, to be here in case any of you wish to do just that." I waved my hand toward where Shannon sat at the back of the room. Her silver hair was tied up in a loose bun, and her silver eyes shone from the sunlight streaming in through the window across from her. The long, seafoam-green cloak she wore pooled around her, making her look ethereal.

She smiled and I heard a few swoons from the crowd. It was the same effect she'd had on me the first time we'd met. But we'd never been anything more than friends.

"What happened to the Stones?" one of Brom's crew asked.

Stiffening, I braced myself for what would come next.

Finn answered, "As I said, the less you all know the better. The Stones are gone, and that's all we will ever say on the subject."

"How do we know *she* doesn't still have them?" the same man said, his gaze meeting mine. "She's the one who killed with them, and yet she's more trusted with information on them than we are?"

I held my breath, trying to contain my panic. We'd been preparing for this. This was the first time I'd been around anyone other than our core group and my sisters in the four days since the fight, and we knew this was bound to happen.

"She doesn't know where they are either," Viv argued on my behalf. "None of us do. And the Stones were more sentient than we realized, which is truly what killed those people, and why we've determined the Stones are too dangerous for this world."

I took a deep breath. "If it makes you feel better, I'll be the first to have my memory of the Stones wiped by Shannon," I said.

Someone scoffed.

"So you can forget the people you killed?"

I had walked into that one. "No, that's not what I want—"

"An easy out for the princess," another voice chimed in.

That triggered something in me. I *was* a princess, soon to be a queen, and this was no way for a queen to behave. Scared and guilt-ridden.

"Enough," I demanded, jumping down to the floor and standing in front of these people. "I understand how this all may look to you. I was never innocent *before* using those Stones, and now, even less so. I've killed people, and I remember each and every one of them." I closed my eyes as all those faces flashed through my mind.

"Lia," Viv murmured, cautiously.

"But we've *all* killed people," I said. "Maybe those people were sirens, or enemies, or it was self-defense. Maybe you did it for fun," I paused, fisting my shaking hands. "This is no excuse for what I've done. Whether the Stones influenced my actions or not, I commanded the siren queen to create that tidal wave, and I will live with the consequences of that for the rest of my days."

A few people gasped as if they hadn't realized the truth of that statement before. It was too late to take any of it back.

"I will have Shannon remove my memory of what happened to the Stones after I took them off. So, I will never forget the harm they caused and their dangerous nature. Will that satisfy you?"

A few murmurs of approval came from the crowd, and I took that as my confirmation.

"Now that that is taken care of," Finn said, coming to stand beside me. "There is the matter of Brom's crew and ship."

Callum stood from where he sat and Tally stood beside him, as if she wanted to be a part of whatever came next.

"We have all agreed that the ship in Sylvane belongs to you, Captain Finn. And we will follow your command if you will have us as your crew," Callum said. Tally gave a little salute that melted my heart.

Finn glanced back at Viv and Jami. Facing Brom's crew once more, he spoke. "I am grateful for your loyalty and would be honored to take Brom's place as your captain." They started to cheer, but Finn interrupted them. "However," he yelled over the crowd. "I no longer wish to spend my days on the water. And so, I would like to propose that you accept Jamison as your new captain, and his brother Charles as his first mate."

Confusion replaced the cheers, questions coming from all sides of the room, not just Brom's crew.

"What do you mean?" Garrett asked, standing from where most of Finn's crew sat. "You're not our captain anymore?"

"It should come as no surprise to you all that Jami would take my place, since he was first mate while we sailed on the *Leona.*"

"Why Charles? Where's Roland?" Jack asked, speaking for Brom's crew.

Charles walked to the front of the room from where he'd sat among Finn's crew. Jami joined him. I'd known this was coming, but tears pressed against my eyes, and I fought the urge to wipe them away.

Jami spoke first. "Roland will be returning with us to Sylvane, but he will be remaining there. He hopes to spend his days with his loved ones, whom he has spent too much time away from. I've chosen Charles as my first mate, because my first choice is no longer with us." He wouldn't say Marley's name, because he didn't want to arouse suspicion as to her whereabouts. He looked to Finn instead, letting people believe what they wanted about his statement.

"I will understand if you don't want to accept me as his first mate," Charles said. "But I will prove to you all that I am worthy of your respect and loyalty."

Murmurs broke out again among both crews, who would soon become one.

Callum spoke for Brom's crew once more, "We will accept this change. However, if we don't agree with the way things are run, we reserve the right to take Brom's ship back and sail it our way."

Finn opened his mouth, looking like he might argue, but Jami spoke.

"Fair enough. That's all we can ask of you."

With that settled, all that was left was to let people choose whether they wanted their memories altered or not. More people than I thought lined up beside Shannon to have her work on them and, as promised, I joined them at the front of the line.

"Lia," Shannon said, taking my hands and squeezing them tight. "I can pretend, if you want," she whispered low enough so only I would hear.

"No. I have to do this so I can regain some of their trust." My gaze flicked to Korra who spoke with Viv at the bar. She'd been distant since the fight and had barely spoken two words to me. I knew she'd been wary of me before, because of my decision to choose Viv over Thalassia, and I needed to prove to her that I would never put anyone above my kingdom again. Which was why Jami and I had chosen to part ways. For now. My heart ached every time I looked at him.

"I'll only remove your memories of the Stones after you took the necklace off," she promised. "Now, close your eyes."

I did as she said and felt her soft fingertips against my eyelids as she murmured a strange incantation. For a few seconds, I thought I was dreaming, and when I came to, I couldn't remember why I was standing in front of Shannon.

"Next," she said, winking at me before lightly pushing me away.

That was weird, I thought, shaking my head.

Brom's and Finn's crews, or what was now Jami's crew, had all headed outside to begin preparations for their journey to Sylvane. They'd find a ship with the same destination and bring aboard their own provisions. It would be tricky since the tidal

wave had destroyed a lot of the ships, but not all of them had been at port when the wave hit.

Rebuilding had already begun, and we'd been helping the past few days. But now we had to return to our own lives.

Jami and Charles had stayed behind, and they were talking with Finn by the bar. I stared at Jami openly, having no shame that he might see me watching him. We'd all watched him closely the past few days, thinking he might present some kind of ability to wield magic now that he was no longer linked to the wards around the island, but nothing happened. He'd assured us all that nothing had changed. The wards had leached him of his magic for so long, it was most likely that he'd never be able to wield it or shift. But I held out hope for him that after enough time passed, his magic might replenish enough for him to shift.

Either way, he'd recovered well from his injury, and now I only watched him because I knew it was going to be far too long before I was able to see him again.

"All good?" Viv asked as I joined her where she sat beside Finn.

"Huh?" I asked, unsure what she meant.

She laughed and took my hand. "Never mind. Are you headed back to Thalassia?"

I swung our clasped hands. "Will you come with me?" I asked, even though I knew her answer.

"I'll come visit soon," she said. "Finn and I are going to remain here a bit longer."

I understood, but I couldn't say the words. It hurt to be losing so much all at once. Half of my magic was gone, Viv was willingly choosing to leave my side for longer than a day for the first time in twenty years, Jami would be captain of his own ship,

293

and Nix ... I couldn't remember what had happened to her, but something told me I'd see her again.

"I'll miss you," I said. "Send me updates on your travels and I'll come meet you when I can."

Viv pulled me down into her lap and hugged me tight.

"I love you, Lia, and I know you'll do great things for Thalassia. I promise to come visit as soon as things are settled."

"Sorry to interrupt," Jami said.

Viv and I broke apart and I looked up at Jami, hope blooming in my chest.

"Can we talk? I didn't want to leave without saying ..." He stopped abruptly, like saying *goodbye* was as hard for him as it was for me.

Viv practically shoved me off her lap, and I landed on my feet, laughing.

"Yes. Come on, let's go somewhere quiet." I took Jami's hand, trying to memorize the feel of it for when he was gone. I led him to the entryway, and we sat on the stairs. My throat constricted as I tried to fight back tears.

"I know we're taking a break," he started, and before he could finish, I'd leaned forward and kissed him. His hands wound in my hair and held me there.

I'd say it was my subconscious taking over, and I had no idea what I was doing, but I knew exactly what I was doing. It was impossible not to kiss him one last time before we were separated for gods knew how long.

"Sorry," I murmured as I pulled back.

He chuckled. "Don't be. I've been thinking about doing that all day."

"I know we decided on taking a break from each other, and seeing how we felt a few months or years down the road ..." The tears finally won, and a few slipped down my cheeks.

"I love you, Lia, and that will never change. This break is so that you can take care of Thalassia. Once you've found your balance, I'll be waiting for you." He wiped my tears and kissed my cheek.

"I love you, too, and I *will* find you after things have settled in Thalassia," I promised.

"I'm looking forward to it."

Epilogue
Viv

The table was set, and the food was prepped and ready to be cooked. It had been eight years since we'd all been together. Nix and Marley had been in the wind since the day they'd left to hide the Stones, and though Finn headed into port whenever Jami's ship was docked there, I hadn't seen Jami in two years. Lia stopped by more frequently, and I'd been able to visit Thalassia a few times since they'd dispelled the boundaries.

I sat down, winded from such little exertion.

"Don't overdo it," Finn warned, poking his head into the dining room from the kitchen.

I stuck my tongue out at him and pressed a hand to my swollen belly. "I'm fine. This isn't my first rodeo." My hand grazed where my scars used to be. After Humer used the Azurean Stones on me, my scars had disappeared. Some days I missed them because they had become a part of me. But it was nice having a fresh start without that constant reminder of him.

Moving to stand in front of me, Finn crouched down and cupped my face in his hands. "You're right. You can handle

anything. But that doesn't mean you shouldn't rest occasionally." He grinned at me, and I bent down to kiss him.

Marley entered the room, wrinkling her nose at us. "Ew, get a room." She took a grape from the bowl on the buffet and popped it into her mouth.

"Where's Nix?" Finn asked, standing, and sitting on the edge of the table to face Marley.

Casting a glance at the doorway, Marley whispered, "Hide and seek."

I covered my mouth as I laughed. "Oh, this will be good. Atty and Leo are *very* good seekers. Leonora not so great, but she's learning from the best."

Callum had come to us about a year after Brom's passing and asked if we would take in Tabby and the twins. Thankfully we'd already found a house at that point, so they'd have a stable roof over their heads.

At the time, even though I knew deep down I'd be able to bear Finn's children because of Humer, I was terrified to even contemplate it. So, I figured Tabby and the twins were my only chance of ever having children. Until Leonora came along, as a complete surprise.

We'd planned on waiting for her to present either mer or lion shifting abilities before having any more children, but once she turned five and still presented neither, which was uncommon for a mermaid, we figured it was safe to have another.

Our assumption was that Leonara, if she was a shifter at all, would be a lion-shifter, because they often didn't shift until later in childhood, or young-adulthood. I secretly hoped she was just a late mermaid-bloomer.

"Found you!" I heard Leonara's little voice and my heart swelled with joy.

"Amazing!" Nix cheered. "My turn to find you."

"When is Jami arriving?" Marley asked, popping another grape into her mouth. "I haven't seen him in eight years and I'm dying to make a wager with him."

Finn put his hands up. "So long as I'm not involved in your wager, then have at it. He should be here any time now."

"Knock, knock!" Lia's voice rang throughout the house. She'd let herself in, as always. Her footsteps paused in the hall. "Aunt Lia brought you a treat," she said.

I groaned. Last time she brought a 'treat' for the kids, they were up until midnight jumping on their beds pretending to be pirates fighting monsters.

"Lia!" I yelled at her. "Don't you dare!"

Her laugh was answer enough.

She waltzed into the dining room and kissed me on the cheek. She'd cut her hair up to her shoulders, almost as short as it had been eight years ago. "You missed me, admit it," she said.

I pulled her in for a hug. "Of course I did. I always miss you." Living on land was strange enough but living without my sisters had been a whole other obstacle. I was so used to having them to lean on and talk to all the time, it had been an adjustment. Finn had made it easier, though, and when Tabby and the twins moved in, it was almost like having my sisters back. But instead, a horde of needy wild animals. Equally as loving, but twice as much work.

After everything that had happened with the siren queen, Finn and I agreed we needed a break from the ocean. So, we moved inland. There was a lake nearby that I could swim in whenever I wanted, but it didn't quite compare to the ocean. Occasionally, we'd make a trek to the ocean to relive the days when we'd called it home. Now our home was wherever our growing family was.

"You're glowing, dear," Lia said, patting my belly. She was one of the only ones I'd allow to do that. "She's going to be here soon. I can tell."

"Oh please," I murmured. "I'm not ready yet."

"Don't worry, I'll be here to help! Aunt Lia, Queen of Thalassia, at your service!"

"Oh yeah! I forgot! You're all fancy now," Marley teased. "Crowned Queen of Thalassia. Don't forget us little people."

Lia waved a hand at her. "Hush. I would never. Besides, dear old dad is still doing most of the work as king. I won't be *officially* queen until he's gone. Which won't be for a very long time. Which means I was able to get a month-long vacation to the Harper residence."

I jumped up, invigorated with more energy than I'd had in months. "Really?" I grasped both of her hands in mine. "Oh, Lia." I hugged her tightly.

Hugging me back, Lia said, "Really."

"This means so much to me, Lia, truly. The Harper residence is open to you anytime." I kissed her cheek and pulled away. It was strange using Finn's last name, considering he hadn't even used it since leaving Sylvane over a decade and a half ago. But I loved sharing it with him now that he'd decided he didn't mind having the same last name as Brom anymore. Even though his mother had never married Brom, she'd given Finn his last name. Maybe it was some hope that one day they'd resolve things.

"I have some business in Asmara as well, so it will give me plenty of time to stop in and pay my yearly visit with King Danforth." She gave an exaggerated sigh. "He just can't accept that the Stones are gone, even though every group he's sent to find them has come back empty handed."

Marley chuckled. "It's almost like they're constantly changing location or something."

Lia gave her a weird look but shook her head. Marley liked to mess with her since Lia had her memory of the Stones wiped after she'd used them.

I shot Marley a withering glare. It wasn't fair to Lia to confuse her like that, even if it was entertaining sometimes.

"Wherever they are, or aren't, it doesn't matter. At least the king will never find them," I said.

Lia nodded her agreement and leaned against the table.

"Sorry I'm late," Jami called out from the entryway. "It's a bit of a hike from the port to the middle of the country."

"It would make more sense for you to come in from the North," Finn said, walking out into the hall to meet Jami. "You're making it harder on yourself."

"Maybe. But my crew appreciates having some time without their captain in port, so I couldn't deprive them of that."

I glanced at Lia. She was biting her lip and twisting the ends of her hair as if she were going on a first date rather than reuniting with the man she'd loved for over eight years.

"It's been over two years," she murmured to me. "I've been so busy back home."

"And I'm sure nothing has changed," I tried to reassure her, but she continued twisting her hair.

"Tabby's spending the night at the Asmaran Library to do some research, since she shifted for the first time." It had caused a few days of tantrums and fits because the boys wanted to shift, too, but it would probably be a few more years for them. "So, her room is open if you want to borrow it." I smirked at Lia, and she rolled her eyes. "Justine also said she misses you."

Lia guffawed. "That's a lie. She'd never say such a thing."

"She hasn't seen you since she helped us find this house. She might come off a bit stand-offish, but she truly does care about you." The library was only about a ten-minute walk from our house. There weren't many residences out here, which was nice, but made it difficult for the kids to make friends. Tabby loved spending time at the library, though.

"I'll have plenty of time to visit while I'm here." Lia patted my arm placatingly. "And I'm taking you up on that offer for Tabby's room." She raised her eyebrows and jerked her head at the doorway. Jami walked in, Finn behind him.

I'd admit, he only grew more handsome with age, same as Finn. They both sported fuller beards now, which I kept telling Finn was like kissing a porcupine, but if he ever shaved, I'd leave him alone with the kids for a week.

Without so much as a hello for the rest of us, Jami walked straight up to Lia and took her into his arms, kissing her tenderly. It was as if they hadn't spent any time apart.

"It's almost like we aren't the reason for your visit at all," Finn teased.

Jami pulled away from Lia, but slid his arm around her waist.

"Well, there are a few other things on my mind." He smirked at Lia, and I almost wanted to leave them alone from the heat in his gaze. "One of which is a new development." He pulled Lia's hand, and she followed him outside. Finn, Marley and I weren't far behind.

Jami stood in the yard, smirking, but before any of us could guess what he was about to show us, he shifted into an eagle, his wings flapping and keeping him aloft.

"Oh my god!" I exclaimed.

Lia gaped at Jami, a grin spreading on her face. She laughed and clapped her hands as she watched him fly up above

us and over the trees. I walked up behind her and wrapped my arms around her.

"Amazing," she breathed.

Jami came back down to the ground, shifting once more and moving to stand in front of Lia. I took a step back.

"I hadn't told anyone yet because I can only shift for an hour or so at a time before I'm drained and can't shift back. I got stuck as an eagle the first time for almost an entire day and I think my crew thought I'd abandoned them. But that's how I was able to get here from the port."

Lia threw her arms around him.

"I'm so happy for you," she said, pulling back and kissing him.

"I'm going to play hide and seek with the kids," Marley said. "But we're going flying later." She disappeared inside.

"And I'm going to show my wife some appreciation in the kitchen," Finn said, taking my hand. We left Lia and Jami alone and started up the ovens in the kitchen.

"What kind of appreciation did you have in mind?" I asked, eyeing him as he rolled up his sleeves, baring his well-muscled forearms and newest tattoo. He'd gotten mine and Leonara's names tattooed there. Tabby and the twins had picked out tattoos for him that he'd gotten in honor of them on his calves. A beautiful purple flower for Tabby, and a two-headed cat for the boys. I'd been a little concerned when they'd come up with that one, until I saw the book Tabby had brought home from the library with a drawing in it that looked exactly as they'd described the cat to Finn.

Finn crossed the kitchen, taking my hand. "I'll start here," he said, kissing the back of my hand. "And work my way up, and then down ..." A low growl in his throat had my toes curling.

"Momma!" Leonara ran into the kitchen, making us laugh. "I can't find Auntie Nix or Auntie Marley!" She tugged on my hand, and I let her lead me out of the kitchen.

"I don't think they want to be found, sweetie," I said. Finn laughed behind me.

Lia and Jami were suspiciously absent, and Leo and Atty were playing a card game on the floor in the hallway.

"Let's go outside for a while. I think everyone is taking a break," I said. Opening the door wide, the fresh air rushed in and swept over me.

Finn stepped outside beside me. "Don't worry, I won't forget to finish what we started later." He winked. "Aunt Lia can take a turn with all the kids. Maybe they'll even do us the favor of shifting for the first time on her watch"

Smiling, I leaned my head on his shoulder. "Oh, I look forward to that."

Atty, Leo, and Leonara all ran out into the yard, tumbling into the grass and laughing. I closed my eyes, savoring the moment.

Ruthless Tides

About the Author

H. M. Huntress is a self-published author and content creator. She has been writing stories since grade school and is driven by the desire to share her writing with the world while encouraging others to do the same. All her books are currently available on Amazon. If you want to connect with her on social media, find her at the handle below!

TikTok & Instagram: @authorhmhuntress

I'd love if you left a review for *Ruthless Tides* on Amazon, Goodreads, or social media!

Scan here for updates on future projects and events!

Ruthless Tides

H.M. Huntress

Check out my other books!

Haunting Memories

The Forbidden Waves Series:

Forbidden Waves
Ruthless Tides

Beneath Venomous Sails

The Broken Angel Series:

Broken Angel
Condemned Angel
Forsaken Angel

The Unbound Series:

Unbound
Disgraced
Awakened

307